Dedication

Each one of us has one or more things or people that inspire and help us to keep going when we're ready to throw in the towel, or in our cases, the keyboard.

To inspiration, muses and music. We thank you.

Never stop dreaming, never stop creating and don't let anyone or anything get in the way of your goal.

Introduction

The Ink Slingers Guild is a group of like-minded individuals who come together for support and encouragement. Since its inception the Ink Slingers have continued to expand membership, filling their ranks with some of the best and brightest up and coming authors of our time.

This, the Ink Slinger's second anthology, is aptly named Into the Abyss. As with the first anthology, Beyond the Threshold, this collection of short stories is based on one of the writing exercises done at every ISG meeting. The exercise is to have three members each pick one word. Members have five minutes to compose a story with the chosen words. As with any creative outlet, members take each other into new worlds the way only writers can.

The words that were chosen this year were:

• Gravity
• Innocuous
• Perilous

Each story is a journey created just for you, so sit back and enjoy as the Ink Slingers welcome you **Into the Abyss**!

The Ink Slingers Guild

Presents

Into the Abyss

A Collection of Short Stories
Volume Two

Contributing Authors

Alden Scott
JM Paquette
Nicole DragonBeck
Erika Lance
Rhiannon Matlock
Lisa Barry
Robert Broughton
Anne Cargile
Dinah T.R. Shatter
Désirée Matlock
Angel Woolery

Witching Hour Publishing, Inc.

Witching Hour Publishing, Inc.

ISBN-10: 0-9885799-4-4
ISBN-13: 978-0-9885799-4-1

Ink Slingers Guild crest: Nicole Dragonbeck
Ink Slingers Guild crest digital artistry: Desi Matlock
Cover Design: Lisa Barry
Editor: Courtenay Dodds: www.CourtenayDodds.com
Proofreading and Creative Writing: Erika Lance

Contents

The Scarab

By Alden Scott

I immediately regretted the last punch. I ain't hard-boiled like most of the mugs I had the pleasure of associating with. My knuckles throbbed and shouted their agreement. Vigorously moving an injured part of the body had no scientifically proven healing ability, but that didn't stop instinct from making me shake my hand in the air. The attempt was in vain. My hand still hurt.

Jake blacked out again. The two bit, rag-a-muffin could disgust me on a good day, but now he made me physically ill. Blood poured from his freshly broken nose, and nauseating bubbles popped from his left nostril when he exhaled. A familiar smell wafted from his corner of the room. I recognized the smell in the same instant I saw the dark stain spread from the crotch of his pants. He started to snore, which added to the chaotic dance of bodily fluids that leaked from his face.

"God dammit, Jake," I muttered and fetched Colonel's bowl of water from across the room. I threw the water in his face and said, "First you try to bump me off, now you piss on my floor."

Big Jake sputtered to life. He spit out water and German Sheppard saliva as Colonel watched passively from his corner of the office. The mutt almost raised his eyebrows with interest, but obviously had more important plans for his energy. I wondered if Colonel would have lifted a paw to help his old master had the fight taken a different direction. I doubted it. As long as Colonel and I had kicked around, he never showed an abundance of motivation. Hell, I've been tempted to flour the office floor to see if he actually got up at night to eat, or if he somehow willed the food bowl straight to his mouth. Either way, whether I would have seen paw prints or a sliding path, the food was always gone in the morning.

Jake struggled against his handcuffs. In hindsight, I should have used rope to tie him to the chair. Furniture was usually the first thing to go in the fireplace on cold, winter nights, and he was scraping the cuffs up and down the armrests of my last good chair. Wood shavings collected at his feet. I couldn't afford to replace the chair, but the good news was no one could afford to hire a private dick these days. I doubt I would be entertaining potential clients any time soon.

"Who was the Jane, Big Jake?"

Life flowed back into Jake's eyes as he blinked himself fully awake. He stopped struggling and gazed around the room. When his eyes settled on me, the realization struck him that the situation, and the horror that led to our current predicament, was no dream. He thrashed again and uttered animalistic growls that would have been better suited in a jungle.

"Who was the Jane?" I repeated.

"I... I don't know. Honest I don't!" Big Jake's demeanor transitioned from a trapped panther to a whipped puppy. He relaxed his arms and his shoulders slumped. "I was just followin' the broad to shake some coins out of the money tree, that's all. I wasn't gonna hurt no one."

"Oh, you weren't gonna, huh?"

"I didn't hurt no one!" he quickly added.

"Then who was your friend?" The question leapt into the forefront. I had been preoccupied keeping a grip on my sanity after I saw that mangled corpse. The woman's hair and evening dress matched the description I'd been given by The Gentleman, but any resemblance ended there. Her skin was gray and wrinkled up like a raisin. Her body had no substance at all. It was as if she'd been sucked empty from the inside until the only thing left behind were bones held together by an aged, leather bag. And her face... I shuddered to think about that eyeless, twisted face forever locked in an agonized death scream. That face would keep my imagination company for many years to come. I had barely noticed the second figure flee the scene. He, or she, dissipated like a phantom after a hard day of haunting. Ice-spiders danced up and down my spine.

"Ain't no friend, boss. I told you what happened. I told you we gotta scat or we're next!" Jake started to test his bracelets again.

"You told me nothing that makes sense," I said. I heard a humph from behind me. Apparently my little interview was disrupting Colonel's much needed sleep. "Start over, and this time keep it civil."

"We don't have time! That thing... that thing is comin' back to...," Jake trailed off and stared at a nonexistent wonderland in a dimension only he could see. I snapped my fingers in front of his face to break his concentration. Jake shook himself back into reality and inhaled deeply. "Okay. Okay, alright. I see this broad standing outside that swanky hotel. She's got the jewels; she's got the fur; she's the perfect mark, right?" I nodded, not in agreement, but to keep Jake talking. "So I go up and try talking, ya know? Just tried to see what could come of it. She starts gettin' huffy and uppity, so I start gettin' brave. I know she's gotta be a whore 'cause there ain't no woman like that standing out by herself."

Actually, I reflected, she was out by herself because I was late. Jake or his buddy could have done the deed, but there would have been no deed to be done if I'd been on time. Her final scream could have been meant for me.

"So she brushed me off like I ain't even there!" Jake guffawed. How dare she. "Just turns her back on me and starts walking off. Up till then I was being nice, so I followed her. 'Sorry to offend you, your highness,' I says. She walked past an alley so I gave her a little bump to get her inside. I wasn't gonna hurt her, you gotta believe me! I was only gonna shake her up a bit. Maybe take any spare dough she didn't need. Next thing I know, the broad reaches in her purse so I slap it away incase she's got a piece. The purse hit the ground and everything dumped out, but there wasn't no piece." Jake's voice quieted and he whispered conspiratorially, "There was this trinket that spilled out and rolled down the alley. It almost looked like it was hoofing it all on its own."

Now this was new, and also added to the crazy factor of previous versions. While Big Jake rambled, I retrieved a bottle of hooch from a locked drawer in my desk. Since my office doubled as my living quarters during these tight times, I had creature comforts scattered throughout the sparse furnishings.

"It was gold," he paused for a moment, exhaled slowly and continued, "and loaded with glitzy gems. One big green one on the head, and a fat red one on the back. I left her and went after it. Even if it wasn't real, I could've offloaded it to someone."

"Head and back?" I asked. I obviously missed something. "Back up and explain that."

"The trinket!" he exclaimed angrily, as if it was my fault I couldn't fill in the blanks with my imagination. "I ran over and snatched up the trinket. It was this big beetle thing. And that's when I heard her scream from behind me, and when I saw you coming around the corner," Jake's voice trailed off and he murmured, "We're gonna die."

Big Jake looked defeated as he sat in the chair. He tucked his chin into his chest and grew silent. The gravity of the situation took a literal toll on his face and pulled his sagging cheeks downward. I tugged on my bottle a few times and pondered my recollection.

From two blocks away I spotted Jake hassle the Jane into the alleyway. By the time I came around the corner Big Jake was about ten feet from her body, and a man shaped shadow high-tailed it down the alley. If only I had walked faster, or left earlier...

I stopped the thought before it added more layers to the foundation of my guilt. The Gentleman, I realized, was still in the dark about what happened. How much time had passed since I left? It wasn't a glamorous gig, nor did it have anything to do with my chosen field, but money was money and The Gentleman had a lot of it.

The Gentlemen's real name was Carter. The nickname comes on account of him being from London, and extravagantly dressed in glad rags every waking moment of the day, no matter the weather conditions. He probably slept in a three-piece suit and top hat. Carter was some sort of treasure hunter from what I could gather and a few years ago stumbled across his payday in Egypt. Now he toured from country to country, city to city, and showed off his loot. It may be apparent how little I care for the man or what he does. Us insignificant folks have been more focused on minor things, like discovering creative ways to avoid freezing to death in winter. Suits in the news talked about how economic indicators warned of a great depression. The Gentleman referred to it as a 'minor financial setback' and that 1929 was a strong year in the US. He predicted by October the banks would be back on their feet and the stock market would soar. Hell, he had an accent and an armory full of words I'd never heard of before. He was probably right.

I was contacted by The Gentleman after an old buddy from the precinct gave him my number. Apparently it was our city's turn to be graced by his treasures and he needed a bodyguard, tour guide and manservant. Lucky for me, I was able to fill all three roles.

I escorted him to and from speaking engagements, interviews and meals. I sat patiently as he organized events, and ran small errands for him when he rested. The Gentlemen wasn't much of a talker when we were one on one, but from what I heard he enthralled audiences of every kind for hours. People regarded his lectures and viewings as brilliant and enlightening.

Tonight he surprised me when he requested I pick up a lady friend and bring her back to the Continental Towers hotel. I spent most hours of the day in his presence and didn't recall him making any dates. Maybe Big Jake was right and the Jane really was a whore. I wasn't given a name, only a description, and was told to pick her up in front of a different hotel. The Gentleman fidgeted nervously and paced the length of the living room when he relayed the instructions. An 'innocuous task', he had called it. I chalked his odd behavior up to anticipating a sexual encounter with an unknown woman, but there seemed to be more to it. The base of his nervousness was fear.

Big Jake was getting to me, that was all. I could tie up this entire package with a neat little bow if I could figure out how that corpse came to be. I toyed with the idea of the dame working with Big Jake. When they entered the alley, the petrified corpse would be staged to take her place as she fled, but why? Were they trying to set me up? It didn't explain Jake's panicked expression and the fact he was rooted in place, unable to move. There was no reason I could conceive to even go through the trouble of such an elaborate escape.

The alternative was the corpse and lady were one and the same, but it would be easier to convince a kid that an alligator wearing rabbit ears was actually the Easter Bunny. The corpse was so old and drained it could have never been that twenty-something dame with gams straight out of a teenager's imagination. There had been rumors of chemical warfare from the Great War with similar, nightmarish results, but the war had been over for nearly a decade, and people-shriveling-gas guns have yet to surface on the black market.

I was floundering for answers and I knew it. I decided to keep riding the Jake train.

"Where's this beetle, then? You said you snatched up the trinket, where is it?"

"Promise me on the straight. Promise me if I tell you, you'll cut me loose," Jake pleaded. He looked up at me with tears in his eyes. The bum was serious.

"I can't promise anything, Jakey. If I do that I'll have a dead broad, a gold bug, and I'll be out my only suspect. What kind of sense does going in cahoots with you make? I patted you down and nothing turned up, so is it back in the alley?"

Jake sighed and lowered his eyes back to the ground. The light at the end of his tunnel was extinguished. "It's in your coat pocket," he admitted softly.

"My what?"

"It's in your coat pocket. When you jostled me around, I slipped it in your coat pocket."

I subconsciously rubbed the front of my pocket and felt a lump. It was about a quarter the size of a baseball. "Why would you do that?" I asked. Something forced my brain to advise my hand to not, under any circumstances, reach into that pocket and touch the object within.

"When the girl screamed I spun around to see her. I figured she was hollerin' for help and I was gonna shut her up," Jake took another one of his dramatic pauses that tempted my urge to choke the life out of him.

"And then you see the mystery man sucking the life out of her," I impatiently finished for him.

"I told ya, it was like they were kissing but the girl just shrunk up. Then," Jake gulped and made eye contact again, "this voice said 'the scab' or something like that. The guy turned around and looked right at me." Jake trembled in the chair.

I rolled my eyes and sat on the corner of my desk, losing what little there was left of my patience. "Are you making shit up now? Now there's a bug and the guy said scab."

"No, you ain't listening. The guy didn't say scab, some dame's voice said scab. Her voice came from inside my head."

"And this female voice told you about her scab," I sighed.

"The Scarab," said a distinctly female voice with an unrecognizable accent. Her voice echoed from everywhere, which made it impossible to isolate the origin. I leaped to my feet and spun around to find the intruder. To my surprise, Colonel was on his feet and lurked around the office maliciously. His guttural growls made the hairs on the back of my neck stand up and salute.

We were still alone, but Colonel decided to focus on a shadow in the corner. He faced the shadow, sat, and whimpered. So much for his temporary display of bravery.

The shadow appeared to gain substance, if that was even possible. It was darker than a shadow should have been with the amount of lighting my modest office offered. Before my mind consulted fear and coordinated our next move, I found myself approaching it. Anything capable of making Colonel nervous enough to move would fill any man with the heebie-jeebies. I heard wet, slurping noises behind me.

I turned to see Big Jake, helplessly handcuffed to my chair. His legs kicked out uselessly as a shadowy form leaned over him, face to face. It was the kiss Jake had described. The alien form inhaled something from the inside of Jake's body. Bluish wisps of smoke passed from Jake's mouth into the mystery man. Jake's face started to resemble the corpse from the alley. I noticed a distinct lack of romance in the act.

"The Scarab," repeated the voice. My hand instinctively went to my pocket. Just as Jake had described, the mystery man stood erect and faced me. He was almost as unidentifiable as the shadow Colonel was guarding. There was a rough outline of a man, slight of build, and about five feet six or seven inches. His head appeared to be elongated and his limbs lacked muscle and definition. In fact, his entire body lacked definition. It was an outline of a small man, and inside that outline was blackness. Oh, and did I mention golden, glowing eyes that wanted to devour my soul? As he walked toward me I saw what was left of Jake. The puzzle of how the alley corpse came about was solved.

"This one survives," said the voice. I hoped this was an order, and that it was about me. The voice definitely came from the shadowy corner this time. When I was certain the mystery man had stopped his advance, I turned to face the general direction of the voice.

"The Scarab," she thundered again, "release it to the Boy King."

At some point between witnessing a supernatural horror and considering the hell I would soon be part of, I must have reached into my pocket and grabbed the trinket. I held it out in front of me as if it were a protective amulet. For all I knew, it was.

The mystery man, or the Boy King as the voice referred to it, was suddenly in between me and the talking corner. He lunged at me, and being the brave tough guy I am, I closed my eyes and screamed.

After some time I realized magic smoke wasn't being sucked out of my body. Since the weight of the trinket was no longer in my hand, I decided the screaming wasn't helping my situation. I stopped and opened my eyes.

The Boy King creature was gone, and so was the trinket. All that remained was a pruned up corpse, an edgy German Sheppard that nervously guarded a talking corner, and a private investigator in desperate need of some clean britches.

Staring directly at the corner produced no results. I found that if I looked at it through my peripheral vision, I could see shapes moving in the darkness. I decided it was my duty to be the ambassador for the entire human race and open talks with this alien entity using my gift of words.

"Uh, hello?" Masterful, mister Ambassador.

"Your animal annoys me." Now that death wasn't staring me in the face well, directly in the face, I noticed the thick accent was strange and exotic. Her tone was sensual. It took me and my libido a minute to grasp what she said.

"Colonel!" I barked at the dog. Colonel looked at me over his right shoulder. Reluctantly, he rose and trotted over to his usual spot beside my desk. He did not cease the whining altogether, but at least it was not constant. I shortened the gap between me and the corner. "Who... what are you? And why did you kill the whore?" I asked, coming up with nothing else to say.

"You may refer to me as Maia, and the woman was much, much more than a whore." The voice sounded amused, "but she is no concern of yours. Your concern must be focus. Your skills are needed again. It is why I spared you."

"Uh, what?" I continued to amaze myself with my linguistic skills.

"The Boy King's treachery has cursed our afterlife. There is no paradise for us to claim. He turned his back on the gods, and so have they returned the favor. Our prayers go unanswered.

"Seek out the grave robber named Carter. Tell him what has transpired here. Tell him the wet-nurse still watches over her child."

I definitely saw shapes moving in the shadow now. They began to coalesce into a single figure. The figure of a woman. She stepped down from a nonexistent stair as her tanned, scantily clad body formed from nothingness. Black hair flowed down her back and blended into the abyss behind her. The woman had almond shaped, golden eyes that glowed as the Boy King's had. The glow settled to dark brown as she approached me. Her features were nothing short of perfection. She closed the distance between us and looked up into my eyes.

"But, why me?" I asked.

"You are the only one that can save us. You must remember," she said softly.

Maia reached up to take my face in her hands. They were soft and caressed my face lightly. The movement of her fingertips against my cheeks numbed my fear and eased my excitement. I felt relaxed, and was hardly even worried when her eyes began glowing again.

The glow intensified and enveloped the entire room. I tried to step backward to avoid a burn, as one often does when standing next to a small sun, but the attempt was ignored by my own body. It remained in place, patiently awaiting orders. Maia's hands continued their calming charm on my face from somewhere within the blinding light.

The light began its retreat and revealed Maia, inch by inch, in the same position as before. This version of the foreign bombshell wore a conservative linen dress decorated with beads and feathers. The look in her face was desperate and sad.

"Please," she said intensely, "the Grand Vizier is evil. He means to make himself Pharaoh."

Maia's little lightshow trick had not only changed her clothes, but managed to transport us to some kind of desert. I could make out a few trees and shoddy buildings from the corner of my eye. My body continued to ignore my requests for control, but it did manage to look down. Oh hell on a stick, the boys at the precinct would get a kick out of this. Was I wearing sandals and a skirt?

"He is an insect, and a cheat, but evil?" The words came from my mouth unbidden. "Sweet Maia, Tutankhamun's body is weakening, but his mind is strong."

"He has forsaken Aten in favor of Amun-Ra!" she whispered harshly. She balanced the necessity for quiet with the sense of urgency quite well. "The priesthood has already been restored, and the rituals are sure to follow."

"Bah, the gods," the words flowed from my mouth once again. "Old gods or new gods, it makes no difference to me, my love. It is not the gods that aide me in battle. It is not the gods that I fight to protect."

"You should not say such things." Maia dropped her hands from my face and looked downtrodden. "Amun-Ra is the nemesis of our people, and with the Vizier's assistance he now controls our King."

"Ah, General, there you are," said a new voice from behind me. I've met a few politicians in my time, and I instinctively knew this had to be one. The words were pleasant enough, but they sounded as if they were raised in a sewer by lizards, and low-crawled through pigsties their entire life.

I saw a momentary look of panic cross Maia's face, but it vanished in an instant. My eyes flicked down toward the handle of a sword on my belt, and back up into Maia's face. She shook her head very slightly. My body turned to greet the newcomer. I'd given up on trying to control any physical actions. As far I was concerned, I was just along for whatever ride this turned out to be. A passenger in someone else's body. A body that happened to be wearing a skirt.

My eyes squinted to avoid the harsh glare from the sun setting on the horizon. The stranger wore what I would normally call a dress, but considering my current attire, I'll call it a robe. His hands were clasped behind his back, and he wore a smile like a bum would wear a bowtie. It sat on his face uncomfortably and looked as if fangs were ready to spring out. There was something oddly familiar about the man's facial features. My head bowed almost imperceptibly while my mind scrambled to match that face to one from recent memory.

Carter, I thought. "Grand Vizier Ay," my body said.

The Vizier returned an equally insignificant bow. He looked over my shoulder and took notice of Maia. "Leave us, woman. I must speak with Commander General Horemheb in private."

I could feel Maia's glare pierce my body to get at this wormy fellow, but nonetheless I heard footsteps signal her departure. My gaze never left Ay. It was a shame, because I'd give anything to watch the south end of a north bound Maia.

"Your King needs you Commander General. While the priests prepare for the festival, your duties as Lord of the Two Lands require you to take the army east."

"And what festival would this be?" I asked. The skepticism in my voice's tone matched what I was thinking.

"The restoration of Amun-Ra back to supremacy, of course. The priesthood plans to bestow upon him the sacred Scarab," Ay said. His eyes gleamed unnaturally. "It is said the Scarab may even heal him of his physical illness. I am sure once our King accepts the Scarab, he will be forever changed. He will never let it out of his possession."

"I'm sure the King will be fine," I said while I unsuccessfully tried to coax my body into punching him in the throat. If this was the same jeweled bug that was responsible for Big Jake pissing in my office, I wanted it destroyed.

"Be that as it may, General," he spat the title as if it tasted like week old cat turd, "make your preparations. The army marches in two days. Plenty of time to settle your affairs with the wet nurse."

"My army marches upon my orders, Vizier." Atta-boy, I told my body. Now punch him in the throat! Hurry, he's walking away!

Grand Vizier Ay waved his hand dismissively as he turned to leave. The sun shot out from behind his egg shaped head and made my eyes water. Since the throat punching wasn't going to happen, I tried to convince my body to turn its head before the sun melted my eyeballs instead. Not surprisingly, it was a futile attempt. I watched the man's form grow distant, while the sun appeared to swell. It seemed to cover the entire horizon and reach for me with limbs made of fire. Suddenly, the sun shot towards me as if it were launched from God's slingshot. I mentally screamed and reeled back, while I physically stood there to greet my own personal apocalypse.

I was engulfed in heatless flames. The yellow and orange inferno softened into a golden hue that slowly shrank to two points directly in front of my face. Those two points transitioned into Maia's beautiful gold eyes. She still held my face in her hands. A quick glance verified that I was back in my office, and had total control of my body once again. As much control as I could hope for with my body nearing a collapse from exhaustion, anyway.

Maia smiled at me with an amused expression. The black portal she stepped from pulsed slowly behind her. She turned and looked into the void, and then met my gaze one last time. Her amused expression was replaced with sadness.

"I must go. Your perilous journey begins, now," she whispered. Maia kissed me lightly on the lips and added, "I have missed you, General."

Maia kissed me again. The sensation I felt was something only a poet could put into words. I closed my eyes and let the passion flow through my body. While my eyes were closed, she licked my lips. It was odd, I know, but she obviously wasn't from around here. As her tongue grew more insistent, I opened my eyes and discovered Maia's head had taken on the shape of Colonel's massive noggin. To add to my confusion, I was also lying on the floor instead of standing and holding the girl of every man's dreams. It didn't take long to realize I had passed out. There was a bottle of hooch not too far from my hand.

I sat up and rubbed my head with one hand and pushed the dog away with the other. I didn't want to think about anything he'd licked previously before he molested me in my sleep. I was surprised, but not shocked to see the body of Big Jake still handcuffed to the chair. Somewhere deep inside, I knew I wouldn't be lucky enough to pass this off as a dream.

To tell the truth, I wasn't exactly hitting on all sixes after coming to, but I knew enough to know I didn't come back to my senses alone. The evil, little creature that accompanied me back was the type that often haunts me. It sits on my shoulder and whispers harsh truths into my ear, humbling any notion I may have about being brave, or smart, or worth my weight in salt. It was memory; cold, heartless, unforgiving memory.

This memory was different from the usual run of the mill flashbacks I experienced. I thought about the ride I took in the General's body, and wondered what happened to him after Carter, or Ay, walked away. Instead of speculating, I remembered clear as day. I sought an audience with the king and requested he delay the festival until my return from the east. He was leery of the Vizier as I was, but the king felt confident in his control of the situation. Leading the army through successful military campaigns bolstered the boy's confidence to dangerous, even foolish, levels. On the Nubian battlefield, the guy wearing different armor is trying to kill you. In the king's own land, it was a different story.

I remembered the boy's face in detail. The face contained features of a man, but beneath the façade sparkled the excited eyes of youth. The boy I raised; the boy that raised me. The more I tried to recall from the memory of the General, my memory, the more I was shown.

I remembered a scared child, freshly deprived of his father and surrounded by powerful advisors; few of whom cared about him or our lands. He held Maia in high regard, and rightly so, though she did not fulfill an official capacity and was silenced whenever she spoke in a public setting.

I remembered how he accepted me, a commoner, based on merit and not blood. He argued with his board of advisors to have me recognized as their peer based on years of lesser service with his father, and a year with him. You should have seen him go. Barely ten years old and forty pounds soaking wet. He trembled as he ordered Ay and Maya to accept me, and held his ground against their protests.

I remembered him look at me with love in his eyes throughout the years, which I returned unconditionally. He was my friend, my son, and my fellow soldier. He was my King; the first and only one I ever acknowledged.

I remembered what it was to care for another person. The level of caring that could break the bonds of time, and apparently lives. My recollection of the mystery man, the evil soul sucker, softened. The dread I felt earlier when my agonizing death was imminent evaporated. The picture of the boy in my mind's eye filled in that featureless figure. It wasn't a ruthless shadow. It was a scared kid running on instinct and pain.

He will be forever changed. He will never let it out of his possession. Ay's words slithered through my head and fueled a dark rage deep within. He would pay for this curse.

I tossed the key to the handcuffs in Jake's lap. I'm not entirely sure why. He sure as hell wasn't going to do anything with them. Maybe it was a premonition that I wouldn't be back, and eventually someone would need to clean these digs up. Maybe it was to add a bit of comedy to such a strange day.

In any case, I cursed my luck for a few minutes, and then rose to retrieve my piece from another locked drawer. I made sure it was loaded and threw the remaining ammunition in my pocket. I covered Big Jake with a blanket and looked at my furry sidekick. The dog hadn't moved since I yelled at him for antagonizing the shadow, but his ears were perked up and alert.

"Looks like I outrank you, Colonel." The German Sheppard twitched an ear and licked his nose in response. He was clearly intimidated by my newfound military stature. "Just in case you'd rather starve to death to avoid moving, I'll leave a note for Janice to come check in on you."

I composed a quick note for Janice explaining I would be away for an indeterminate amount of time, and to please check on my mutt. I would slide it under the door of the Williams, DeVito and Glitch law office on my way out. I said my final goodbye to Colonel, grabbed my hat off the stand and departed the office. It was at that exact moment when the most bizarre thing of the day happened. The sound that exploded from behind the door was so strange and surreal I had nothing in my memory to compare it to. It almost sounded like...

I opened the door to my office. Colonel sat at attention behind the door and looked at me expectantly.

"Did you just bark?" Colonel cocked his head to the side as if to ask if I were crazy. I wondered the same thing myself. "And you moved twice in the same day?"

Colonel barked again. I swear on a stack of bibles, he opened his mouth and barked. Plain as rain. The dog that I normally have to check throughout the day to see if he's breathing let loose a bark that would send an intruder over the edge.

He stood and padded through the doorway. I simply watched him, unable to do anything else. He stopped and looked back at me. He glanced in the general direction of the Continental Towers, whined, and then faced me again. It was the international language for dogs that means I want something that is over there.

"Alright then," I said and closed the door for the second time. It couldn't get any weirder than this. I didn't even own a leash. "Shall we?"

With my dog, that many believed to be a rug, trotting by my side, I ventured out into a world I once thought was simple.

About Alden Scott

Growing up in the howling wilds of Wyoming, Alden Scott was forced to develop an imagination to stave off the boredom of small-town life. Later, he got what he had always hoped for and found himself careening through an increasingly bizarre life. He soon began to long for the dangerous boredom once again. Hoping that writing ridiculous stories might let him avoid having to live through them, he began his journey down the dark path of becoming a writer.

Connect with Alden Scott:
www.aldenscott.com

Sending Sally Home

By JM Paquette

"How much farther is this place?" Sally asked Peter as they followed the overgrown, twisting path through the woods. The canopy was heavy overhead, the dim light of late afternoon drifting down to the ground in hazy, golden streaks. Sally paused, letting Peter move a few steps ahead, one hand brushing stray strands of light hair out of her eyes as she paused to adjust the messenger bag slung bandolier style across her chest. She contemplated taking off her sweatshirt, letting her heated skin drink in the breeze through her thin t-shirt, but the late afternoon light made her reconsider. It would be cool soon enough, and she would want the sweatshirt then, she thought, taking in the ancient trunks around her. She had never been one to stare at trees before. The feeling was uncanny, like something calling to her at the same time that it was trying to warn her away. She resisted the urge to check her phone, knowing that the screen would still tell her that they were well out of cell phone range. It was funny to think that pockets like this still existed in the world, places where all of the conveniences of modern technology ceased to function. Sally hadn't been away from the city for months, and she was amazed at how much it showed.

"Peter, this tower of yours," she began, moving again and almost immediately stumbling as the path dipped suddenly beneath her feet. Her friend was there, his strong hand on her upper arm, steadying her as they made a final turn around the rough-hewn trail and coming into a small clearing.

"Here it is," he said, his free hand gesturing to the meadow and the innocuous building in the center. It was a tower—tall and stone and spiraling upward with tiny slits for windows crawling up the walls. There was a small archway at the base, and a single and well-worn stone step leading to what must be the front door. She wondered how long it had been here in this strange place—it seemed ancient.

"Peter!" she cried, ignoring the sudden jolt that told her to run away. Why would she want to leave such an amazing sight? She stepped towards the building instead, leaving Peter behind for once, his hand drifting off her shoulder as she moved away from him. "It's amazing," she said in a voice hushed with awe. "What is it called?" Sally paused. What an odd question to ask. Did towers like this even have names?

"Scorem," Peter said as Sally turned to look at him. Her lanky companion was still standing where she had left him, feet locked as if he were unwilling to leave the path, a nervous hand running through his short blonde hair.

Sally cocked her head curiously, wondering why alarm bells were going off somewhere deep in her mind. "Seriously?" When he nodded, she asked slowly, "Peter, why does this tower have my last name?"

"It's important to your family," he told her. Sally tried to decipher the look on his face. She had known Peter almost a year now, and she had never seen him at a loss for words. If Peter could do anything, it was talk—he had convinced her to come out to the middle of nowhere with him to see some fabled tower, after all. Sally looked back at the building, that same odd feeling of pulling and pushing possessing her once more. Peter continued in a low voice, but something about his words seemed practiced now, like a speech he had given many times. "It's always been here, waiting for you to return. Your family needs you."

"My family, huh?" she asked, her mind wandering to the kind faces of the people she had only just started to call mom and dad. "You know I'm adopted, right?"

When Peter said her name again, there was some urgency in it, and Sally realized that she was much closer to the tower. She didn't remember walking towards it, but she must have. There was a sharp hiss behind her, a curse, and then she was standing on the top step, hands reaching out to the wooden door. "Can we climb to the top?" She put her hands out to touch the metal latch that served as a doorknob, and a small part of her was surprised to see that the door was in perfect shape. The wooden door looked as smooth and as newly crafted as if it had been installed that very week. Even the stones seemed fresher up close. Looking at the tower now, Sally wondered how she could have ever thought it old and worn.

"Sally!" a voice called out behind her, but the sound was distant, muffled somehow, and Sally pressed the latch and pushed the door open. It moved easily, as if on oiled hinges, and she stepped through.

"Come on!" she shouted over her shoulder. "I want to see the view from the top before it gets dark." The interior of the tower was dark, darker than it should be with all of those windows. Maybe there were solid floors between her and the windows, or the curve of the tower's ascending stairs blocked the light. She squinted, taking slow steps forward as she waited for her eyes to adjust, but then she heard something that made her stop.

A clinking sound, like metal against stone.

"Is someone in here?" she asked, and then mentally harangued herself. Really?! How much of a horror movie would you like this to be? Anxious, and slightly embarrassed for thinking those things, she waited silently for the noise to come again.

She peered intently into the dim area where the sound had come from, and then the shadows coalesced into a shape that her eyes could identify. It looked like a person, a lean figure spread-eagled against the far wall. It's just a homeless guy, she thought. They must have disturbed a drifter squatting here. "Sorry," she told the man in the dim light. "We didn't mean to bother you."

She looked back over her shoulder then, hoping to see Peter's tall form coming through the door. "Pet--!" but the word died in her throat.

The door was gone.

She spun in a slow circle, certain that she must have somehow gotten turned around.

No. She wasn't confused. The door was gone. All around her were stone walls.

The shape across from her clinked some more, and then a cultured voice said, "Don't suppose they gave you a key, eh?"

Sally stared at the wall, her brain refusing to register what her eyes were telling her as they adjusted to the dim light, details filling in the gray edges of her vision. The man was chained against the far stones. He was bare-chested, lean with muscle and pale skin smeared with soot. A sword leaned against the wall just out of his reach.

And he was staring at her, his green eyes blazing cat-like in the gloom. He must have been chained there for a long time, Sally observed, noting the dirt embedded in the creases of his face. His hair was a mass of waves falling just below his shoulders, and his chin was bearded and unkempt. Her first impulse was to cross the room and try to free him, but then she paused. They didn't always chain up the wrong man.

"Who are you?" she asked in a voice that was far calmer than she felt. Her hands pressed the wall at her back to steady herself, and she found reassurance there, a cold certainty in the stones.

The man's eyes narrowed at her question, and he looked her up and down slowly. She could see his confusion at her jeans, his curiosity at the school logo on the t-shirt she wore, and then his cool assessment as he noted her black sweatshirt and the messenger bag. "I am someone who could use some help, Lady." He eyed her bag again, wrists clanking against the wall as he gestured towards her. "You don't happen to have the key in there, do you?"

"Key?" she repeated dumbly. Who did he think she was? Some kind of magical warden appeared to release him? She felt the wall behind her again, wondering just what the man had seen. Had she just walked through solid stone to his eyes, or had the door been there the entire time, taunting him with freedom just out of reach? She took another look around the room. There was nothing on this level, but there were stairs along the wall to her left, a spiral disappearing into the ceiling and what must be a second floor overhead. Dim light filtered through, and Sally realized that she was standing in a dungeon with a chained prisoner. Peter had led her here and then left her.

The prisoner shook his head slowly, hair like a mane around him, and she realized it was a deep, rich brown when it caught some stray beams of the fading light. "Key," he said again, wrists clanking against the stone as he gestured. "Traditionally used for opening locks?" He paused, then heaved a long suffering sigh. "He never sends me the smartest lackeys, does he? Not that I expect anything else from him…"

"Who is he? Do you mean Peter?" she asked.

The man looked at her, his green eyes suddenly gleaming, his face alight with excitement. "Peter! Peter sent you? Then there is hope! Let me see you, Lady. Come closer!"

Sally didn't understand his sudden optimism, but she obliged, stepping into the center of the room to let the dim light illuminate her features. "Who are you expecting?" she asked him, one hand nervously pushing her hair behind her ear, the other clinging desperately to the strap of her bag.

The stranger studied her features, then wrinkled his brow in confusion. "You say Peter sent you here?" he asked again. Sally nodded, uncertain. "Are you Sara Scorem, then?"

Sally shook her head. "I'm Sally Scorem. Who is Sara Scorem? Is she the one whose family built the tower?"

"In a manner," he said, sniffing the air and squinting at her. "You are not the right one, then." He turned up his lip then in an odd mixture of shaking beard and flashing teeth. "Why did Peter send you then? Did you wrong him somehow?"

"No! We are friends!" She looked around at the dungeon that Peter had sent her into. "Well, I thought we were friends…"

"You have the name," the prisoner said, "and you resemble the old queen a little. All that golden hair, and definitely in the eyes, but no," he said decidedly, "you are not the true Scorem."

Sally chafed a little at that. "Well, I may not be the Scorem you're looking for, but I'm Sally Scorem, and I'm not the one chained to a wall right now. I'd say I'm the one you need right now."

His eyes softened with shame. "I apologize. It's been a long time since I had…decent company."

"How long have you been here?"

He shrugged, the movement a little awkward as his chains rattled. "Long enough, I suppose, to forget my manners around a lovely Lady. Forgive me. I'm not usually so crude."

"No worries," she said, her default response to apologies. Sally glanced around again at the empty room. "How are you still alive? Does someone bring you food?"

The man sniffed dismissively. "He brings me scraps sometimes, but only to tease me with the memory of taste. The place is magic. I can live for a very long time here without food or drink. It's a prison, after all."

"Who? Peter?" Sally asked, trying to envision mild mannered Peter as some kind of demented jailer.

"No!" he insisted. "Peter would never do me harm." He looked at Sally for a second, then grinned, an unspoken memory running across his face, and added, "Well, nothing permanent of course, but no, Peter didn't lock me in here."

"So…?" Sally let the question hang in the air.

"Perhaps you should try to find a key, which might be somewhere upstairs, let me loose, and then I can tell you the entire story on our way back to Garant?" Sally looked up the stairs, listening for any sound up there.

"You think the key is up there?" she asked, head gesturing to the yawning gap where the stairs disappeared into the ceiling. She walked towards the bottom stair as she awaited his reply. "Is anyone up there?"

The man shook his head. "No. The Baron only sends his people every few days or so. They never stay long." Something in his tone made Sally wonder just what happened during those brief visits. The prisoner gestured up the stairs, chains clanking. "I think there is probably a spare key up there though. Just in case."

Sally decided not to press the issue. "Ok," Sally said, taking a few tentative steps up. Still, she never could stop herself from asking questions. "Do I want to know who this Baron is?"

"If you were Sara Scorem, he would be your arch-nemesis," the man said gravely. "But since you are not, he is simply a very bad and powerful man with a lot of influence at the moment. If he finds you here, well…let us just say that there are stories about what the Baron does to the women who fall into his hands."

Sally shuddered. "Well then, let's not stick around to meet him," she said, ascending. She tried not to imagine running into guards up there, seeing them drag her across some distant castle foyer to face a red-faced man with empty eyes.

The room on the second floor was simple, the stairs continuing up the wall, a small table and chair, and a wooden door that resembled the one she had walked through downstairs. The ceiling here was much taller, but there was another wooden ceiling above her head. She didn't see any keys, nor was there anywhere to hide them, so she took the stairs up to the next level.

This room was smaller, but only because it was crowded with furniture. An old bed and blankets gray with dust and cobwebs, sat near a tall wooden dresser. She was about to search the inside of the dresser when she spied the small wooden box on top of a small table next to the bed. The lid opened easily enough, and inside was a key ring with two keys on it. They were old keys, made of iron and crafted after the fashion Sally imagined a medieval key must have looked like. One of these had to be the key the prisoner needed. She scanned the room once more, then glanced at the stairs. If the tower was the same as the one she had walked into with Peter, then the stairs going up would reach the top.

She climbed quickly, thinking it was probably foolish but knowing that she would probably never get another chance, and when she stepped out on the top floor, it was empty. She stepped over to one of the window slits, gasping as she peered out.

Trees, so many trees, and a river glimmering in the distance like a satin ribbon draped across the land. Beyond the forest and the river was a castle. An honest, straight-out-of-a-fairy-tale castle. Sally pinched herself to be sure. She grunted at the pain, but she didn't wake up. The castle was still there, gleaming white and gold in the distance. She wondered if the castle came with a prince. The man had mentioned an evil Baron. There had to be a handsome heroic prince to match.

Yeah, and there is probably a princess to match, her mind retorted. You're not the Scorem they are looking for. No doubt any prince here is waiting for her. Sally thought of her foster parents again, and how eager she had been to please them. She had learned the names of all of their family, aunts and uncles and cousins, but no one had ever mentioned a Sara. Sally wondered if Peter and the prisoner had made a mistake somehow. Maybe they really were looking for her.

Yeah, because you're really some long lost princess. Sally pictured her biological mother, face streaked with mascara and glitter as she tossed back yet another shot before heading back on stage. Ok fine, she admitted. I'm no heroine. But I can certainly rescue a man from a dungeon. And that's pretty cool for a Tuesday afternoon. She nodded once, taking in the view one last time, before turning back to the stairs. Now that she had a plan, she felt more in control of the situation. Besides, she was the one with the key.

As she made her way back down to the dungeon and the prisoner, Sally reminded herself that not all fantasies followed the rules. Just because this place looked like something out of the many J.R.R. Tolkien stories she'd read through the years did not mean that she knew what to expect.

She stepped cautiously back down into the dim light, noting how time seemed to have slowed down in this place. She thought the sun should have set by now, and yet it was still the same hazy afternoon sun under which she and Peter had walked while traveling in the woods on their way to the tower. The man had mentioned magic.

Maybe time was affected by it.

"I found some keys," she announced, hopping down the last two steps and walking close to him.

"I knew it!" He moved his wrists the few inches in her direction. "The Baron will be furious when they find me gone. I wish I could see the look on his face when they tell him!" He was grinning now, eager.

Sally paused, keys in hand. "Why did he lock you up anyway?"

"I was waiting for her," he shrugged, clanking again. "It's what I do. The Baron said if I was determined to linger about the tower, then he wanted to be sure that I would always do my duty. It was a big joke." There was bitterness in him now, a long suffering anger.

"Your duty to wait for her? Sara Scorem, you mean?" When he nodded, she peered at him. "If you're supposed to stay here, then what does it matter if you're locked up?"

"That's something the Baron would say," he observed, his eyes squinting, taking measure of her again. He paused, and then sighed, defeated. "I would wonder at your loyalties, Lady Sally, if I hadn't seen you appear out of nowhere. Then again, the Baron does employ several very good magicians."

"You think the Baron sent me?" she asked, leaning down to pick up the sword leaning against the wall near him. "Why would he do that?" The weapon was heavy.

The man sagged in his restraints. "Who knows? Perhaps it would amuse him to taunt me with a different tactic."

"I am not a tactic," she declared, fumbling with the sword to get it in front of her in some sort of defensive position. "I'm the woman with the key, and I am going to release you." She held the sword out in what she hoped was a menacing way. "And I have your sword, so don't try anything."

The man gave her a look, sighed again, and said, his voice formal, "I will not harm you, Lady."

Sally stepped forward and grabbed his manacled wrist. There was a jolt that ran through her arm and she yelped. She didn't let go, but she was suddenly very aware of him there in the dim dungeon, a bare-chested man chained to a wall, dirty hair framing a face that might be handsome if exposed to soap and water and maybe a razor. He was staring at her with fascination, eyes wide, and she took a slow breath, sword lowered to her side.

He wouldn't hurt her, she knew suddenly. Kannin wouldn't hurt anyone without cause, least of all her, her mind told her.

The sword fell to the floor with a loud clang, but to Sally, the sound was distant, far away and unimportant.

Kannin? She knew that was his name. Kannin Song, her mind supplied, as if she had known it all along. He was looking at her, intense eyes burning into hers. "Your name is Kannin," she said in a low voice, her hand holding his wrist as her other hand shoved the key home. She had to release him. It wasn't right for him to be chained to a wall. "I know you," she said, wiggling the key in the lock, fiercely working at the metal as she waited for the small click of release. "How do I know you?"

"You are not Sally Scorem," he replied, eyes locked on her face. "You are Nevada Sally Harris." The manacle came open with a pop, and Sally jerked away from his words.

"My name is Sally Scorem," she hissed, memories surfacing of the awful years in foster care, carrying the burden of her mother's stage name. The Scorems had taken her in, claimed her, loved her, shared their name. She hadn't been Nevada Harris since she was ten years old. How did this stranger know her real name anyway?

Kannin caught her wrist as she moved away, his first motion as a free man to wrap long, strong fingers around in her in a gentle, but firm grip. She was very aware of him again, every one of her senses recognizing him. She had expected his hands to be rough, no doubt calloused from using the sword, but his skin was smooth. "Yes," he agreed, "and no." He seemed to have forgotten that one arm was free, caught up in some moment that Sally didn't really understand.

Maybe it was magic. It must be magic.

"You are yourself," Kannin said after a pause, "and you are my kevashin."

"What is a kevashin?" she asked, and refused to listen when her mind tried to supply the answer, but the moment seemed to be ending, the world catching up with them again. He let her go then, grabbing for the manacle still swinging from the wall. He removed the key, and used it to free his other wrist. Sally moved away from him, head still reeling from the unexpected mental connection. "And what the hell was that?"

The second manacle bounced loudly off the stone wall, and Kannin stood straight against the wall, arms stretched above his head, a low groan of pure satisfaction escaping his throat as he moved. "Come on," he told her, gaining surety with each step he took away from the wall that had been his prison cell. "They will know that I am free and come this way. We should not be here when they arrive."

"Who? The Baron?" she asked, and then he grabbed her hand, tugging her up the steps behind him. "Wait!" she said, gesturing to the sword that she had dropped at some point during the weird episode, "Your sword!" She had half turned around to retrieve it, but he did not let go of her hand.

"It's not my sword," he said, and she stopped, turning back to face him.

"But…" she let the words trail off.

"I don't use a sword," he said, as if she should know that, and then tugged gently on her fingers. "We should go."

She followed, but her eyes went back to the blade once more before they cleared the ceiling. "Whose sword is it then? Why was it leaning against the wall next to you like that?"

Kannin shrugged, climbing slowly but gaining confidence with each step. "I imagine it belonged to the former prisoner of this place. I think the Baron left it there to taunt me, not that it did much good. A sword is nothing but a few feet of metal to me. I am as likely to stab myself with it as anyone else." As they reached the top of the stairs, he glanced around then walked purposefully to the door. Sally followed numbly, still joined to him through their linked hands. He seemed to have forgotten that he was holding on to her, and until she had crossed over to the door with him, she hadn't noticed either. It seemed perfectly natural to hold on to Kannin. Sally tried to figure out what that meant as he reached for the door handle, raising the dark metal with a snick of release that was suddenly loud in the room.

When the door slid open easily, he sighed, a relieved sound that betrayed his tension. After establishing that they could in fact leave this place, he looked around the room again. "Did you go upstairs?" he asked, head gesturing towards the ceiling.

"Not much there. A dresser and a bed. And then a tower room with nothing at all."

"A dresser?" He looked down at their hands, seemed to decide something, and then released her. "Wait here," he ordered, and Sally bristled a little at his tone. He ran up the stairs before she could respond, lithe and graceful as if he hadn't just spent a long time chained to a wall. Something really weird was going on here, she thought, but she would wait until they got outside to figure it out. If the Baron knew she had released his prisoner, he would come to investigate, and Sally wanted to be safely back home when he arrived.

Home.

She looked back down the stairs into the gloomy dungeon. She had come into this place through the wall down there. She heard Kannin returning down the stairs, light feet practically running.

"Hey," she said without looking up, "shouldn't I go back down there if I want to go home? That's where I came in."

"You can't get home that way," Kannin said.

"How do you know?"

"It's the magic," he told her, as if that should explain everything. "Portals don't work that way, especially portals inside watch spells."

Sally looked up at him then. "English, please?" She had planned to say more, but she stopped at the sight before her. He had returned wearing a dark blue robe, a black tunic peeking out from beneath the collar, a thin belt tied at the waist. The long sleeves tapered to a point over his wrists, and she could see the dark outline of his pants where the material split in the front and back. He looked like a wizard.

"Where is your hat?"

"My hat?"

"Your hat," she repeated, unable to stifle a little giggle. This was really getting to be too much. "Your pointy wizard hat." Castles, dungeons, barons, wizards. What the hell had Peter gotten her into? At that, she started to really get going, laughter erupting in sudden, heavy snorts. It wasn't that he looked silly. He didn't. He actually looked quite nice. He had somehow managed to clean himself up in the last moments as well. His hair was brushed, falling gently to his shoulders, and his face was shaved, revealing a jawline and thin lips that were quirked up at her hilarity.

He ran a hand through his hair, then cocked his head at her, "I do not customarily wear a hat, Sally." He paused, "Though I suppose I could if you want me to."

"Oh no," she managed between peels of her now-fading laughter.

"You're good. How?" Then she was laughing again, nervous and a little unhinged. "How did you do it?"

"Do what?"

"Get clean?"

He huffed, shoulders straightening a little. "I'm a wizard, Lady, and if I can't clean myself up with a simple spell, then I should go back downstairs and chain myself back up against that wall."

"So why didn't you use your magic to escape?"

His face grew distant. "It's a bit more complicated than that." At her blank look, he added, "Opening portals within containment barriers can lead to infinite loops. You can't really go anywhere if you're still inside everywhere. Magic like that is quite perilous."

Sally felt like she had walked into a physics lecture in the middle of a review for finals. "Oh," she said, laughter fizzing up again, "well, that explains everything." She put a hand to her eyes, trying to block out the gray haze of laughter-tears that were threatening to overcome her vision.

"I assure you that it was quite impossible to escape that place without the key," he said, but the offended tone had left his voice.

"Oh, well in that case," Sally took a few hiccupping breaths, calming down, "can you magic me up a drink of water? I'm a little light-headed here."

He was next to her immediately, hands grasping hers. He flipped her hands palms up, and held her wrists with gentle fingers. "I am so sorry," he whispered. "I forget how the magic affects others." Sally nodded, finding it comforting that he seemed to be taking her pulse.

"It's been a strange afternoon," she admitted, head swimming. "I'll be fine in a minute."

"Come," he said, and then his arm was around her back, his other arm swinging down to her legs, and he lifted her with a smooth gesture Sally had never experienced outside of a romance novel.

"Seriously?" she asked, her head pillowed against his chest. He smelled good for a man who had just gotten out of a dungeon. What had she been thinking to moan about promised princes? She could definitely get used to wizards.

"It's probably the magic," he said, walking to the door. "It can be overwhelming the first few times."

"Ok," Sally said, closing her eyes, happy to sink into his arms and just exist for the moment without thinking about the future. She felt him moving, but his arms were solid around her. She had never been carried as an adult before. It was quite pleasant for the time being, but she could see how it would get old after a while. Maybe, she decided, feeling the sunlight hit her face as they left the tower. He continued walking, much farther than she thought necessary to reach the surrounding forest, and she opened her eyes. His face was calm above her, and the sky above him was dim, the last of the evening light above them. She turned to her left and saw the tree-line approaching, but there was something hazy between them and it. They approached the haze, and then he set her gently on her feet.

"It's better if you walk through on your own," he told her. "That way the magic knows to release you."

"Release me?" Sally repeated. She was tired of not knowing what was going on, but she obeyed without further question. She took a few tentative steps forward into the haze. There was a low popping sound that she felt deep in her ears. She swallowed hard and kept walking, and then she was free. Her limbs moved normally again, and she took a few halting steps away, surprised by how much she had been affected inside the radius of the magic. Her head cleared, and she turned around. The tower was still behind her, but distant and clouded behind a swirling mass of color. She saw Kannin standing just on this side of the line, face serious as he studied something. She still felt oddly drawn to him, this strange man she had freed, and she frowned a little. She had thought maybe that was part of the magic too.

What had he called her—his kevashin? The word meant something to her, deep in her subconscious, but it was different now, harder to call to the surface, and she let it lay. The day had been long enough.

"Are you well?" Kannin asked, studying her as he approached.

"I feel much better now."

"Good."

Sally stood there, awkward in the fading light. They seemed to have rejoined the regular world of time. "Ummm…" she tried, then stopped. What next?

Kannin smiled a little. "'Um' indeed, Sally." He gave the woods and then the sky a calculating look. "No doubt you want to get home, yes?"

Sally nodded, desperate to get home to things familiar and

expected. She ignored the tiny voice inside that cried out in protest at the idea of being somewhere that this man was not. So what if he had carried her out of the magic tower like some fairy princess? She was being ridiculous. "Can you do that?" she asked him. "Can you send me home?"

Now it was his turn to nod, and the confidence expressed in that single gesture made her stomach stop spinning. She nearly sagged with relief as her unspoken terror faded. She was not stuck in this strange place. She would go home. That tiny voice shrieked a little, but she ignored it. "The portal spell is quite simple," he told her. "But it cannot be done right away," he added. "I need supplies."

Sally looked at the trees around them, then back at the tower. "Where can we get these supplies?"

He gestured deeper into the woods. "The castle is that way, but we do not want to go back there." He looked in the opposite direction, and Sally could just see the tops of a distant mountain range peeking over the trees. "I will definitely need a better spot to cast. The spell works best in certain locations. There is a place that will serve, but it's not nearby – a few days' journey from here."

Sally tried to ignore the small thrill that ran through her at the thought of spending a few days in the woods with Kannin. She was not a teenager, she reminded herself. She was a woman who needed to get back home. Still, a few nights by a fire with a handsome wizard could be nice.

"And what about these supplies?" she asked.

Kannin looked at her and smiled. "We will be walking through the Hanlin Forest," he said. "Jerem will find us."

~~~

The mysterious Jerem found them on the second night. Sally was sitting in front of the fire, huddling against the chill evening air. Kannin had sat next to her the previous night, sharing body warmth and closeness that eased Sally's mind in a way that went beyond practicality. His very presence soothed her. She wanted to ask why, to demand he tell her everything, starting with this kevashin business, but that first night she had just slept instead, tired and out of sorts. The entire day had passed without much conversation as they walked, and Sally hadn't complained. Kannin had fed her a warm soup that he concocted from some shrubbery in the morning, and throughout the day they snacked on berries. It had been a pleasant journey, though Sally wanted to know more about her traveling companion. She had decided to talk to him when they camped that night.

She helped Kannin gather wood for their fire, glad to contribute in some way, and watched as he stacked it in a little tripod, each stick crossing the other at an acute angle. He let her help a little, seeing her interest, but when she shivered in the growing gloom, her sweatshirt already zipped up and the cold seeping through, he said a word and held his hands over the pile. There was a flash of light, and then the sticks were on fire. She laughed in delight, amazed at such magic. They had used her lighter the first night, a device that excited Kannin so much that she had told him to keep it. She didn't smoke after all. It was just an old habit to carry a lighter in her bag. You never know, she had told friends. It might come in handy someday, you know, when I have to burn the ropes and escape! The idea of her using a lighter in some clever way had been funny then, a fantasy, and yet here she was in the middle of the woods, giving her fire to a guy that could use magic.

"So," she said as she sat back from the fire, not willing to wait any more and lose her nerve, she asked, "who are you really?"

"I am Kannin," he replied, folding his legs and sitting beside her, arm going around her shoulders.

"I know that," she said. "But that's all I seem to know." She considered for a moment, her list of questions surfacing as she stared into the fire, and then ran with the first thing that came to mind. "Peter," she said simply, glancing over at Kannin. "What is Peter's role in all of this?"

The wizard nodded. "Peter is looking for Sara Scorem. He is tasked with bringing her to the tower to send her home."

"So, Peter is from here then?" She glanced around at the forest, so similar to the woods back home and yet so very different. "Wherever here is?"

Kannin nodded again. "He is, but he has been gone a long time." He held her hand up to the light cast from the fire, fingers gently caressing her palm. "You should be flattered, you know. He obviously thought you were the Scorem, or he would not have sent you through."

Sally tried to ignore the small stirrings of desire roused by the wizard's gentle touch and focus on his words. "So he's a wizard too?" she asked.

Kannin scoffed, putting her hand down on her lap and sitting back, hands stretched behind him. "Hardly. Peter is good at finding things, but he cannot use magic. Some would say that Peter's gift is what remains of magic these days."

"What do you mean? You seem to have plenty of magic."

Kannin gave a pleased laugh, sitting up and grinning at her. "That I do, Lady. There are few with my skills alive these days."

"And so modest!" she laughed, pushing him away with mock disgust. She considered, "So, Peter's gift made him ideal for finding Sara."

"Yes, but he is not the only one looking." At Sally's look of complete confusion, he added, "Several people with similar gifts were sent to find her. The tower is a standing portal—people can come back here through that one, but they need someone like Peter to help them find it. The magic is very good at hiding itself from the natives."

"Oh," Sally said, trying to follow his meaning. "It did feel odd when we got close to it, like it wanted me to come closer and also wanted me to go away."

"That makes sense. The magic would be erratic. It is not likely that the Scorem is there anyway. In fact, I think Peter is the only one in your world right now," Kannin explained, as if Sally should understand what he meant. It took her a moment.

Sally stared at him, pieces falling into place. "You say that as though there are other worlds." Kannin gave her a look then, and a smile crossed her face as she considered the possibilities. "You mean there are other worlds?"

"Of course," he replied. "I suppose your world hasn't discovered that yet, or the tower there might be in danger. There are other towers, too, echoes of this one, placed in as many worlds as we can find."

"You have no idea where Sara Scorem is, then?" Sally shivered at the thought of being lost in another world, and then smirked at the irony. Kannin put an arm around her shoulder again, pulling her close. She snuggled against him, grateful for his company.

"It's a long story. Suffice it to say she was lost in the chaos, and people have been trying to find her for many years." He paused, and seemed to contemplate his next words. He shook his head again, saying, "No one has found the real Sara Scorem yet."

"But you said you were waiting for her in the dungeon. Were you actually expecting her? Are you supposed to…I don't know…rescue her or something?"

Kannin laughed at that, arm tightening around her shoulder. "Oh no! I am no rescuer of the Scorem. No, I am just a simple man who needed a job."

"A job?"

He tensed as if embarrassed, but then shrugged. "They needed someone to watch for her. I said I could do it. Easier for a wizard, after all. It's not like the time is going to affect me, or the magic."

"What do you mean?"

"The tower is magical," he explained. "Time slows way down there. As a wizard, I'm not affected by it. Others…well," he looked down at her, "you felt it. What was it like?"

Sally had spent most of the day thinking about her time in the tower, that is, the rest of the time she hadn't spent staring at Kannin's back and thinking ridiculous thoughts. "It was weird," she said, knowing how feeble that was. "I was fine at first, but then everything seemed to stretch out a little bit. And then I touched you…" her voice trailed off, and then she gave him a serious look. "Kevashin," she repeated the word. "I touched you, and I knew your name without asking, and you knew mine, and you said that I was your kevashin. What is that?"

Kannin paused, seeming to weigh his words before speaking, but then he nodded. "It means—"

A throat cleared behind them, and a voice said, "Am I interrupting anything here?" Kannin and Sally whirled around. When he saw the speaker, Kannin's face broke into a smile.

"Jerem!" Kannin said, raising his arms in a gesture of welcome and warmth. He stood and walked to greet him. "I knew you would find us, old friend."

Sally stared at the newcomer with wide eyes, taking in the elongated ears that peeked out above a shock of brown hair. An elf, her brain insisted, like out of a fairy tale. While she struggled to process this new shock, her mind continued to assess Kannin's old friend. Jerem wasn't bad looking, she decided, a bit bigger through the shoulders than Kannin, his shape accentuated by the leather armor covering his black tunic. His hair was a bit shaggy as he tucked it behind his ears, his light eyes carefully taking in the scene, and she saw that he carried a lot of weapons—a sword at each hip, a bow slung over one shoulder, a dangerous looking knife in his hand as he idly cleaned his fingernails. His face was serious in a way that made Sally wonder if the elf ever smiled.

"You are lucky that I found you," he observed, with a look at the fire. "What are you thinking, man, to build a fire in the middle of these woods?"

"I knew you would find us if I did," Kannin smirked, and then shifted so that he was facing both Sally in front of him on the ground and Jerem to his left. "And it is cold. Jerem, I want you to meet Sally Scorem."

The elf jerked a little at the name, and he gave her a closer look, but then his face relaxed, his eyes narrowed in scrutiny, "Sally, you say?"

Kannin nodded. "Peter sent her through the tower. I can see why. She does resemble the old queen, but she is not Sara."

"No, she is not," the elf agreed. He gave Kannin an appraising look then. "Did something happen, then?"

"The Baron happened." He grimaced. "I was sleeping. I know I should have set a watch, but nothing had happened in so long…." He sniffed, "Well, they caught me."

"How long?" Jerem asked, his face a mask of concentration and deep concern now.

Kannin shrugged, gazing into the dark forest. "It is passed May Day already, yes?"

Jerem's face was suddenly very pale. "Halfway to All Hallows."

Kannin took a slow breath and let it out with a puff of air. "I thought as much."

"How long, man?" Jerem knelt before them, concern blossoming into something like horror. "I have not seen you since the spring festival. I did not know you were gone…I did not think to ask."

"It is fine," Kannin assured him. "Why would you?"

Jerem shook his head. "I should have come to check when you were not at the May Day ceremony. I just assumed…" The elf looked at Sally and then at the way Kannin's hand had found hers at some point during the conversation, and let the thought end there. "Four months?" he asked, shoulders sagging.

Kannin nodded. "It is fine, I said. You cannot be responsible for me. I am a grown man!" Sally felt something deep in her stomach turn over at the thought of four months chained to that wall. She would have lost her mind.

The elf gave Kannin a look that spoke of a long friendship. "Barely out of nappies," he muttered. Sally got the impression this was an old joke between them, and she wondered if elves here lived as long as the ones she had read about.

"Hardly," the young man next to her snapped, a broad grin on his face. "And I am a wizard," Kannin added, his face sobering. "I should have been fine. I just got sloppy."

"And this Lady rescued you, then?" Jerem glanced at Sally, a polite inquiry on his face. It wasn't friendly, nothing like the camaraderie she had glimpsed during his banter with Kannin.

Kannin grinned proudly. "I am going to send her home," he said. "But we have to get to Hisselak Mountain. That's where the lines are stronger. And I need some help," he paused, then a silent look passed between the two men, "for after."

"Sure. I can help." He looked at their small campfire, at their lack of camping gear, and unslung his bow and bag. "Here." He rooted in the bag and came out with some dried jerky. Sally's mouth watered. Herb soup and berries were enough to live on, but her stomach growled at the thought of meat. She took a small bite, uncertain at first about the strange set of spices, but when it proved to be delicious, she ate the rest in a few quick bites.

"Thanks," she said, and when the elf tilted his head in response, she decided to ask, "So is it your job to watch these woods the way Kannin is supposed to watch the tower?"

Jerem shrugged. "I suppose. It is my job to watch this kingdom, and this forest is a big part of the kingdom."

"So you travel these woods often?" she asked, and when Jerem nodded in assent, she added, unable to help herself, "And you haven't been here in four months because…?" Jerem winced at that, and he glanced again at their joined hands, then up at Kannin. The man studiously avoided meeting the elf's gaze.

"Forgive me, Lady," Jerem said. "I should have come sooner."

"Yes, you should have," Sally snapped, slow fire of anger burning in her chest at the thought of Kannin chained to that wall day after day. Part of her knew that this reaction wasn't right, that she shouldn't care so much about a man she just met, but she couldn't help herself. The anger was there and so real it couldn't be ignored.

"It's not his fault," Kannin said, giving her a pointed look as he raised her hand to his lips and kissed it. "I told you that time is different there. He couldn't have known." Yes, she thought, time was slower there, which meant that he had been there even longer than four months. How could he possibly be so cheerful after that? She tightened her hand on his, glad to feel his reassuring squeeze.

Later that night, as Sally fell asleep snuggled next to Kannin, a small part of her was annoyed that Jerem was there to disturb the time she had to ask questions, but she was relieved to know that someone was standing guard at the same time. She was sure that Kannin could protect them, but Jerem had a lot of weapons, and Sally had seen the casual way he handled them. There was an elf who knew how to use a sword. She was glad that Kannin wouldn't be alone after she went home. She tried not to think too hard about her sudden protectiveness for a stranger. It must be magic of some kind, and when she got home, if she ever got home, she hoped she would forget all about it.

~~~

They traveled for two more days, and Sally learned a little bit more about her strange companions. She learned that she was not the first almost Sara Scorem to come through the tower over the years. She got the distinct impression that neither man wanted to talk about the others, and she let the matter drop, deciding that she didn't really want to know either. She forced herself to stop wondering about them, and focused instead on what she could learn. Jerem wasn't nearly as forthcoming as Kannin, but the former prisoner opened up even more as they drew closer to the mountain he needed to call the portal that would send her home.

He had known Jerem since childhood, he had told her. The elf was like a brother to him, an older brother who had long since given up teaching him how to use any weapons.

"Besides," Kannin said, flashing Sally a bright smirk, "once I got my magic under control, I didn't need weapons."

"So if you don't even need weapons, how did the Baron manage to catch you?" Sally quipped.

Kannin shrugged in the offhand manner she was growing to know. "Well, that's magic. No comparison to the weapons Jerem uses. No one can cut me with a sword, if I'm paying attention," he boasted, "but someone can hit me with a spell, and if they know their business, I may be in trouble."

Sally nodded, trying to understand. He had shown her some of his magic, the fire he could conjure, the light bolts he could fire that stuck trees with a meaty thunk, the way he could lift her off the ground to hover in the air before setting her back down again. He had cleaned her clothes and fixed her hair with a few words. "I appreciate it, really, but it doesn't beat a shower and a washing machine," Sally had told him, looking down at her clean clothes and feeling her tangle free hair. "Not to mention a bath…"

Kannin had winked at her then, and Sally had grinned back, both of them thinking of hot soapy water and sponges squeezed over bare flesh.

She tried not to think about that now as they took a short rest while Jerem scouted ahead. She seized on a random subject instead. "So, what's May Day?"

Kannin glanced at her sharply. His hand ran through his hair, a nervous gesture she was starting to recognize, a sign that he didn't really want to talk about the topic. "It's a festival," he said vaguely, then turned to scan the trees for Jerem. When the elf didn't return immediately, Kannin sighed, then turned to face her and sat down heavily in front of her. "He told you, did he?"

Sally looked around at the surrounding trees. "Who—Jerem? Told me what?"

Kannin nodded meaningfully at her, both hands holding hers. Sally leaned in to him, serious now. "He told you about May Day."

Sally shook her head. "No, you mentioned it when he first arrived." She glanced in the direction the elf had gone. "He wouldn't tell me anything," she said. "He barely notices me. I was just curious."

Kannin seemed to doubt her for a moment, then his gaze went to their hands, and Sally suddenly knew that he knew that she was telling the truth. It was an odd feeling, and she resisted the urge to pull away from him. He seemed to sense that too and he released her hands, letting them rest on her crossed knees. He was nodding again, face solemn. "May Day is a special festival," he said, "for couples."

Sally had an idea of where this was heading. "And Jerem didn't expect to see you there because…?" She let the thought trail off, her mind filling in the blanks with all of the normal responses. Because I am afraid of commitment. Because I can't get involved with anyone right now. Because it's not you, it's me.

"Because I had not found my kevashin," he said instead, "and there were some who thought that I was foolish to wait."

"What do you mean? You were foolish to wait for what, Kannin?"

"Wizards live a very long time," he said, trying to explain, "and some people think that we should…" he paused, face reddening a little, but then he forged ahead, "Some think that we should try to spread the magic around a little more freely than I was willing to." He looked at her then, face hard with some remembered outrage. "I will not lie with women desperate for a magical bloodline. I will not serve as stud for someone willing to betray kevashin for a bastard child who may not even have the gift."

Sally stared at him, shock fading as his words sunk in. "Magic is precious here then? And rare?" she asked. Kannin nodded, obviously relieved that she had understood him. She smiled at him then, "You sure that you didn't go to the May Day Festival just once maybe? Just for a good time, maybe?" She winked at him, trying to lighten the mood. He furrowed his brow in mock-contempt and snorted.

"Well, as I said, wizards live a very long time, and I was not always as wise as I am now. I was once a very young and foolish wizard." He gave her a serious look then, as if feeling the sudden jolt that went through her at the thought of him with another woman. "I have never participated in the ceremony," he told her, a finger tracing her chin as he lifted her face to his. "I was waiting."

"Waiting?" she asked in a hushed, breathless voice. His face was very close to hers now. "For what?"

"For you," he replied, and then he kissed her. Sally barely had time to register the feeling of his lips on hers when she heard the unmistakable sounds of the elf's return.

She cursed as Kannin pulled away, biting her lip as she imagined sneaking away with him after the May Day festival and finding a secluded place where no elves could interrupt them.

~~~

It was foolish, Sally told herself. She was leaving this man in a day. So what did it hurt to fantasize then? It didn't matter what she told herself; Kannin was growing dearer to her every hour.

So when they finally reached the mountain, and Jerem led them up and around to a cliff overlooking a sheer drop, Sally felt her skin grow cold.

"Well, here we are," Kannin said, and his face grew tight. "Let me get things ready." He let go of her hand reluctantly, but then his expression grew stern, and he left to kneel down by the edge, no doubt checking to see if the portal spell would work. Sally tried to blame her sudden chill on the heights, but she couldn't hide her disappointment. She would be going home soon. She would leave Kannin behind.

"Do not worry," the elf said behind her, "He is very good at portals. He will get you home in one piece."

"Oh, I know that," she replied, "I trust him."

"I see that." He paused, glanced over her shoulder at where Kannin still knelt, head bowed in concentration, and then gave her a hard look. His long pause suggested some kind of inner battle, but then he added, "You more than trust him."

Sally felt her cheeks coloring in embarrassment. Was it that obvious? "He's sending me home," she defended. "I appreciate him."

The elf smirked, and it was the first hint of humor she had seen from him. Jerem could be coolly polite and friendly, but he wasn't exactly a beacon of hilarity. "You do not need to lie to me, Lady. I know what I am looking at." Sally stared at him, waiting for him to continue. "I know he feels it, poor fool, but I was not sure about you until just now."

"Sure about what?" Sally asked, turning to face Kannin's back as he continued to kneel on the edge. He seemed to be whispering some words, hands moving in a careful way.

"You love him," Jerem said. It was not a question.

Sally sighed.

"So what?" She turned away from Kannin's back, not watching the hair flying around his head in the light breeze. "I mean, it's ridiculous. I just met him."

"And yet," Jerem said, and his face was soft then, lit with an expression Sally didn't think often crossed the elf's face, "there it is. Kevashin."

"That word again," Sally groaned. "What is it? No—I don't want to know." She bit her lip, looking at her feet. "I'm going home. I can't…"

"I see," Jerem agreed. "This world is no place for you. You have to go."

Sally looked up then, meeting Jerem's gaze. There it was then. She had known that there was no real way for her to stay, no reason to stay, but hearing it from the elf had doused some small fire of hope that still burned in her belly. "I know," she said, and her voice was a hoarse whisper. She gave Jerem a searching look then, "Will you take care of him?"

The elf nodded.

"I'm serious," she demanded. "Take care of him. Make sure he's ok. Do not forget about him for four months."

"I will, Lady," Jerem said, hand raised to his breast in a formal oath.

"Thank you." Sally walked away from him then, moving closer to where Kannin knelt. The height made her dizzy, but she sat a few feet from the edge, waiting for her kevashin to finish his preparations. She watched the wizard work, seeing the intensity of his concentration as his fingers traced arcane patterns in the air, and soon she saw a slow swirl of energy appearing before his hands. He continued, and the small patch of light stretched out in a long cord to a space a few feet away from the cliff's edge. The space began to spin a little, hazy at first, and then the air itself bubbled into a slow whirlpool of power that made Sally's skin prickle. There was a hum as well, a low sound that made her ears ache a little until she swallowed.

She must have made some small sound of pain, because then Kannin was there, his hand holding hers again, reassuring in its simple presence, and he finished his work with one hand. The wind picked up slowly, tangling her hair.

When Kannin made the last gesture, there was a loud popping sound that echoed in Sally's teeth, and he turned away from the edge. His face was drawn, exhausted with effort, and she moved towards him, hands pulling him down to sit before he fell down.

"Kannin!" she shouted at him. "What is it?"

"'S fine," he slurred, eyes out of focus. "I made sure it would be safe. Portals…tricky things. I made sure."

Jerem knelt next to them, and she gave him a desperate look, "Is this normal? Does he always look like this?"

"No, portals come easily to him." The elf shook his head, lip curling up in a proud smile. "He did this for you, Sally. He exhausted himself making sure that the portal was solid, that there was no chance for you to go somewhere else."

Sally gaped at him. "Somewhere else? When were you guys going to tell me about that?"

"There was no need," Jerem tried to explain, but the wind was rising, and Sally had to strain to make out his words. "He could be sure. Most wizards would not risk it though. It took a dozen wizards to make the portal that brought you here—and they killed themselves in the process. Now, wizards make a connection and you just hope it gets you where you want to go. It is the price people pay for quick transportation, but there are ways to be sure. Kannin knows them. It takes a lot of energy though." Jerem gave her a pointed look. "He did it for you."

Sally nodded, heart tweaking a little more as she realized that this man, this stranger, had risked his life working a spell to send her home. "Thank you, Kannin," she told the man sitting on the ground next to her. Kannin was still far away, face dazed, but at the sound of her voice, his eyes focused, and he stared at her, a look of such longing creasing his face.

"I would have proudly taken you at the May Day Festival, you know," he told her in a dreamy voice. "I would have seen you standing with the other women, lighting a candle for me, and then," and here, his voice dropped lower, and Jerem stood up, walking away to give them some privacy, "Then I would have taken you to my bed," Kannin finished, a gleam in his eyes that Sally could learn to appreciate.

"I wish you could have," she told him, that feeling of ridiculousness fading away. What did it matter anyway? She was leaving. Even sitting on the ground so far away, she could feel the portal pulling at her, insisting that she go that way, that she stand up, gravity be damned, run and jump into the yawning emptiness that would lead her home. There was something else tugging at her as well, a solid cord leading from her wrist to Kannin's, and for a moment, she thought she might be torn in half by the two forces.

"I will miss you!" she yelled at Kannin, memorizing his face as she felt herself being pulled away from him. Her body was standing up, her feet taking slow reluctant steps away. He rose with her, his whole body wobbling, and she was suddenly terrified that he would fall off the cliff. She clung to his hand, pulling him a few steps away from the edge, away from the magic pulling at her to run.

Kannin said something, but the wind was too loud for her to hear. She tried to ask him to repeat himself, but then everything slowed down, time doing a strange pause, and she heard his low voice in her head. His lips weren't moving, but she heard him quite clearly.

"You were not the one everyone is waiting for, but you are the one I need."

She smiled at him, nodding in agreement. She was going to say something, to reply, but then he was pressed against her, lips meeting hers in a kiss that Sally felt in her entire body. It was soft and sweet and everything she had ever dreamed of in a kiss, and then she was being pulled inside out, and everything else was silence.

~~~

Kannin stood there for a long moment, skin tingling with the magic all around him, lips still warm where Sally had been before she was drawn into the portal. He knew she was safe. He could feel it. Just as he could feel the empty place inside himself where she used to be. It was a small thing now, he knew, but it would grow. It would consume him.

"Kevashin," a voice said, and Kannin turned to look at Jerem.

"So?"

"So?" The elf shook his head. "Silly little brother. You find your kevashin and you just let her go?"

"What else could I do?" Kannin asked. "She wasn't Sara Scorem. You know how it is. I had to send her home before they found her." He looked out over the abyss where the portal still swirled, the magic slowing, but still very present. He would suffer for the magic he had used today, but it was worth it. Sending Sally home was worth it.

"You know what will happen to you now," Jerem observed. "Without her, you will fade."

"It is alright," Kannin told him. "I have had a good life."

Jerem grabbed his shoulder then and shook him a little. "Without you, she will fade."

"Her world has no magic. She will not be affected by it," Kannin said, but something in his stomach ached at the thought.

"Are you sure of that?" Jerem asked.

Kannin nodded. "She told me. They have technology."

Jerem shook his head. "And in this world without magic of any kind, Peter managed to send her through the portal to the tower."

Kannin gave the elf a desperate look then, a horrible thought surfacing. "What are you saying?"

"I am saying that you are a foolish little man, but lucky for you, I am here to help you." The elf looked at the portal, the circle a little smaller now, still spinning a few feet away from the edge. He pointed his finger at it. "Go."

The power was magnetic, the portal tugged at him as they always did, but he gave the spell a critical look. He had made a strong connection to her world, sure, but it should have faded away by now. The magic wasn't supposed to work like this; it must be a glitch in the spell. Glitch, he thought with a grin—it was one of her words. He had known her only a few days and already he was picking up her odd turns of phrase. He stood in the midst of the flood of magic, suddenly heavy with the knowledge that her words would be all that remained of her now.

"She would want you to follow," Jerem suggested. "She felt it too."

"And how would you know?" Kannin snapped at his old friend.

"I know kevashin when I see it," the elf said, "and I have seen what happens to those who deny it." He put both hands on Kannin's shoulders then, face grave. "It is not a fate I would wish on anyone."

"She could be fine without me."

"Are you willing to risk that?"

Kannin glared at him. The elf knew the answer to that. Of course he couldn't risk it. When it came to Sally, he could risk everything except her safety. "Dammit," he sighed, turning to face the closing portal. "Wish me luck, old friend."

The elf patted both of his shoulders and made a little shoving motion, as if to hurry him along. "You never needed luck before."

Kannin faced the edge, gritted his teeth, and let out a slow breath. The dying wind whipped his robes into a final frenzy, and he judged the distance. He would have to run and leap. It seemed fitting somehow. The opening was still there, a shrinking swirling mass just beyond the edge of the cliff.

"You are not the one they wanted, but you are the one I need," he heard himself saying to her.

He took two deliberate running steps towards the edge, and jumped silently out into the abyss.

About JM Paquette

JM Paquette hails from upstate New York, so she misses the snow, but not the shoveling, and now lives in Florida, where she hates the heat, but not the beach. She has an embarrassingly large comic book collection that is only shamed by her ever growing horde of cheesy romance novels, and she openly admits to being both a fantasy enthusiast and a roleplaying aficionado—both of which have earned her solid stamps on her Geek Card. She lives in Clearwater with her husband, her daughter, her big-boned dog, and a cat who occasionally appears at mealtimes.

Connect with JM:
Facebook.com/AuthorJMPaquette
Email: authorjmpaquette@gmail.com

The Heart of Ballion

By Nicole DragonBeck

The old man looked over the sea of faces with white-filmed eyes, a small smile on his lined, brown face. The murmuring of the crowd increased until the harsh clang of a gavel rang through the smoky room. An expectant silence stretched out.

"Whiliam the Elder of Cast'Gluim, Apprentice to the Warden of the Eastern Border, Wordsmith of the Fortress!" the dark and shadowy Judge called out, pausing only slightly on the last of the titles, the tone of his voice saying what he could not. What could the Wordsmith have to do with a trial of treason?

"Just Whiliam, if you please," the old man said, his smile widening ever so slightly.

"As you will," the Judge said and looked down his long nose at the small man with the shock of white hair sitting, hands in his lap, blind eyes gazing out with serene patience. "You told the Sorcerers they were mistaken in their finding regarding the young Thryn Cawll and Alièll Hamer?"

"The finding of treason was mistaken."

"You have personal testimony to back this up?"

"I do."

Another pause, this one longer. "Let it be heard."

For the first time the smile blossomed into a grin and Whiliam the Wordsmith began to speak.

~~~

At the Border fog cloaked the trees and ate the road in greedy grey swirls. In the distance a raven gave a croak, but all else was silent. Thryn Cawll blinked drops of dew from her eyelashes as she peered about, heart pattering in her throat, sending fiery blood coursing through her veins.

Allowing the refugees past the Borders of Ballion had always been the most exciting thing about being a Sorcerer. In fact, it was really the only exciting thing about being a Sorcerer. Everything else was simply riding, sleeping on cold, hard ground, eating cold, hard food with only brief stops at the Fortress to break the monotony.

But when the Border was open, one might catch a glimpse of the worlds the refugees were fleeing, strange and awesome worlds covered in ice or fire-mountains, where the sky was held up by marble columns or the rain never stopped. Born in Ballion, Thryn had never known any other world and the concept of having a home to leave was foreign to her. Unlike her fellow Sorcerer, Alièll Hamer.

Her eyes turned to the young man who stood beside her, his grey eyes narrowed as he studied the road. Dark hair framed a gaunt face and he still wore the drab clothes of his world, tight pants, a shirt with sleeves to the elbows and an open vest. His world, a world he named Slyvf, was a world the Overlord had taken and crushed with his black fist, as he had with so many others, as he had done with the lands the refugees would be leaving when they came to the sanctuary of Ballion.

The road was still empty and the mists yet swirled.

"They're late," Thryn whispered. "Where are they?"

"They'll come," Alièll said. His voice was low with a slight accent, even after all these years in Ballion. "The Tower has never lied."

Thryn shifted restlessly. What he said was true. The Tower of the Wardens' Fortress was the only reason the Sorcerers could still open the Borders, despite the fact that the Wardens had disappeared many years ago.

The rumors would have her believe the Wardens had left to distribute crystals to other worlds, or that the Overlord had somehow imprisoned them, or that they were somehow in cahoots with the Overlord, but Ballion was still here, so that one couldn't be true.

At least Thryn hoped it was not true, but there was no way to confirm or deny the rumor unless one consulted a Wordsmith, and they were difficult people to find nowadays. Just like Sorcerers, Thryn thought. The protectors of Ballion were a dying breed all around.

A shape moved in the mist, no more than a darkness shifting even as the mist did, then another and then another, interrupting Thryn's musing.

"They're coming!" Alièll said as he bounded forward, throwing up his hands.

His maroon fire-lightning arced forward and pushed the mists back, opening the Border and Ballion. Thryn joined him, her own pale blue fire complimenting his. People staggered into sight, wrapped in tattered blankets. Children with bare feet clung to women with burns on their faces, men with missing limbs pulled overloaded travois filled with strange metal contraptions and various strange creatures with scrawny limbs and singed fur limped by.

Thryn and Alièll leaped into action. He grabbed a flagging child and she took the arm of a woman with a bloody bandage over her eyes to guide her past the Border. Though her attention was on getting people through before the Border closed, Thryn spared a glance through the mists, hoping to catch sight of something spectacular. She was rewarded with the sight of bright orange fields and a dark, star-filled sky, not unlike that of Ballion. Then the mists swirled past, obscuring it and she heard Alièll curse.

"There's too many of them!" he yelled. "We have to wedge it open!"

Thryn paled. Wedging open a Border was perilous; it would give the refugees time to pass, but it held the risk of letting in other things, unwelcome, unwholesome things. But Alièll was already widening the gap, urging more people through and Thryn had no choice but to take the other side, for otherwise he would be crushed along with the refugees when the Border closed.

Thryn Cawll would not be able to live calling herself a Sorcerer if she stood by and allowed that to happen without doing a single thing.

~~~

Sweat poured down Thryn's face, her back ached and still she held the Border open. The stream of people had no end, but Alièll's face was set; he would not leave them to die in their world. After what seemed like an age and a half, just when Thryn thought she could hold it open no longer, the last refugee staggered past, leaving the misty Border empty. With a gasp Thryn collapsed, allowing the Border to close on her.

Cold mist clamped on her body like the jaws of an icedog and she would have let it crush her but a warm arm pulled her out and she found herself on the ground, a thick bed of leaves under her, the trees of the Northern Forest standing silent guard. Alièll stood bent over, his body shaking and heaving with each breath he labored to take.

"It was too long," Thryn admonished as she slowly sat up.

He flashed her a rare grin. "I know. But what would life be without a little excitement?" He pulled her to her feet. "Come on, our work is done. Let's get out of here."

With legs that were barely strong enough to support her, Thryn staggered back through the trees. The mist had disappeared when the Border closed and the midday sun shone down, gold and white. Their horses stood where they'd left them, and snorted an equine greeting at the Sorcerers.

Alièll helped her mount and then leapt upon his own steed. They watched the faint line of people winding out of the trees and trudging across the hills.

"Where do you think they'll go?" Thryn asked softly.

"They'll go wherever it looks most like home and settle there," Alièll said. "Just like all the refugees."

"Like you did?"

"Like I did."

Thryn knew from the tone of his voice that the discussion was over. Alièll did not like to talk about the destruction of his world or the fact that he was once a refugee like the ones they had just let into Ballion. Thryn would not press him, but deep down inside she knew he would not let a second home fall to the Overlord. It put a streak of recklessness in him that was hard to argue with. It would be his undoing one day.

She tried to think where in Ballion the refugees might find orange fields. "Perhaps over the San'Drai Belt," she said.

"What?"

"I was trying to think of where they might find something that looked like home," she confessed.

Alièll considered her words. "Perhaps. It's a little too red, I think. Though, if they have a wizard or another magic-wielder, perhaps they can shape the land to their desire."

"But we didn't tell them that could be done," Thryn said, her eyes following the line of refugees that was no more than the faint scratch of a pencil across the green hills.

"They're here, aren't they?" Alièll asked. "They must have heard of Ballion to get here. I've no doubt they know the basics. Come on, let's get going. We're days overdue already."

Riding hard over the varied land that was Ballion, Thryn Cawll was too lost in her thoughts of that morning to noticed the stunning and diverse beauty that surrounded her. The blue green fields of Eldar County gave way to the Retan, a forest of sculpted trees, quartz, amethyst, jade and tiger's eye sprouting from the ground like their living counterparts; skirting the D'Uluth at sundown, the fiery sun brought out the blue and purple tones of the black sand which ran to the horizon and the Gorlomn Mountains, sharp spires of glittering silver.

They reached the Pensar, plains of fuchsia grass that Thryn heard came from a land called Pensar as well. As the moon began to rise, the Sorcerers made camp beneath a stand of Pensar Pine, their vivid red needles providing a much softer bed than was usual. However, the sweet wood would not light, so they were forced to go without a fire.

Thryn's stomach grumbled at the last stale bits of fare they'd brought from the Fortress, but Alièll ate with gusto, rolled out his blanket and was soon asleep, his scimitar at his side. Sleep did not come so easily to Thryn as she tried to find a comfortable position on her own thin blanket. She ended up on her back, staring up at the starry sky searching for patterns.

Ballion had no constellations, as the stars in Ballion were not fixed and drifted about aimlessly. Thryn remembered it had something to do with Ballion, being an unnatural creation of men long after the gods had formed all the worlds, was not itself fixed in space.

Alièll, who understood it much better than she, had attempted to explain it to her once, but all that came of that was Alièll rolling on the floor laughing as she mispronounced the complicated words he'd said.

The memory made her smile and she drifted into sleep. Her dreams were soon filled with burned people falling out of an orange sky. When she opened her eyes she saw a dark shadow outlined in silver moonlight watching her.

Thryn bolted upright, her fingers automatically grasping for her straight-edged sword, a cold hand clutching her throat, forcing the air from her mouth in a strangled moan. The shadow moved closer to her with a gliding motion that betrayed no steps and Thryn thought she heard a whisper. Though she could not discern any words the sound numbed her mind and froze her body against any command she tried to give it.

The thing moved closer.

~~~

Alièll woke at once when Thryn screamed, his scimitar already in his hand. "What is it?"

In the time it took for Thryn's eyes to flick to him and back to the shadow, the shadow had disappeared. The only remnant was the cold stiffness in her limbs and the echo of the whisper in her ears.

"I...had a bad dream," she told Alièll, still looking for the watcher, but there was no one.

Perhaps it really was just in my dream, Thryn tried to tell herself, but her eyes kept flitting back to the place where she had seen it. Alièll gave her a searching look and Thryn was glad when he didn't press it, slipping his blade back into the sheath. He looked at the horizon growing lighter in the distance. "Well, we're up. We may as well start."

In the sunlight, the memory of the darkness faded, the sound of the horses' hooves on the dirt road soothed away Thryn's agitation. She found herself dozing in the saddle. When the horses splashed across a wide stream, the cold water on her thighs startled her into wakefulness and she looked across to find Alièll laughing silently. He seemed to be in an extraordinarily good humor. Thryn loved the way his face lit up when he smiled and she smiled back.

"Why are you so happy?" she asked.

"It's my birthday today," he said. "I am two-and-twenty."

It was one of the customs he'd told her of his world, to celebrate the day one was born. In Ballion, there were a thousand different customs, but none were native to the land itself. It was a lonely sensation, and Thryn dove into the ones Alièll shared with fevered interest.

"What does one do on a birthday?" Thryn asked.

"There is a large meal, of all your favorite foods, everyone sings a song in your honor, and gives you gifts."

"If I had known, I would have gotten you something," Thryn said.

Alièll smiled. "And what does a Sorcerer need with gifts? All he needs is a horse and a sword." After a pause, he cocked his head. "What would you have gotten me?"

"Dry clothes," Thryn said as she splashed him in the face before urging her horse out onto the bank and to a gallop, laughing as she heard Alièll spluttering behind her.

The land undulated under her and copses of trees sprung up like clutching hands. As Thryn crested one hill she came upon a sight.

White stone carved in the likeness of a large, bare-chested man, his beard flowing to his navel, wise eyes smiling beckoned the looker forward with one hand. Standing many times the height of an ordinary man, the statue was a work of strength and beauty.

Now it lay in large pieces, the head severed from the body, its face scorched black and its beckoning hand pointed forlornly at the empty sky.

Stillness pervaded the air and the sky held a fragile appearance. It seemed as though Thryn could reach up and punch through it. She felt an electric surge race though her, setting off tingles in her fingers and the tips of her ears. Alièll reigned up beside her, his mouth open to offer a rebuke for the splash, but the words died on his lips and the smile fell from his face as he beheld what was in front of them.

"What is it?" he asked in hushed tones after a long moment.

Something tickled the back of Thryn's mind, a story she had heard sitting on her father's knee from a Wordsmith in Conamori. The Heart of Ballion, the Wordsmith had said, leaning forward with a conspiratorial look in his eye, is kept safe by nine Keystones, nine locks...

"It's a Keystone," she whispered.

"A what?" Alièll looked as though he had not heard her properly.

"A Keystone," Thryn said with more confidence, a thrill.

In all her travels she had never encountered a Keystone, indeed never expected to. The Wardens had hidden the Objects themselves from prying eyes, hidden their location in the sands of time. The Keystones were now more myth than history.After a moment the thrill died and was replaced with a queasy mass in her stomach. Something was not right.

"It's broken," she whispered. "I don't think it should be broken."

~~~

With the smooth grace of a gymnast, Alièll slid from his horse and strode towards the shattered Keystone.

"Wait!" Thryn said, sliding off her horse. "This is very complicated and powerful magic. It could be dangerous."

Alièll waved his hand at the shattered statue. "That? It's been destroyed! What could possibly be dangerous about it?"

Before Thryn could answer Alièll took another step forward. A blast of power carried him a good dozen paces back and set him on his back, coughing and choking on the dust. Thryn ducked behind her horse and only a breath of warm air rustled through her hair. When she was sure it was done she hurried forward to where Alièll lay and helped him to sit up. He looked at her with watering eyes, rubbing the dust out.

"Don't," she said, taking his wrist. "That will just aggravate it."

She took the hem of her still wet tunic and gently wiped his eyes clean. "You still have a lot to learn about Ballion," she told him. "That was a Keystone. It is very old, very powerful magic."

Alièll looked at her. "I know what a Keystone is. What I wanted to find out is why is it in pieces?"

"Perhaps it was a prank," Thryn said, but even as the words came she knew it was not so. A mere prank would not topple a Keystone of Ballion. Not if the stories were to be believed.

"Who would be able to do this?" Alièll wondered aloud, his eyes tracing the cracks in the stone.

Thryn sifted through her knowledge, all the stories she'd heard, the legends the Wordsmiths told and gasped as the answer came. Alièll turned to her and grasped her shoulder, the same thought she'd had reflected on his face.

"It's not possible," she whispered, gazing into his eyes.

"What other explanation is there?" Alièll said.

"How...?" Thryn began and then froze. "It couldn't have been us, could it? The Border wasn't wedged open for that long..."

"No," Alièll said, looking at the cracked figure with narrowed eyes. "This work is days old. Maybe even a week."

"But if they have been here for a week..." Thryn said.

"We have to get back to the Fortress. Now," Alièll said.

Thryn nodded. She glanced back once at the violated giant king and followed Alièll as he mounted his horse and raced across Ballion to the Fortress, only one thing on both their minds: Blackfire Riders, the image of nightmares used to scare children into good behavior and the servants of the Overlord, had somehow managed to get into Ballion.

~~~

Rising up like a dark fountain the Wardens Fortress sat upon cliffs over the Lake. In the setting sun shadows made figures and faces in the stone, and they watched the two weary and distraught Sorcerers fly through the gate to the courtyard. The horses were taken by stable boys and Thryn and Alièll ran through the halls. Reaching the doors to the Hall four paces ahead of her, Alièll turned and grabbed her arm. "We need to gather the others. Go to the bell tower and sound the bell three times."

Thryn nodded. In the days of the Wardens the bells had been used to send messages as they could be heard across the entirety of Ballion. Nobody bothered to keep it up since the Wardens had gone. The bells were rarely used and the bell tower was dusty and in disrepair.

"One day something is going to have to be done about that," Thryn said to herself, as she covered her mouth with her hand to avoid being choked with dust. She gave the rope a good yank. A metallic cacophony sounded, deafening her. She winced as she pulled twice more and then ran from the bell tower.

At least an hour was spent pacing tightly in front of the fireplace before the other Sorcerers began to shuffle into the Hall. Alièll tapped his foot and glared at the door, and even Thryn, who was usually the more patient, began to chew her lip and wring her hands.

"Well, what is it?" a voice called out.

"This is everyone?" Alièll asked, raising an eyebrow as he looked over the small group of no more than a dozen.

"Some of them have turned in already, and others are in the Pleasure Rooms or the Recreation Hall," the voice said. "What is it that you sounded that dratted bell for?"

Thryn squinted into the crowd and made out the form of Sorcerer Verio, a fat and careless man who, like her, was born of Ballion. Before Thryn could say anything, Alièll was standing in front of him, grabbing his collar and shouting. The other Sorcerers went into an uproar and it was a few minutes before Thryn could restore any amount of order. Alièll was glowering and Verio was rubbing his neck with a petulant expression.

"Blackfire Riders have returned to Ballion," Alièll said without preamble. "They have to be found and killed."

"And you know this because?" Verio asked, unimpressed.

"The Tower sounded six days ago around midnight. We went north to let refugees through the Border," Alièll said, "and on our return journey we found the remains of a Keystone that had been destroyed about a week ago."

"A Keystone?" Verio said, raising an eyebrow. "You're certain of this?"

Alièll looked at Thryn and then nodded. The other Sorcerers looked at each other uncertainly, shuffling about in their slippers and dressing gowns. Thryn could almost read the thoughts running through their heads. The Keystones were a myth. They couldn't be seen by ordinary eyes. Only the Wardens knew how to find them. The silence stretched, thin and brittle.

"A Keystone was destroyed," Alièll repeated, each syllable forced out with precise care. "Ballion is under attack."

"That is impossible!" Verio said. "No one could destroy a Keystone and we simply remain oblivious! We would feel something. Besides, no one can see them!"

"A Blackfire Rider might," Thryn chimed in and the gazes moved to her.

"There hasn't been a Blackfire Rider in over a hundred years," one Sorcerer said. "The Wardens handled the last one. There aren't any more!"

"Besides, even if there were, they'd never get across the Border," a young and arrogant voice seconded.

"Because you are all so busy watching them?" Alièll said, his voice thick with contempt. "Instead of sitting on your well-padded behinds, eating and drinking, and playing Seven-square and Man-in-the-Corner-Man-in-the-Middle? When is the last time any of you answered the Tower?"

"Now listen here, young man," Verio said, waving his finger in the air. "There is a lot more to being a Sorcerer and the running of Ballion than gallivanting around, opening Borders and letting all manner of riff-raff in. Not all of them are as innocuous as they might appear, you know. There has to be some organization, someone has to administer, manage, and oversee all those people you so casually let in..."

"The Blackfire Riders destroyed a Keystone," Thryn interjected before Alièll could say anything. "They have to be stopped."

"What are we supposed to do about it?" Verio said. "We're just Sorcerers. That is a job for a Warden!"

"There aren't any more Wardens!" Alièll said through gritted teeth. "They're all gone. There are only us!"

"Well, then, I move that you go out and confirm your suspicions and then we'll see what should be done," Verio said. "All in favor say 'aye'!"

A chorus of ayes followed Thryn out of the Hall as she ran after Alièll.

~~~

"How did they get so stupid?" Alièll fumed as he stormed through the halls. "Their entire world could end, and all they can say is 'aye'!"

Thryn followed him silently, letting him rant. Something inside him had reacted to what the other Sorcerers had said, something that Thryn suspected had to do with fact that he didn't want to contemplate the destruction of his second home.

In the courtyard, Alièll put his hands on his hips and stared at the now dark sky sprinkled with little glowing stars. His breath misted as he heaved a sigh and turned to her.

"I am going to find the Blackfire Riders and what they are up to," he said. "You don't have to come if you don't want to."

"You're not supposed to go out without a Second. Besides, why should I let you have all the fun?" Thryn said. "Not a chance."

A raspy voice from the other side of the courtyard made them both jump. "Blackfire Riders are not fun, my dear."

"Who is that?" Thryn called out.

"My name is Whiliam," the voice said and an old man with white hair followed it out into the light, his arm waving in front of him, his steps hesitant.

"How do you know about the Blackfire Riders?"

"In the days of the Wardens three bells could only mean one thing," the man smiled.

"Whiliam the Wordsmith," Thryn said suddenly, grabbing Alièll's arm, putting her lips close to his ear and spoke softly. "He's been here since the days of the Wardens, or so they say!"

"My dear, I may be blind but my hearing is in perfect order," Whiliam said. "But she speaks the truth. A Wordsmith I am, gods be gracious."

Thryn and Alièll looked at each other, eyebrows raised meaningfully. A Wordsmith was as powerful as a Warden, maybe even more so, depending on the Wordsmith and the Warden. Their power was in their words, keeping the history of the worlds, the myths and legends and the truth of things in sight, binding the world in ways that even the Wardens could not.

"Can you help us find the Riders and defeat them?" Alièll asked and Thryn could feel the excitement coming from him.

"No, that's not right," Thryn said. "The Blackfire Riders are on the move. They will be difficult to find and we can't waste time and energy chasing after them. We have to find the Keystones. Then we will find the Riders."

"But we don't know where they are," Alièll said. "Or how to get to them. Will you help us?" he asked again.

"Boy, you must be desperate indeed if you think a blind old man will be any help," Whiliam said. "But if you will have me along, why, I'll help any way I can."

He raised his hand and scratched his temple. A mark on his wrist, a small crescent that looked as though it had been cut or burned into his flesh, caught Thryn's attention. She knew what that was. It was a Binding-Mark, a mark of recognition of service, something only a Warden could bestow.

A little memory tickled at the back of her mind, a story from a minor Wordsmith who passed through Conamori just before she left to become a Sorcerer, something about the legendary Silverflame, the last Warden, who had disappeared into the shadow of words, and Thryn began to wonder if perhaps the old Wordsmith would be more help than he let on.

~~~

"We'll need some way to find the Keystones," Alièll said.

"There is a map of sorts," Whiliam said. "But it is very old. It is possible some of them may have moved or changed. It is in the Vaults."

"It's the only thing we've got to go on," Alièll said. "Even if it is not exactly accurate, we must take it."

"But only a Wordsmith can get into the..." Thryn started to say then stopped. "Oh."

Whiliam smiled at her.

"I'll get it," Thryn said. "I can read better than Alièll can."

"She's right," Alièll said. "I'll get fresh horses and supplies."

"I will go with the young lady," Whiliam said. "If you would be so kind as to help me, we'll be going to the Tower, at the very top."

Thryn knew better than to point out that the Tower had no top, or at least, no way to reach the top, so she simply took Whiliam's arm and led him. They entered a small, round room lit by torches in regularly placed sconces that burned endlessly with a black flame.

A jagged shard of crystal on a dial in the middle of the room sat milky white, for which Thryn was glad; she did not know what she would have done if a message had come through the crystal to announce refugees waiting to be let through the Border. Verio certainly would not have answered that call.

"We're here," she told Whiliam.

The Wordsmith walked over to the wall with his hand outstretched. No lever was pulled, no handle was turned, but a door opened in the stone, revealing a winding stair. Thryn took Whiliam's arm and led him up to the landing where he ran his hand over the wall and another door appeared, this one opening directly to the Vaults. It was old and musty but somehow still pristine, not a speck of dust or cobweb was to be seen.

"You will find what you're looking for in the trunk in the Crimson corner," Whiliam said, gripping the edge of a table.

"How do you know?" Thryn asked, watching him closely, though her eyes kept darting to the mark on his wrist.

"Because I put it there," Whiliam said with a smile. "A long time ago."

Thryn was curious exactly how long ago, but she refrained from asking and went to the trunk. It was not locked, but the lid was heavy and made her hands tingle. On top, as Whiliam had said, covered in strange symbols and rolled with fine gold velvet, was a map of Ballion.

Under it lay many more long, rolled papers. Curious, Thryn pulled back a corner, and then more, revealing a diagram, lines and angles marked, with long equations in strange runes across the top and conversion tables in the corner. The next one and the next were similar to the first. Some showed magnifications of complex contraptions, others depicted wave patterns, swirling vortices and puzzle-piece shapes on warped grids. Her breath caught in her throat as she realized these were the original plans for Ballion, drawn up by the Wardens' own hands. Suddenly afraid of the immensity which she held in her hands, Thryn rolled the papers back and hastily closed the trunk.

Taking the map to Whiliam, she had to hold the edges on the table because the stubborn curl of time wouldn't allow it to lay flat. Whiliam's old fingers gently traced a path, his fingers pausing over each of the Keystones depicted in an ink that seemed to fade when she stared too long. Thryn thought she saw his Binding-Mark glow faintly, but she wasn't sure.

"How are you doing that?" Thryn asked.

"Some things even a blind man can see if he cares to look. But it is more than that. This is magic, which is seen least by the eye and most by the mind," Whiliam said, and then he frowned as his attention turned to the map and the Keystones. "There are seven..."

"Six," Thryn said. "Less if the Blackfire Riders got to more."

"Which was it?" Whiliam said.

"It was a giant man carved in stone," Thryn said.

A frown crossed Whiliam's face. "The third, the Giant King," he muttered. "We do not have much time." Before Thryn could ask, Whiliam explained. "The Keystones are like a series of locks. One cannot get to the second before the first has been unlocked, the third will not appear until the second comes, and so on."

"And when they get through the last, they'll find...the Heart of Ballion!"

"So the legend says," Whiliam said. "It would be best if we never find out."

"Why?" Thryn said.

"Because at that point Ballion will be lost."

~~~

In the courtyard, the predawn silence made the world seem heavy, as though it were sinking into a great sea of black water. Alièll waited with two horses saddled, the same two horses they had ridden to the Border. "The stables were empty," he fumed. "What are these people doing here?"

"It's fine," Thryn said soothingly as she took one of the horses from him. "Whiliam and I can ride together."

Alièll blew the hair from his face and gave a sharp nod. Thryn watched the way his eyes flicked to the gate every few moments, the way his jaw tensed. We need to get going, she thought, before he explodes.

"Look what we found," Thryn said as she handed him the map. "Or rather, what Whiliam found."

"A map. Good," Alièll said, pursing his lips in determination. Unrolling it, he held it out in front of him, his gaze narrowing as he followed the lines of ink showing mountains, rivers, endless plains and dark forests. "This is very old. I...I don't recognize most of this."

"That's because it's upside down," Thryn said.

"Right," Alièll said, turning it around.

"Here's where we saw the giant," Thryn pointed. "Where is the next one?"

"The Fourth is the Lightbreaker, but it is all the way on the other side of Ballion, last time I checked," Whiliam said, "in the Cart'Illon."

"That could take a fortnight," Alièll said, an unhappy frown settling over his eyes.

"The Blackfire Riders can already find them somehow, so it matters little. It would do no good to gallop around one or a hundred steps behind them," Thryn said, and then paused. "We could just sacrifice it. Find the closest one, and stake out there?"

"That plan would be more certain to work," Alièll said, though the corners of his mouth turned down at the word sacrifice.

"If my memory serves me that would be in the Valley of Yester," Whiliam said. "It is north, not too far from the Fortress."

"Let's go," Alièll said, rolling the map up and sticking it in his belt.

The sky lightened as the trio rode north. The trip was silent as they flew unhindered over flat plains, but when they reached Blost'Onor, an expanse of treacherous marshland, their pace slowed to a slow crawl as the horses picked out each step with care, mud pulling at their hooves. The grey-green waters were thick and sluggish, and plants with glowing lights that sped from leaf to leaf and plant to plant like snakes of lighting marked the areas of firmer ground. At times Alièll and Thryn dismounted and led the horses when the weight and the danger of sinking became too much.

It was at one such time that the Wordsmith began to speak, telling of the Creation of Ballion.

"Many years ago, seven brave and wise men from the Firstworlds, known as the Wardens, banded together when the Overlord began his ascent. They built Ballion in secret, as a temporary harbor, a failsafe. To protect it from the Overlord they secured it with seven Keystones, one from each of the Firstworlds.

"The people of those worlds were not willing to give up their homes and flee, but Ballion would be open to anyone whose home the Overlord had destroyed. Then, as a feat of that nature could not be kept secret forever, the news of what the Wardens had done reached the ears of the Overlord.

"One by one the Overlord tracked down the Firstworlds, thinking that if he destroyed them, he would be able to reach Ballion and destroy it. After many years of conquest, Amab was the last of the Firstworlds to fall and the Overlord waited for Ballion to appear so he could crush it too."

"But that didn't happen," Thryn said.

"No," Whiliam agreed. "And so we are still here."

"At least for now." Alièll clutched the map in his hand as he squinted at it and Thryn had to fight the urge to take it away from him. "How much further does this muck continue?"

"It ends here, then the Valley," Thryn pointed.

The Valley of Yester was in the crater of a volcanic mountain. Steep rocky sides surrounded a perfect circle of emerald grasses, marred only by a charred black circle roughly in the center. Faint traces of smoke curled up to the rim and the horses snorted softly.

"It is here," Whiliam said softly, his face turned up to the sun. "The Tree of Life. Or what was once the Tree of Life."

"Give the horses their heads," Alièll said. "They'll get us down safely."

He spoke correctly and a few minutes later they stood on the floor of the valley. The Sorcerers dismounted and looked over the charred remains of the great oak tree, its ashes bright blue and violet. The air tore into icy strands, enveloping them as a spiderweb would. As they walked closer the sky pulsed with a syncopated heartbeat of its own. There was no doubt it had been one of the Keystones of Ballion.

"The fifth," Whiliam said.

"That leaves only two," Thryn said.

Alièll knelt down and scooped a handful of still-glowing coals, letting them slip through his fingers. The blood tinged wood did not burn his hand. "This is recent, no more than an hour," he said. "We missed them."

"Can we make it to the next one in time?" Thryn asked.

Alièll looked at the map, tilting his head. The way his brow furrowed when he was puzzling something out made him look softer and Thryn couldn't help but smile. Alièll glanced at her.

"What?" he asked.

"Nothing," Thryn replied. "Where do we go?"

Alièll frowned and then pointed. "That way."

~~~

The grassy hills flew under their hooves as the volcano diminished behind them. Above them the sky had a faint green tinge and smoke to their right indicated the presence of people. Thryn wondered if their wizard had made the sky that color intentionally to remind them of home. Personally Thryn preferred the blue, but to each their own.

Winter's Well was an elaborately sculpted structure of silver-white clay. It lay under a copse of long-leafed trees, dappled in shadows. The Sorcerers gazed at it, wind rustling the grass around their boots.

"It's intact," Alièll said. "They haven't gotten here yet."

"Wrong," Whiliam said softly. "They are here right now."

As Alièll and Thryn turned, six shapes materialized out of the trees, clothed in black fire, and glided gracefully towards the Well, ignoring both Sorcerers and the old man. Thryn felt a familiar cold seep into her flesh, rooting her in place.

"Stop them!" Alièll sprinted forward.

He got no more than four steps. Only one of the Blackfire Riders turned to deal with him, in an unhurried, nonchalant way that Thryn knew Alièll could only find very insulting. The thing parried a slash from his scimitar easily.

Thryn joined him against her body's frozen protests, her own blade straight and serrated on one edge, sparkling with pale blue energy, and engaged another Rider. Whiliam stood straight, his blind eyes staring over the Blackfire Riders heads waving his hands in slow circles as a third Blackfire Rider stepped towards him.

The remaining three Riders made for Winter's Well, and the Sorcerers pressed harder, trying to break through to intercept them. The more savagely Alièll and Thryn attacked the slower and lazier the Blackfire Riders seemed to become. Alièll's eyes were icy slits and Thryn's teeth were bared, but nothing they did had any effect on the Riders. Back to back they circled, jabbing sporadically at their foes, their muscles becoming more and more leaden.

One of the Blackfire Riders chittered something at its companions and motioned towards the map in Alièll's belt. All three Riders descended on him, hands clawing. There was nothing Alièll could do. He threw up his hands up, trying to block all of them at once.

"No!" Thryn cried out as a Rider reached around him, its fingers twitching for the map.

The map seemed to light up and shrink away. Thryn brought her blade down hard but it passed straight through the arm of the Blackfire Rider. To her relief, its arm passed through the map, but three more grasping hands took its place. Alièll twisted away. Thryn saw an opening and grabbed the map, lightning quick, clenching it in her hand and protecting it against her chest. It only confused them for a split second, and then they turned on her.

The map was warm in her hands, and some part of Thryn knew the Blackfire Riders must not get their hands on it. There was more to the map than just paper and ink. Hesitating for just one interminable moment, Thryn thrust the map forward into the black flames surrounding the Riders, where it was incinerated in an instant.

The Blackfire Riders drew back as if hit and screeched angrily. An explosion engulfed everyone in heat and purple smoke. When Thryn could see again, the Blackfire Riders had disappeared; the only trace was tiny black flames dying in the ground. Winter's Well looked like a burnt candle, twisted and stunted.

With half a glance at what was left of the Well, Alièll leaped forward. "We have to get to the last one!"

He reached down for the map. "Where is it?" Alièll said, patting himself frantically.

"I burned it," Thryn said. "It was the only way to keep it from them!"

"How are we supposed to find the last Keystone before the Blackfire Riders?" Alièll shouted.

"I don't know," Thryn said, glaring at him. "But at least the Riders won't be able to use it!"

Who knows what would have happened if Whiliam had not stepped up and placed a hand on each of their shoulders? "Come now. It does no good to stand here arguing about that which has passed. I know where the last Keystone will appear."

~~~

The Milkway was a sea of white grass. To the left, an abyss dropped into blackness. The final Keystone sat on the edge of the precipice, still glowing faintly. An elaborately carved pole of rich amber wood, as they walked closer, Thryn could see pictures with symbols under them winding around the pole like a ribbon.

"It's beautiful," Thryn said.

Alièll said nothing for a moment, his face pale as he gazed at it. "The Gravity Plane," he breathed.

"What?" Thryn asked. "What is it?"

"It is something we have...we had in Slyvf," Alièll said as he walked up to it. Putting his hand on it, he traced the symbols, his lips moving silently. They were unfamiliar to Thryn.

"What does it say?"

"It is the tale of Celdonai, one of the Old Heroes that built Slyvf before time began. It sat in the capital, in the Hall of Light," Alièll said, wonder in his voice. He turned to Whiliam, his gaze both curious and accusing. "But...what is it doing here?"

"Ballion was build out of other worlds. There is something of each of them in Ballion."

Thryn looked sideways at Alièll, who was staring at the pole. "I used to sit for hours and read it when I was a kid," he said, his eyes fixed on the engraved pole.

Black flames began to creep towards the base of the pole.

~~~

The Blackfire Riders appeared suddenly, leaping out of the black flames like wraiths of smoke. Alièll, Thryn and Whiliam stood against the Gravity Plane, between the Riders and the Keystone. Alièll pulled out his scimitar, maroon lighting streaking down its length.

Six Riders gathered, coated in black flame, their eyes burning white. Long blades of silver ice appeared in their hands. Hissing malicious words only they understood, the Blackfire Riders advanced.

"Stay together," Alièll said, dropping into a crouch.

Thryn took Whiliam's hand and pulled him closer. "There are too many," she said, looking between the shadows that multiplied as they advanced.

Whiliam shook his head, his blind eyes fixed on the Blackfire Riders. "Six there are, as six there were. It is just a trick."

Alièll's eyes burned as he looked at them. "Then six I am going to kill."

"You cannot kill them," Whiliam said. "They are not alive, and so cannot die."

Alièll's glare intensified. "I'm going to kill them anyway."

"You can't," Thryn said suddenly, remembering the last time that glare had been directed at the Blackfire Riders. "If you fight them, they just wear you down until you can't fight anymore. That's how they do it."

"So what do we do?" Alièll asked through gritted teeth. "If they destroy the last Keystone, the Heart will be laid bare and the Overlord will come swooping down. Ballion will fall."

The world froze. Thryn saw each part spinning around in an infinite pattern that was simple and beautiful, and everything made sense. She grabbed Alièll's arm. "You're right. If they destroy it, they'll get to the Heart. But we can use the power of the Keystone to destroy them."

"We'll have to unleash it..." Alièll said, catching onto her plan immediately.

"How?" Thryn asked.

Alièll looked back at the pole. "We have to destroy it."

~~~

Alièll grasped Thryn's hand tightly, his scimitar lowering even as the Blackfire Riders came closer. "We'll have to get out of the way quickly."

Thryn looked at him. "I..."

"What?"

"I hope we don't die," she said, and then she pulled her hand away and put her arms around the Gravity Plane.

Pale blue lightning raced from her palms, illuminating the pictures and symbols. Almost instantly it was joined by a deep maroon light. The two pulsed like an erratic heartbeat as the Sorcerers pulled at the fiber of the Keystone, trying to unravel it.

"It's too strong," Thryn said, her voice a hoarse whisper. "We can't undo it!"

"No," Alièll said. "We can do this!"

"We need Whiliam's help!"

But the old, blind man was nowhere to be found.

Thryn's strength began to flag and she swayed away from the

pole. Alièll let go with one hand and the heartbeat coursing up and down dimmed. When he grabbed her left hand tightly the lightning took on a violet hue and surged up the Gravity Plane in a blinding glow that threw Thryn backwards. She would have lost touch of the pole if Alièll had not been holding on to her.

Bony fingers with an unnatural strength grabbed the back of Thryn's tunic and began to pull her away. Her fingernails dug into the old wood and blood began to run down her hand, making her hold even more slippery.

"Hang on," Alièll said through gritted teeth. "We've almost got it."

Giant cracks began to run through the pole, glowing white. A moment later the Gravity Plane exploded, throwing large chunks of wood into the air which spun in a tornado of icy wind. Wails filled the air as the Blackfire Riders were assaulted by beams of white light and purple lightning.

Thryn closed her eyes and rolled over through the air, praying to whatever god may be in the vicinity that she didn't die. Landing with an organ-jarring thud, she groaned. The winds did not die, but a chilly silence pervaded the air. Thryn was scarred to open her eyes. Eventually she did, slowly lifting first one eyelid then the other.

She sat up with a gasp.

~~~

Thryn looked down. Alièll was semi-unconscious next to her, blood running down his temple. Though a four-inch splinter protruded from his upper arm, his hand was still tightly griped in hers. Extricating her hand, Thryn stood up, her bones humming with pain.

"Let's never do that again," she said and Alièll mumbled.

Eyes the color of the blue-grey predawn horizon opened and stared at her, glazed and disoriented. "What just happened?" he asked.

"I think we destroyed the final Keystone of Ballion," Thryn whispered, offering him a hand up.

Alièll grabbed it and winced as he stood. Thryn pointed wordlessly to the splinter and he gritted his teeth and yanked it out, discarding the shard of bloody wood.

The pair stood and beheld what had become of their home. Surrounded by a great blackness, the tiny finger of land upon which they stood had managed to survive the explosion unscathed and the rest of Ballion lay before them.

The great skies no longer resembled anything either of them had ever seen. Huge arcs of silver metal and blue light crisscrossed the air above them, and the stars, visible even though it was midday, were impossibly large in the spaces between.

Crackling with visible energy, the air blew in a sucking wind that pulled at their hair and clothes. The entirety of Ballion looked like a patchwork quilt, badly stitched by a fumbling child. Made entirely of magic, the stitches themselves were a wonder to gaze upon, dark light and icy fire entwined, binding the fabric of the lands together.

"The Heart of Ballion," Thryn whispered.

"It feels terribly drafty!" a familiar voice complained.

"Whiliam!" The pair turned.

The blind old man took careful steps towards them and Thryn dashed forward to take his arm.

"Where did you disappear off to?" Thryn asked.

"I have no idea," Whiliam said. "I am blind, remember? What happened?"

"We sort of destroyed the Keystone," Thryn said. "We can...see the Heart."

"What does it look like?"

"It's beautiful," Thryn said. "So...big."

Alièll was frowning. "There is something I don't understand. I remember sitting in the Hall looking at the Gravity Plane as a child. But you said the Keystones were from the Firstworlds. How can that be? I didn't leave Slyvf until I was three and Ballion is older than that!"

"Yes," Whiliam said. "It is as you say."

"You're a Wordsmith," Thryn said. "You know what happened."

"Tell us," Alièll demanded.

~~~

"When the Wardens secured Ballion with the Keystones, they took one from each of the Firstworlds: the Iron Ring from Coron, the Window from Amab, the Giant King from Doriel, the Lightbreaker from H'Tash, the Tree of Life from Virstilial, Winter's Well from Ipp..." Whiliam pointed at the chunks of charred wood around them. "...and the Gravity Plane from Slyvf.

"But the Wardens were wise and had not left the Keystones in their respective worlds, they brought them to Ballion itself and replaced them with replicas. Even if the Firstworlds fell, Ballion would remain. When Amab fell, Ballion was safe from the Overlord," Whiliam said.

"Until the Blackfire Riders showed up," Thryn said. "But how did they get in? The Borders shouldn't have let them pass..."

Alièll's mouth hung open in shock. "The Keystones!" he said. "They got in through the first Keystone!"

"How?"

"I don't know," he said. "Maybe...maybe because they are from the Firstworlds and not of Ballion so they could be... isolated and traced? But I'm sure that is what happened, like smoke slipping through the keyhole of a locked door!"

"It merits looking into," Whiliam nodded. "But first a new Keystone must be made. You have some time, I imagine, as the Riders will not be taking news of this to the Overlord. But now Ballion is unprotected."

"Us?" Thryn asked in a squeak. "But...what...what about you?"

"I do not have that power," Whiliam said. "I am only a Wordsmith, my dear. This is a job for a Warden."

"But...there are no Wardens!" Thryn said.

Whiliam smiled. "There are the two of you."

Thryn and Alièll looked at each other.

"What do you say?" Alièll said. "Do you think we can do it?"

"We have to try," Thryn said with a nod.

As one the Sorcerers turned and gazed around at the dazzling and frightening spectacle that Ballion had become.

"What do we do?" Thryn said. "How do we just...create another Keystone?"

"The same way we destroyed it," Alièll said, taking her hand with one of his, maroon lightning tingling at the tips of the other. "But we need an object, something to encase it in."

"What shall we use?" Thryn said. "What about your sword?"

The Scimitar had fallen from Alièll's grip and tumbled away when the Keystone was destroyed. Alièll went to retrieve it. Unscathed but for a nick in the pommel, it shone brightly in the half-gloom.

"Fitting," Alliel said as he held it aloft. "It was my fathers and his before him, truly of Slyvf. Where shall we put it?"

Thryn pointed. A large chuck of the Gravity Plane had landed right at the end of the precipice, balanced like a bird ready to take flight. Thryn and Alièll stood on either side of it, holding the sword together, her hand above his on the pommel. Blue and maroon fire-lightning danced down the blade and together they plunged it into the petrified wood. It slid in easily, like sliding into water and then jerked into place, as if a hand inside the wood had grabbed it. Thryn and Alièll let go simultaneously, took a step back and looked around.

A film of star-studded black had filled in overhead, the magical seams disappearing into rolling green hills and a sparkling ocean of sapphire and cobalt.

"It's really quite beautiful," Alièll said. "Worth protecting."

"Yes it is," Thryn agreed. "Now we have to go back and explain to the others what happened."

Silence filled the court. Even the judge had nothing to say for a long time, and then he folded his hands and looked down his nose. "This is the truth?"

"Yes," Whiliam said.

The Sorcerers shifted and muttered between themselves.

"He could be lying," Verio said.

"A Wordsmith cannot lie," Whiliam said, serene as ever. "You should know that."

"This is preposterous!" Verio said. "They destroyed the last Keystone! Ballion is vulnerable! Someone must pay!"

"Perhaps," Whiliam said. "But it is not Thryn Cawll and Alièll Hamer, for it is they who will create Keystones so Ballion will once again be fully protected."

"Impossible!" Verio spluttered. "That would mean..."

Whiliam smiled. "Indeed. There are Wardens once more in Ballion."

<<<<>>>>

About Nicole DragonBeck

Nicole was born in California one snowy summer long ago, the illegitimate offspring of an elf and a troll. At a young age her powers exploded and she was banished to the wilderness of South Africa because her spells kept going inexplicably awry. There she was raised by a tribe of pygmy Dragons and had tremendous adventures, including defeating a terrible Fire-Demon that had been tormenting a sect of Dwarf priests. In gratitude they taught her the arcane magic of writing and the rest is horribly misinterpreted history. She reads as much as she writes, is obsessed with dragons and Italians, enjoys cooking, listening to music and can often be heard fiddling on a keyboard or guitar. She currently lives in Clearwater, Florida, is a member of The Ink Slingers Guild and is working on several novels, all of which have at least one mention of a dragon. She lists friends, music and life among her greatest influences.

Connect with Nicole:
www.NicoleDragonBeck.com

facebook.com/nicolebeckauthor

twitter.com/DragonBeck

Other books by Nicole DragonBeck:
Beyond the Threshold (Anthology)

.

Jimmy

By Erika Lance

Part 1

The sound of beeping began to penetrate Mike's dream. The noise was faint at first, like it was in the distance, but as it continued it became louder. He felt in his dream he should be able turn it off, but there was another beep, this time louder than the last.

Before opening his eyes, he reached his hand over to where his alarm clock should be. He knew he could hit the snooze button three times before he had to actually open his eyes. As he moved his arm he was only able to raise it four inches off the bed before something stopped him. He tried to pull his hand to him and again he met resistance. He told himself to not panic.

He took several deep breaths as his eyes opened and adjusted to his surroundings. He looked down at his wrist. There was a canvas strap attached to a padded cuff around it. Glancing further down, he saw that it was attached to the railing.

His bed didn't have a railing.

He tried to sit up suddenly but couldn't. There was a sharp pain in his stomach and as he attempted to sit. He was just about to panic when he felt a stabbing pain on the right side of his head and fell back on the pillow.

As he lay back down, his mom was standing over him.

"Slowly sweetie, you're still a little weak," she said with a smile. Her voice sounded a bit hoarse and as he looked up into her eyes, he realized she had been crying. Her hair was pulled back into the ponytail she wore around the house when she was cleaning or relaxing. She never went out like that.

"Where am I?" he heard himself say. His own voice cracked and his throat burned as the words came out.

"You're in the hospital," his mom said as she brought a straw to his lips. He took a drink. The cold water shocked his system and he began coughing. He tried again to bring his hand to cover his mouth and failed.

"Hospital?" he heard himself ask between coughs, as if it was a complete question. He saw his mother's face shift. It was so subtle, but he had become familiar with it in the last few years. She was worried. She looked at him, her lips parted as if she wanted to say something, but as quickly as her mouth opened, it closed again.

She offered him another sip from the straw. He took it and then she placed the cup down and took his hand. "Mike, baby, do you remember anything from the other night?" Her voice was almost a whisper. She kept looking down at his hand, refusing to meet his gaze.

He closed his eyes and tried to remember what had happened. He remembered school; he remembered coming home. It was just a jumble of pictures.

He tried to think if he had been in a car. Had he been in an accident? Had he been driving somewhere?

Then his stomach cramped and he tried to jerk his hand away. His mom's hand just tightened around his, as if she thought that would somehow offer support as the memories came flooding back.

"I don't...." he began out loud and then his voice trailed off.

He had been sitting in his room reading the page he had just written in his journal.

He remembered the note he had written to his mom.

He opened his eyes and looked into his mother's hazel ones staring back at him, tears streaking down her face. He realized he had ones to match.

"I'm sorry," she said to him. "I am so sorry Mikey. I am so, so, sorry. I didn't understand. I didn't realize…"

He closed his eyes again and turned his head from hers as she tried to comfort him.

He remembered now. He had taken the entire bottle of pills, the ones for his "depression," with a bottle of wine he had stolen from his parents.

He lay there on the bed, turned as far as the restraints would allow him, listening to the monitors, his mother's sobs, and her soft voice trying to comfort him, numb.

After several minutes he heard a door open and looked up to see who had entered. He attempted to bring his hand up to his face again. It was his father, who looked as if he hadn't slept in days. Following him was a man in a lab coat Mike could only assume was a doctor.

"Mike, you're awake," his father said and smiled.

He attempted a weak smile back at his father but all he could manage was a grimace as a wave of pain hit his stomach again.

After the spasm stopped the doctor asked him, "How are you feeling?"

"Sore," was his only reply. How do I look like I am feeling? He thought as the doctor continued to look at him.

The doctor smiled at him again and said, "You're a lucky kid. If your mom hadn't found you when she did you might not be with us now."

As usual, Mike couldn't say what he was thinking; he wanted to scream that he didn't feel lucky at all and he wished his mom hadn't found him, that the tears he cried were not due to being sad, but were because he failed.

"Lucky I guess," was all he said.

The doctor told him that he had been in the hospital for three days and that he had been in a coma because his heart had stopped. That Mike had, in fact, been dead for several minutes. Mike realized the last part the doctor had stated, not to explain the gravity of his health situation, but to scare him. It didn't. Mike assumed death was most likely less painful than what he was going through now.

As the doctor continued to speak, he began to hear less and less of what was being said. He nodded his head and said the obligatory "uh-huhs" when there were pauses and started to look around the room he was in. To his right there was a small table with some cards, flowers, and balloons. There was even a teddy bear, no doubt from his family. He didn't have any friends.

He glanced to his left, nodding when he heard a questioning tone in the doctor's voice and realized there was a curtain pulled to the edge of his bed. His wasn't the only bed in the room. Just great.

Because the curtain was drawn he couldn't see if it was occupied. As he turned his head back to the right to see if the doctor was almost finished, he had another sudden sharp pain on the right side of his head. Instinctively he reached for the area but the canvas straps still held him in place. Frustrated his pushed his head back into the pillow.

His mom jumped to his side and began to say, "Mike, don't touch it, it needs to adjust ..." but she was cut off by the Doctor who said, "Michael, you fell and hit your head on the desk in your room. There was a nasty cut that required several stitches. If it is hurting, we can give you a little something for the pain."

"When can I get these off?" Mike said as he held up his hands to gesture to the restraints.

"Soon. We just need to ensure you won't try to hurt yourself again," the doctor replied. This created a slightly awkward silence.

Taking some cue the doctor continued to speak with the same innocuous smile he had shown before. "Now that you're awake we can begin your therapy sessions as soon as tomorrow if you would like, and we shall see from there. Sound good?"

"Great," was all Mike could say.

"We're going to let you get some rest now. We will talk some more soon," the doctor added as he injected something into the IV in Mike's arm.

Any thoughts of protesting were moot as he realized it must have been pain medication for his head, it made him instantly drowsy. As his eyes began to close, he heard muffled talking. Something about an introduction happening and then the words became subdued. All Mike could think about was how great another therapist would be. He hated therapy he thought, and fell into blackness.

Part 2

He couldn't tell how long he slept, but it must now be morning because the room seemed brighter from behind his closed lids than it was before. He listened to see if his parents were still in the room before opening his eyes. He heard the hums and beeps of the machines and nothing else. His eyes cracked open.

Out of habit he tried to move his arm to push himself up, only to realize he was still restrained. With an exasperated sigh, he rolled onto his back and stared up at the ceiling.

"Feel like a dog on short leash?" he heard from his left.

The voice startled him. He turned his head slowly to his left, assuming the curtain was still in place. Instead he saw that the curtain on the bed next to him had been drawn back and he was looking at a boy about his age, staring back at him. The boy raised his hand in a mock gesture of shaking hands to show he was similarly restrained. "My name is Jimmy, and you are?"

"Mike," he replied.

"They only keep you restrained for a few days. That is, unless you look like you are going to attempt again and then they may never take them off." Mike realized this caused his anger to rise before he noticed Jimmy was smirking at him. "I am just messing with you, Mike."

Mike didn't know what to say next. "So how did you fail to kill yourself?" didn't seem like a social thing to ask his roomie. Not that Mike was ever very good at the social stuff, just ask all of the friends he didn't have he thought.

He opted for awkward silence instead and looked back up at the ceiling.

"Wondering how I tried to do it?" Jimmy asked after a couple minutes.

Yes, Mike thought to himself as he considered his failed attempt to end his own life. He said nothing, like he always did, trying in some morbid way to be invisible.

"I jumped," Jimmy finally said after another long silence. "I supposed I should have picked a higher place, but of course I thought I would be looking at it from the cheap seats now."

Mike smiled a little at that. He felt the exact same way when he remembered the look on his mom's face. If he hadn't failed, he would never have seen that.

When you're killing yourself, he supposed, you don't think you are going to fail and look back at yet another part of your life you didn't get to go your way. He hadn't.

He was about to open his mouth to make a comment when he heard their room door open. He turned to look at a nurse coming in with a wheelchair. He was about to ask what the chair was for when he saw it being parked next to Jimmy's bed.

As the nurse began to open up a cabinet on the other side of the room she said, "It is time for your first therapy session Michael." He sighed, but Jimmy just winked at him.

Mike took stock, for the first time, of his roommate. Jimmy was thin, with light brown hair cut short, a light completion and blue eyes. He wasn't the type of person most would pick out of a crowd except for one key feature, a scar that ran from his temple almost all the way to his chin on the right side of his face.

As Mike took a closer look he also saw that Jimmy wasn't really moving his legs. They were bandaged in a couple of places, and there were red lines that showed they'd been recently healed.

Mike realized he was staring when Jimmy said, "Gnarly, huh?" He looked up and met Jimmy's eyes. He found Jimmy smiling at him, the scar almost invisible when he did. Mike found himself not looking away, and actually nodded and smiled back.

The curtain was suddenly drawn closed between his bed and Jimmy's. He had forgotten the nurse was there. She moved up the railing of the bed, undoing each restraint in turn.

"Put these on sweetie," the nurse said as she gestured to a pile of fabric at the end of the bed. The nurse had also grabbed a blanket and placed it next to the clothes. She went back out the now drawn curtain and stated, "Just holler for me when you are ready." With that he heard the door close.

He rubbed his wrists and sat up in the bed, swinging his legs over the side, making sure he still could. As he stood up, the first thing that hit him was that he was dizzy and very weak. So much so that he fell back onto the bed and had to breathe slowly through the renewed pain in his stomach and head. As he lay there he heard a faint buzzing.

Do I really have to move? he thought. He knew the answer. The nurse, although apparently sweet in her demeanor, would he was sure, be more than happy to "assist" him in getting ready for his session. He wasn't the least bit interested in being manhandled in his current condition.

He slowly sat up again, the buzzing and pain lessening as he took his time. He placed one foot then the other on the floor and using the bed for support worked his way down to grab the clothes. Then, using the wall to brace himself, he slowly made his way to the bathroom. He placed the clothes on a bench and carefully made his way to the sink, holding on with his right hand and turning on the facet with his left. He didn't want to leave his ability to stand to chance.

He looked at himself for the first time in days. What he saw looking back was terrible. The first thing he saw was that his hair had been cut very short. He was paler than normal, had large bags under his eyes and the entire right side of his face was horrible bruised. He turned his head to get a closer look.

The bruising went from somewhere in his hairline to under his chin. A bandage covered what he assumed was his head wound behind his right ear. The doctor had said he had fallen. He knew he wasn't supposed to, but he pulled away the bandage and looked at the two-inch cut. It had at least a dozen stitches. He couldn't help but wonder, as he looked at his injury, if the desk had survived any better.

He replaced the bandage and closed his eyes and felt the familiar feeling of tears begin to well up in his eyes. His mother had found him. He wasn't going to let it happen, he wasn't going to cry, he wouldn't let Jimmy hear that, he thought.

He took a deep breath in and slowly let it out. Then another.

The deep breaths helped him recover from the flood of self-pity with the realization that his breath was terrible. However many days of not brushing his teeth was nothing short of disgusting. He focused all of his attention on the need to brush his teeth right then.

As he looked around he saw only one toothbrush on the ledge. As he reached for it he stopped. That one must have been Jimmy's. He opened the mirror to find a similar toothbrush as the one on the counter, still in plastic wrap. He opened it up, brushed his teeth and placed it back on the bottom shelf of the cabinet, to keep it separate from Jimmy's. He had never shared a room with anyone before, but it seemed that sharing toothbrushes would be just as gross to his roommate as it was to him, even if by accident.

He dressed and slowly made his way out of the bathroom. The nurse was waiting for him with the wheelchair. He debated protesting but as a wave of dizziness hit him, he realized he was in no position to do anything but accept her help. He sat down and she wrapped the blanket around his legs.

"See you on the other side," he heard Jimmy say as he was wheeled out of the room.

Part 3

As he left the room for the first time he could remember, he was able to determine that he must be on the ground floor of the hospital or close to it. He could see trees out of the small rectangular window at the end of the hall.

The nurse did not stop talking the entire time she wheeled him through the small maze of corridors. As they made a final turn to the right he knew that he was in a series of offices instead of normal hospital rooms. Mike also knew that he would not find his way back to the room without help. All of the offices looked the same and he assumed they were all for therapy.

The nurse opened a door with a press of a button and wheeled him in. A couch and two chairs with a small coffee table in between was the only furniture in the room. The nurse, whose name was Carla he had found out on their brief journey, offered to help him onto the couch.

Realizing he still didn't feel right, Mike took the assistance and said, "Thank you" once he was seated on the couch.

Carla smiled and said, "You're welcome. See you in a bit," and left the room.

He was looking around at the walls when the door opened and the doctor from earlier walked in carrying a small tray with containers on it.

"I thought you might be hungry," the doctor stated with a smile as he nodded towards the food. He put the tray on the table so that it was within Mike's reach.

The doctor reached out his hand to shake and said, "Michael, my name is Dr. Epeton. How are you feeling today?"

"Fine and it is Mike," he replied, shaking the doctor's hand.

"Mike, I know you don't like therapy. Your parents told me that you didn't think it helped," the doctor said as he seated himself. As the doctor continued to talk, Mike opened up the containers to find apple-sauce, a broth of some kind, and finally some chocolate pudding. He took the pudding and a plastic spoon lying on the napkin on the tray. He noticed that was the only silverware available.

"You have been through a lot, and the last thing you want is some doctor telling you how you should feel and that it will all be better. I am not going to do that. I am just going to ensure that you are not going to attempt to take your life again. When I am pretty sure that is the case, then I will release you. If we work together we can make that happen fast." There was a pause in the talking then and Mike realized the doctor was waiting for a response.

"Great," was all he decided he should say.

Dr. Epeton smiled again and asked, "So how about I ask you a bunch of questions, and we talk a bit and see where it goes from there?"

Mike nodded, scooping pudding into his mouth.

He was with Dr. E, as the doc wanted him to call him, for about two hours. He knew how to do the song and dance. He opened up, just a little. He didn't want the Doctor to think it was easy, and, explained how hard life was as a teenager in world that didn't understand him. It was painfully predictable, and so was the diagnosis. He was "depressed."

As usual, the Doctor was able to tell him that "there was hope" and "it actually could get better for Mike," but only if he was "willing to try." It took everything for Mike not to roll his eyes. He had heard it before, almost word for word, and as with all therapy it never changed.

When the session was completed Carla came back, helped him into the wheelchair, and took him back to his room.

Part 4

"You survived," Jimmy said with a little laugh.

Mike shrugged.

"I know, my doctor told me I wasn't crazy. That was a first. Not really. They all say that, don't they?" Jimmy laughed as he grabbed something off the side table. "Hey, I scored us a remote. Wanna watch something?"

Mike did, so he moved so he could see the TV. Being cuffed, it was a bit uncomfortable. They watched movies for a couple hours. When they got bored with the movies they began to play a game of truth. Telling each other personal information in turn, they talked about school, parents, and girls. He found out that Jimmy played most of the same video games he did, and that he had pretty much the same hobbies. Jimmy's favorite movie was Aliens, which was one of his favorites as well.

It was dark out when the nurse came in again to give him some of the pain medication that put him right to sleep, the sound of TV in the background.

When lunch was brought in the next day it interrupted their movie, mainly because the nurse insisted the TV be shut off for mealtime. He was finishing more pudding when his parents walked in. His mom began to smile as she walked up to give him a hug.

"You look good," she said as she squeezed him a little tightly.

"Thanks," he replied.

Mike was about to introduce his parents to Jimmy when he looked over to see that Jimmy had fallen asleep. His mother walked over in the direction he was looking.

"So, this must be Jimmy? Are you going to introduce us to your new friend?" she asked, using her "hostess" voice as she turned back to him.

"He's sleeping" Mike said quietly, looking at his mom a bit confused.

"Oh, well," his mother quietly said as she pulled the curtain between the beds closed, "why don't you tell us all about him then."

He told his parents about his new "roomie." When he finished saying only what he thought he had too, his mother said, "Well I look forward to meeting him." And she smiled again in the direction of the closed curtain.

"How did you know his name?" Mike finally asked, realizing he had not brought up Jimmy to his parents.

"Well, you see ..." his mom started to hesitantly explain before his father jumped in with, "Dr. E. told us you made a friend, so we wanted to find out more about him." His mother nodded with each word.

So, Dr. E. was spying on him, just great. Well maybe making a new friend would convince the great doctor to let him out sooner.

His dad set a bag on his lap. They brought him some clothes, a couple of comic books, and his handheld gaming system so that he could play a little.

As he looked through the bag, Mike noticed there were a few of his favorite snacks as well. His mom always gave him snacks when she felt guilty. He looked up and thanked his parents.

"How long I have to stay here?" Mike finally decided to ask.

His dad told him that the doctor didn't think it would take that long, and he should be able to go home soon. He could tell that this news made his parents happy.

They visited for about two hours, telling him all about the happenings with his family and neighbors. He listened and nodded, as he always did when his mom tried to include him, as if he was involved or interested at all.

It wasn't long after his parents left that Jimmy woke up. When he asked what he missed, Mike told him about his parents visiting and the stuff his parents had dropped off.

Mike shared everything with Jimmy. Taking turns, they challenged each other on the videogame and spend hours swapping stories. They also ate all the snacks by the next day. This did not help the pain in Mike's stomach, but it did cheer him up a little.

Part 5

The days began to roll by. The therapy was mandatory, sometimes two to three times a day he spent with Dr. E. Some days seemed to be better than others, and of course it was always better when he was medicated.

The Doctor had put him on a medicine for his depression and when he wasn't making any progress, the nurses realized he hadn't been swallowing his pills and resorted to administering the medication via the IV.

The new drugs made him tired. They always had some sort of side effect; the last ones had made him nauseous all the time. He supposed it didn't matter what they did to him as long as they made him happy, even if he was sleeping through half of his life.

He listened to Dr. E. speak, hearing the noise of the Doctor's voice, but not the words. Sometimes he did that, just faded out and only heard the noise of people speaking around him. He found that he did this a lot, with teachers, his parents, and the kids he disliked at school. He suddenly heard himself ask, "Are you treating Jimmy?"

Dr. E. looked at him, stunned for a moment. "I can't talk about other patients, you know that." The doctor gave him a fake smile, the kind a person gives when he wants to drop the subject. His mother did that a lot.

"I wasn't asking you to talk about other patients; I was asking if he was in therapy with you?" he persisted.

"Why do you want to know that?" the doctor asked.

"He never has visitors," Mike said, meeting the doctors' gaze perfectly. Dr. E. had a look flash across his face for only a second, but there was something there.

"His dad visits him. He visits him in his physical therapy sessions," the doctor said as he closed his notepad. "We can pick this up again tomorrow. You look tired." He pushed the button at the door that called for the nurse.

When he got back to his bed he found Jimmy playing on the game system. "So, how is our friend Mike doing today? Is he cured?" Jimmy said without looking up from the unmistakable sounds of the Mario Brothers game.

"Yep, all good, should be out of here by the morning," he responded.

He looked up at the ceiling tiles and blew his bangs out of his vision. His hair had grown out. He wouldn't let them cut it. In some weird way it measured his incarceration time in inches. His fingers brushed along the scar. The bump to his head had healed finally. There was a small hard knot that felt flat with little bumps. The doctor had told him it was scar tissue from when they had gone back in to fix something wrong with the way it was healing. It hurt a little when he rubbed it.

As he found himself following the lattice work of ceiling tiles he asked, "Does your dad visit you?" He heard the sound of the game music stop suddenly.

"What?" Jimmy asked, sounding a bit surprised.

"I never see them, your parents, I was just wondering if you saw them." There was pause. Looking over he saw Jimmy staring at him with an unhappy look on his face.

"Sorry dude, I didn't mean…" he began to say, but Jimmy cut him off.

"It's fine. My dad works a lot so I see him when he can, just not as much as… well… not a lot." Jimmy turned back to his game and the sounds started up again.

The nurse came in then for his next dose and within a few moments he let himself go to into the abyss of sleep. It was a convenient way to let the subject drop.

Part 6

When he woke up hours later, Jimmy was not in his bed and his head was hurting again. He must have rubbed it too hard earlier. As he reached to touch the area where the pain was coming from, he found another bandage. He called the nurse to let him off his leash to use the restroom.

When he got up, he was a little dizzy and his mouth was really dry. He slowly stood and made his way to the restroom, where he turned on the water and looked into the mirror. He lifted the bandage to another set of stitches. What had happened?

When he finished, he washed his hands and noticed the toothbrush on the counter was in the same exact place as the first day he had seen it. He held it up and it was dry. This meant nothing until he pulled his own from the cabinet and held them side by side. Jimmy's hadn't been used. He put them both back and made his way back to the bed.

He asked the nurse, "What happened to my head?" All she would say was that the doctor would explain. He asked her to get him some juice or something cold to drink. As she re-attached his restraints, she promised she would.

He closed his eyes. It had been months and he was no closer to getting out of here than the first day he woke up. He had been saying all the right things to the great Dr. E. and yet he was lying in the same bed, restrained, and nothing had changed.

He heard the door open and shut again just as he was about to go into another wave of self-pity.

"Whatcha doing?" Jimmy asked, startling him for a moment. Jimmy, it seemed, was a ninja. He had an ability to be completely silent, and then just appear. Jimmy said it was because he had been invisible to most people all his life that he must have adopted it as a superpower. Mike knew exactly how that felt.

"I would say wallowing in self-pity, but that doesn't sound nearly as cool as thinking about hot sexy cheerleaders," Mike chimed back.

"I like cheerleaders, especially the really bitchy ones. They are the hottest of them all," Jimmy retorted as he propped himself on his side.

"What's with you?" he asked Jimmy.

"Well, besides the newfound joy of never ending sponge baths, I won't walk again. Doctor said the nerve damage will make it so it is impossible, even with physical therapy," Jimmy said as if he was still talking about bitchy cheerleaders.

Mike didn't know what to say, so he stayed silent as he always did.

"You don't have to say anything. I figured it out before they told me, and nothing was changing with the physical therapy so it was sort of a given. Didn't mean to make it weird. Sorry bro." Jimmy winked at him and then smiled.

Mike realized that Jimmy was the only friend he had since grade school. He didn't always know how to act or what to say, but Jimmy did. It threw him off sometimes, but at other times he felt relief.

They watched some action/comedy movie with Bruce Willis for the next couple of hours; the end scene was some guy being thrown off a building followed by some brilliant comedic tagline that was terribly overused. As Jimmy began looking for the remote, Mike looked over and asked, "Do you ever think about doing it again? Jumping I mean."

"Yes, well, I think about how I would do it. I mean, I can't really jump again," Jimmy said, gesturing down to his legs.

"I think I would have to be surer next time that it would really be done. I mean, I can't wake up after my mom finds me. That can't happen again," he said, feeling more emotion then he thought. "Although, I don't see how it will happen if I can't get out of here." He slammed his hand down, and felt the restraint on his arm slide up and down.

"Why would it have to be after?" Jimmy asked, but before he could reply, he heard the door open. Dr. E. walked in.

"Good, you're awake. How are you feeling?" Dr. E. asked.

"Why do I have more stitches?" he asked back, sounding more aggressive than he intended.

"We found something in the scar tissue, the way it had healed, and we had to make an adjustment. This should be the last." Dr. E. smiled the same way he did at each therapy session.

"When can I get these off?" Mike said gesturing to the restraints and ignoring the fact his previous question went unanswered.

"Actually, that is part of what I am here for. You can have them off today. I just need you to understand that doesn't give you permission to roam the halls. But this way you can move around your room comfortably. How does that sound?" Dr. E. sounded like a ride host at Disney when he wanted to, with his perfectly calm voice.

"Great," and Mike faked a big smile to seal the deal.

He looked over at Jimmy, who gave him a little nod for his performance. Dr. E. bought it fully because he smiled back and said, "I am glad to see you doing so well, Mike." As he was turning to leave, Dr. E. patted him on the shoulder in acknowledgement or comfort, Mike wasn't sure which. He was just glad when the doc was gone.

Part 7

It wasn't until later in the evening that the nurse came in to remove the restraints. There was a long list of do's and don'ts he had to sign and initial. When it was finally over, he sat up in bed for the first time, stretching his arms above his head.

"Free at least, free at last," he heard Jimmy chanting beside him.

He looked over and realized that his happiness was slightly short lived; Jimmy was still restrained. He got up and went to the side of Jimmy's bed. He didn't want to leave his friend bound, but when he grabbed the restraints, he saw they were secured with a lock and key. He sat back on his bed.

"Don't worry about it dude. Mine will be off soon. Always happens that way," Jimmy assured him.

"How would you know that?" he asked back, not looking up from his own freed wrists.

"Honestly, well, this is not my first time as a 'guest' of this hospital. This is actually my third round locked away in this tower." Jimmy's voice sounded almost proud.

"What?" Mike said in a whisper. He was stunned.

"They say third time is a charm, right?" Jimmy was smiling, but the smile didn't reach his eyes.

Mike just sat there. He didn't know what to say. He couldn't imagine putting his parents through that kind of pain, over and over, especially after seeing his parents faces the first morning he woke up He would rather see them grieve and be able to move on then put them through that again.

"I didn't think I would get caught. That is why. The last time was a sure thing," Jimmy replied to the unspoken question.

When he met Jimmy's gaze, he could see it then, the disappointment of being here, of being in that bed.

"Is that why I never see your family visit?" Mike asked as he continued to make eye contact. Normally he would look away. He wanted to, but on some level he had no choice.

Jimmy broke the link by looking down, biting his lip for a moment as if he was nervous. "My dad can see me anytime he wants. He works here."

Ten questions immediately raced through Mike's mind. Before he could ask one of them Jimmy said, "Yes, he works here. Yes, you have seen him. You know him in fact." Mike was confused and he was sure it was showing on his face. He tried to remember all the males he had met during his stay and before he could even guess Jimmy stunned him again.

"Dr. E. is my dad, Mike," Jimmy stated flatly.

Mike lay back on his bed, his head swimming, and knew this feeling. When things were about to get really bad for him, this is how he felt just before they did. He felt a sharp pain in his head where the scar was.

"I am sorry. Dude, I am really sorry I didn't tell you before. My father made me promise. He said that it would affect his ability to help you if you knew he couldn't help his own son," Jimmy said as he sighed. "Well maybe not the last part. He thought I was better, you know, but then again, father or no they always think you're better until you jump off the hospital roof four stories up."

Jimmy stated it so matter-of-factly.

"How did you get up there? All the doors are locked." It came out of his mouth before he could even think.

"I got a key from one of the janitors. I told him I wanted to put something in my Dads office to surprise him for his birthday. It was a lot easier than you would think." Jimmy had that proud look again.

"Four floors huh? You survived that?" he asked. He was calming down, his head now more of a dull ache.

Just before Jimmy was able to answer, the door opened and Dr. E. and the nurse stepped in the room, both a bit winded.

An awkward silence followed. Unsure of whom the doctor was eager to speak with, both of them just sat there looking at Dr. E.

The doctor cleared his throat and said, "Michael, are you ok?" The doctor had resorted to using his full name again and that was never good.

"Great," he said flatly.

The doctor walked up to him and pulled out one of those flashlights, shining it in each eye while holding up his eyelids. He then pulled an otoscope out of his pocket and looked in Mike's right ear. When the doctor seemed satisfied with whatever he was looking for, he put both devices back in his pocket.

"You are sure you're fine?" Dr. E asked again. "No pain, dizziness, nausea?"

Although he had all of those moments ago, Mike knew that if the doctor was asking like this it usually meant something was wrong, and it would mean tests or medication at the very least. He was not interested in either.

"Nope, all good," he nodded his head as if this would confirm his words.

"Ok, then. If anything changes, please let the nurse know." Mike used another series of nods until the doctor and nurse left.

As the door closed, he turned back to Jimmy, "He didn't even look at you. What was that about?"

Jimmy shrugged, "I didn't exist much to him before. I guess it doesn't surprise me now."

Jimmy flipped the TV on and lay back in bed. Mike guessed he was done talking about it. Jimmy didn't really speak the rest of the night. He fell asleep to the sounds of explosions and snappy dialogue, which had to be a Michael Bay movie.

Part 8

He woke up to hear the sound of half of a muffled conversation. It sounded like his mother's voice. "Was he hurt? Well how do you know that? I don't think this is a good idea anymore. I want..." the hushed speaking was cut off by him rolling over in bed.

"What is not a good idea anymore?" he asked looking at his mother. She was worried, he could always tell, and she looked from him to Dr. E. as if waiting for approval to respond.

Dr. E. finally took the lead after an awkward silence. "We were just discussing the next phase of treatment." As he finished, Mike's mom looked down to her hands. That wasn't it, he thought, his Mom always looked down when something wasn't completely true.

"So, what is the next phase doc?" he asked, the tension getting thicker.

"Well, Michael, I think the best thing for you right now would be to stay here until we have your medication at the correct level and we have a chance to ensure you are in a good place," Dr. E. answered.

He looked at his mom again. There were tears in her eyes. She wouldn't meet his look. He looked up at his father, whose hand was resting on her shoulder. His lips were pursed. His father held his gaze for only a moment and then he too looked away.

"Great." He rolled over to face away from the crowd. He saw his mother's hand reach out as he moved but never felt it touch him.

Moments later he heard the door close. That was it, he was alone. He was always alone and there was always something wrong with him.

Part 9

"You up?" he asked Jimmy after a few minutes of lying in silence, listening to the machines beep.

"Yup" he heard in reply.

"Tell me how you did it again," he said flatly. Jimmy rolled over and looked at him for a moment. He wasn't sure if Jimmy was going to give him some speech about how he shouldn't even consider what he was thinking. He felt the swirl of emotions start to take hold. As if sensing Mike was near his breaking point Jimmy began to tell him the story in complete detail. Every time a question popped into his head, it was answered by Jimmy before he could ask it.

What Jimmy explained was perilous at times. The plan relied on not getting caught by anyone, because that would result in the restraints going back on. The one thing he knew was that he wasn't staying until the great doctor thought he was in a "good place."

He was about to ask the final question that came to mind when Jimmy said, "I can't" and pulled up on his restraints. Mike nodded. When he thought about it, he knew that the route he would have to take would involve stairs, which Jimmy wasn't equipped to handle either.

He waited until the nurse checked on him at 11:00pm. As the nurse was putting the final dosage for the day in his IV, she said "Sweet dreams." He nodded and rolled over as if the medicine was taking effect. A few moments later, the light was turned out. He sat up in bed, listening to the sound of retreating footsteps.

He got out of the bed, letting go of the IV line which began to empty liquid onto the sheets. He bunched up his clothes and an extra blanket to make it look like he was sleeping, and then pulled the blanket over the top.

He crept up to the door for one last check to see that all was as Jimmy described. As he turned back, Jimmy was smiling at him.

"Thanks man, for everything." It was all he could think of to say to the only true friend he ever had.

Jimmy nodded his head and said, "Good luck, dude." He followed each step Jimmy had laid out perfectly, and everything was exactly as he had stated. Winding through the corridors, he finally found the janitor closet Jimmy described and as he glanced to his left, he found the key hook right where he was told it would be. He took a set of keys and continued to make his way.

As he neared the stairwell, he looked around and saw that he was not near the actual hospital rooms anymore. These were offices. He looked at the nametags and found the second one on the right had Dr. Epeton – Neuroscience. He looked down at the keys and decided he had to try. On the fourth key, he heard the click of the lock and the door slid open.

He quietly entered and shut the door behind him. Taking a deep breath, he walked over to the desk which faced away from the wall that held a huge picture window. The window allowed for a great view of the hospital grounds and in turn, light to flood in from the well-lit hospital grounds.

He sat in the great doctor's chair. While debating if he should leave a note, which did not go so well the last time, he noticed a family picture. It looked like it was taken at one of the family theme parks because it had the park logo. Mike picked it up and held it in the light. It was the doctor, his wife, and Jimmy, and said May 4th 2002. He moved the picture to another angle and looked at the date again.

He placed the photo back on the desk puzzled. Pulling open the drawers, he found the file with his name on it and began to read it. It was all medical terms, mostly medications and dosages. There were references to the surgeries he had, including the most recent one for his head trauma, implant adjustments, predicable software modifications…. He continued reading what looked like version updates when he heard someone whisper, "What are you doing?" He jumped in his seat, his heart racing. He looked up to see Jimmy sitting across the desk from him.

"I was…" Mike started to say when Jimmy said, "I didn't hear any alarms so I wasn't sure if you got caught or changed your mind."

"No," he said, shaking his head. "I wanted…Wait, how did you get up here? Is this you?" he asked, pointing at the picture on the desk.

Jimmy reached out, grabbed the picture and nodded his head, "Yup, last spring, family bonding trip," as he placed the picture back on the desk.

"Better get going," Jimmy said. "You only have about five more minutes and they will be in to check on you." Mike looked down at the phone to see the time; it was 12:04am on 09-04-2010. Nodding back he looked up at Jimmy and then grabbed the picture and headed to the door to the stairwell.

As Mike grabbed the door handle he glanced back one last time at his friend sitting in the wheelchair in front of his father's desk. Jimmy looked exactly the same as the photo in Mike's hand from 2002. Jimmy hadn't aged a day.

Looking back down at the photo Mike guessed why Dr. E. had chosen the Jimmy from eight years ago, and wondered for a moment when the last time the good doctor had seen his Jimmy. He took one last deep breath and headed up the stairs.

He knew that when he opened the roof door, the alarm would sound and he would have two minutes. Mike pushed the door open and in less than a second the alarm triggered. It was louder than he expected. In the next moment, the emergency roof lights switched on. Two minutes, he thought to himself and he began moving again, items in hand.

It only took twenty seconds, thanks to Jimmy.

About Erika Lance

Erika had the unique opportunity to live in several different environments across the country growing up, giving her a colorful perspective on life. Born in Minnesota, she spent most of her formative years in Hollywood, then a ranch in New Mexico on the border of an Indian reservation. With a love of the arts since she was a child (acting, painting, sewing and dancing to name a few!) she found her passion in writing. Beginning with short stories, poems and articles for local papers, "Jimmy" is her first published fiction story.

Connect with Erika:
www.erikalance.com

Email: erikalance@gmail.com

www.facebook.com/pages/Erika-Lance/114388082065099

Twitter.com/AuthorELance

Instagram.com/AuthorELance

The Room

By Rhiannon Matlock

PROLOGUE

Deep within the Vigo quadrant of the universe was a remote planet called Hilo. An opulent world long before, it had been filled with flowers, song and laughter; but all had faded when greed and politics consumed it. When the native inhabitants left they decided to nuke every surface so that no one could have what they couldn't. The area became a dead zone and all trade routes and byways that once frequented it were deserted.

Years later an industrial race called the Truids, who didn't mind the heat, claimed it for their own. Setting up domes along the barren terrain and flushing clean air through, the Truids made it possible for others to come safely, because underneath the carefully constructed domes were dumping grounds. The kind of place where things you didn't want found again were safely stowed. Not many knew of the planet's conversion and those that did kept its secret fiercely. Hilo, a once beautiful planet, was now known colloquially as the Yard.

A ship with folded back wings and a thin, scissor like body cut through the bumpy and hazy atmosphere, diving at an acute 90 degree angle until it nearly collided with the surface. At the last second the pilot pulled the nose up and the plane sped across the deck, kicking up dust and debris. Reverse thrusters kicked in, slowing the plane as it came to the nearest dome. An opening in the glass formed. The plane slid through and came to a sudden yet graceful stop.

A creature not unlike a mole climbed through the dirt and emerged as the plane's engine whirred down. A woman with short, sleek black hair and black eyes descended to the surface, her boots causing an audible crunch in the dirt. The creature quivered slightly. The woman adjusted the glasses covering every inch of her eyes and sniffed the air once before she turned in the direction of the mole.

"Hello Keeper," she said in a smooth voice, "It's always a pleasure to see you again."

It was an old joke between them. They were both blind as a bat under the scorching rays of the sun.

"Yes, tall one," the Keeper replied with a faint smile, "always a pleasure."

Pulling out a wooden token with three crylic symbols imprinted on their face, Jaq pressed it into the Keeper's palm.

"You said you had something for me," she said.

The mole tucked the coin away discretely and nodded. "In the back. I cannot say who brought it in or from where, but it is as you described."

There was something in his voice that caught Jaq's attention. Fear.

"I shall never speak to anyone of your role. You know that Keeper," she stated firmly, gaining a slight nod from the mole.

Without another word he disappeared back into the ground, leaving Jaq to her task. Standing perfectly still, she took in a long breath through her nose and collected every scent she could. Thousands of particles were sifted and categorized. She repeated the action. Automatically her senses disregarded what she'd already caught and looked for anything new. It took a few minutes but she found it. Locking on, she made her way around mounds of rubbish to the back of the dome. She stopped dead in her tracks when she hit the source. Jaq moved carefully to the edge of the pile, cautious because of her reduced vision. The smell of blood, putrefaction and rotting flesh was nearly overwhelming but under that lay something else. The chemical she'd been tracking was in evidence aplenty. The Keeper hadn't steered her wrong and considering the freshness, back tracking where it had been brought from shouldn't be too difficult.

She was excited, but something else snagged her attention. Another smell, something soft and delicate, somehow familiar and yet completely foreign touched her nose. Jaq inhaled again. Like a mercurial flame the fragrance danced around the periphery of her senses until she finally caught it. Cady. She hadn't smelled that scent in a long, long time. She shook. There was no mistaking it, even if it was impossible. Somehow Cady had been in contact with whatever was in the pile at some point.

Jaq touched the side of her head to activate a small chip just under her skin. It was a clumsy device but the mole wasn't telepathic.

"Call Keeper," she said aloud, her voice unsteady and her hands clammy.

"Yes," came the hushed tones of the Keeper inside her ear.

"Shut the panels," Jaq requested, "There is something that I need to see."

CHAPTER 1

The Room. That's what it was called. Stark and plain in design, it had white walls with white lights that illuminated every corner and crevice with blinding clarity. Underfoot one continuous slab of white plastic met seamlessly with the walls. Gleaming equipment and glowing vials sat atop the single counter to the left. Situated in precise spots that never moved, next to them was a sink to wash off. A thick metallic slab rested in the middle of the room. Raised by one twisted spindle of metal and covered on top with a thin, spandex type blanket that molded and held any form underneath it in place. Along one side was a panel of buttons that controlled it.

The room itself was no more than ten feet by ten feet and its innocuous veneer somehow made the perilous undercurrent gushing from the very walls that much more sinister. For just a moment the room was quiet but it was soon disturbed, first by the sound of a door as it swished open, then by a piercing scream, followed at last by the telltale scuffle of someone being dragged across the floor.

A beast, over seven feet tall, with fur and very sharp teeth, dragged along a viciously squirming humanoid female. The subject in question had been in the chair before and knew what was coming, despite the blindfold. No matter how hard she bit, clawed and gouged, nothing fazed the beast as he lifted her up and slammed her to the chair.

"Careful Guard," a voice said. "That thing is more valuable than you are."

It was the Doctor. A squid like creature with eight limbs, a host of eyes and a large brain. The suction cups on his legs moved him along slowly but silently.

As soon as the Guard let go, the woman tried to escape, launching herself with all her might, but the blanket slipped over her before she could move more than an inch. Its molding properties conformed to her and held her firmly down against the chair, leaving her only to yell as a means of defense. The Guard continued to hold the woman down but the Doctor waived him off without further regard. Rather than be offended, the large beast merely disappeared down the same corridor he'd come in through.

Tiny tubes from the side of the chair came out and attached themselves to the woman through generated holes in the blanket. While this was occurring the Doctor made his way over to the counter. A series of readings from the woman appeared on the counter's clear plastic top that doubled as a screen. Scanning over the data in detail, the Doctor soon grew tired of being disturbed by the woman's pitiful cries and hit a button on the counter top that injected a sedative into her system. Blue liquid traveled quickly and within moments the room was quiet once more. Definitely how the Doctor preferred things.

CHAPTER 2

It was cold and dank outside. Not surprising considering Calisis was mostly a water planet, but still Jaq did not like it. She stopped and shook herself, sending the tiny droplets of water that had collected along her body off with a rapid fling. In the denser atmosphere, moisture collected on her more quickly than usual, which in turn annoyed her quicker than normal. With a muted sigh she looked around, mostly to make sure that she had not missed anything while her senses were smothered under the offensive dew in the air. With her faculties quickly returning to capacity, she felt the subtle shift behind her as the one following her ducked behind a nearby building. The other reason she stopped was to give the creature tracking her pause, and she felt some small measure of amusement that she could do it so easily.

She'd known that she was being followed since the Yard, but had allowed the pitiful man to shadow her. She'd wanted to get a reading on him and the cat and mouse game excited her. Upon discovering how his inept his abilities were she'd been greatly disappointed and was now looking for the easiest way to dispatch him. She was in a bit of a rush.

With a sniff of the air, she resumed her stride and continued on down the dusty street. There were no patrons at this late hour of the day and the thickening fog made conditions nearly ideal. Sensing the creature drawing closer and in a bolder fashion than before, Jaq detoured from her intended destination and turned down a side street. The road narrowed considerably and after a little bit she stopped and turned. The fog rolled over her, and covered her completely. This was the one condition of liquid that appealed to her and while it was clear he had trouble seeing through the haze, she certainly did not. He was a few feet away when he stumbled, hands flailing in front of him as he staggered. Jaq smiled.

Mist swirled supernaturally around her as she reached through the fog at lightning speed and latched a hand firmly around her followers' arm. He jumped in shock at the contact, but she held on firmly and tightened her grip like a vice. His scream soon followed.

"Who are you?" she asked.

He did not speak but emitted several pained, guttural sounds.

"This will continue until I either snap off your hand or you speak," she said.

Still, he did not say a thing as bones started to creak. Instead of fighting he sagged into it, ripping more sinew and tendon than she intended. A terrible wail came from him and she loosened her grip. Without the support, he dropped to the ground with a thump and made no move to rise as he held his arm and whimpered. The fight in her died. Not because she felt pity, but because she was repulsed. This man was hardly worth her time. She started to leave him when he raised a hand in protest.

"Please," he said.

She stopped. Something about the way he implored her halted her in her tracks. Dropping to one knee, she came to eye level with the man and nearly hissed. He was like no beast she had ever seen, or rather, no one beast. His face was scarred and disproportionate, housing a set of large insect like eyes, but having a snout jut from his leathery face.

"What are you?" Jaq asked incredulously.

The beast groaned and shifted itself so that it was resting on its hind legs.

"Unnatural," he said again though it was labored. "Please..."

"What do you want?" she asked after he didn't finish his sentence.

"Please kill me," he said and then bowed his head in shame.

Of the things Jaq thought she might hear from this disfigured mutt, this was the least expected. Never before had she been asked by a healthy creature to end its life.

"Why would you want me to do this?" she asked.

"Because it hurts."

"What does?"

"Everything."

Something about the bend of his frame screamed for her to fulfill his request, but alas she could not harm something unarmed that posed no threat to her. She shifted to stand up when he leaned forward, eyes wide and fearful.

"Please," he begged again.

"Find someone else to do your bidding. There are plenty who'd be willing."

He grabbed hold of her arm with his good hand and she felt the strength coursing through him, though he inflicted no hold on her.

"I can't," he said, "no one else strong enough."

"Then do it yourself," she replied.

"I ... I can't," he mumbled.

Jaq knew without asking that he had tried already and, for whatever reason, had failed repeatedly. How he knew a Vadan could execute him she didn't know. She wondered absently if he was just hoping.

"How did you find me?" she asked.

"I didn't. I was at the Yard and saw you."

Her eyes narrowed. "Why were you there?"

"Mourning," he replied simply, his grief almost palpable.

"I see," she said softly.

Perhaps the loss was still fresh or perhaps it was the first time he felt someone really understood what he meant, but either way he started to weep. She allowed his grip to tighten on hers while the sorrow bled from him. After a few moments he looked up at her again, his bewilderment somehow plain on his grotesque face.

"You're not going to kill me are you?" he asked.

"No."

"I don't understand. You're a Vadan aren't you?"

Jaq almost smiled, an echo of Cady's words about that very subject ringing in her mind. Remembering that time was painful though so she smothered it.

"What is your name?" she asked as she pulled out a small device.

"Manut."

"Take this and go to my ship."

He took it but looked at it curiously.

"I did not come here to deal with you Manut," Jaq clarified.

There is another pathetic creature that I'm looking for she thought. When he didn't move, she gave him a little shove to catch his attention.

"Hey, I don't have a lot of time. Go and wait for me. I will help you," she said, "but first you will help me."

He nodded and got to his feet.

"Manut," she said as she rose to her full height. "My ship and I have a long history. I don't think it needs to be explained that I like it just the way it is."

The creature regarded her for a long moment. "I understand your words Vadan," he said and left.

CHAPTER 3

It took a little while for the Doctor to finish going through the testee's readings but the results looked within range. The Doctor smiled to himself. His first thought was to congratulate himself on how brilliant he was. His second was that the Boss would be happy. Rapid movements from his multiple arms input a series of commands into the system. A few moments later, a second liquid started to pump into the woman. Now was the time to see how well it worked he thought as he started toward the testee with his deliberate footsteps.

By the time he arrived to her, the liquid had stopped pumping. The Doctor looked down at the woman, concentrated on her and her alone. There was a delay, but before long her eyes flew open. The Doctor's smile grew in depravity as he touched her hair with pseudo affection.

"That's right my dear," he said, "I'm in control now."

And I don't think you'll like what I have in mind he thought, morose merriment bubbling up from within.

~~~

Outside the Room there was a separate compartment that housed all of its controls. Temperature, air quality, and maintenance were all handled by two technicians who sat behind a set of glass panels and whose sole purpose was to preserve the room. They didn't know what went on inside; nor were they were allowed beyond their own walls. They had a wing off to the left for sleeping and a wing off to the right for eating. No one but the Doctor and the Boss were allowed further. Not even the Guard, who neither spoke nor moved, unless it was to open the outside door to the facility and that was only a few feet from where he stood.

It had occurred to one of the technicians that there should be more than just one Guard for such a facility, even if it was so far removed from civilization that there wasn't even a sign of habitation or vegetation. Someone would eventually go crazy from standing and watching nothing happen all day. The technician never mentioned his thoughts to anyone though, knowing instinctively that it was unwise. Instead, he sat behind his panel, monitored readings from the multitude of sensors in the room and around the facility, and kept mostly to himself. Bored with the lack of activity, Rapht flicked non-existent dirt from under his fingernails and looked over at his co-worker.

"Have you heard anything about when the Boss will be back?" Rapht asked.

The other man glanced up from his panels and shot him an annoyed expression. Jime was his name and he was a short, tow headed man in his middle years. Aside from that Rapht knew nothing else about him.

"No, why does it matter?" Jime replied.

Rapht shrugged, "No reason, I was just curious." Jime looked back to his panels, dismissing the younger man. Rapht kept his sigh in check and went back to his own screens. It had been twenty weeks since he'd arrived at the facility and he had yet to be outside once. He longed to get some fresh air, talk to someone who did more than just answer his questions, and do something besides turn some knobs every now and again.

Before Rapht could ponder once again on how he'd ended up there, a faint buzz sounded behind him. The door that led from the outside world slid open with a faint swoosh. At once a pall settled within the maintenance room, lifting the hairs on the back of Rapht's neck. Dread and inexplicable anxiety beaded his brow in sweat and twisted his stomach into knots. It was always the same. Without having to look up, Rapht knew exactly who had finally arrived.

The Boss.

CHAPTER 4

It didn't take long for Jaq to find her way to the Maison Du Joie. Not only was it the biggest building in the small, dingy outpost of a planet, but it was the only thing that had any sign of life to it. The fog had thinned noticeably which allowed the establishment to be easily seen, along with the two guards posted at the entrance. Squat, burly creatures with leathery skin and claw-like hands, both were mean looking. Jaq hardly spared them a glance as she started past them. One of them grabbed her by the shoulder so she turned and barred her teeth at him. Her serrated set of incisors gleamed in the light of the building. The guard quivered slightly as he turned to his companion. A series of basic grunts passed between them before she was released and waved on.

Without glancing back she shoved the heavy doors open. Music, strobe lights and a thick panoply of aromas immediately assaulted her senses. It was overwhelming for a moment until she felt the fine spray of mist settling over her. For once she was grateful for the dulling aspect of water. Making out more distinct figures now, she saw that there were literally thousands of people packed within the space, writhing in time with the beat.

Along one wall ran a bar filled with patrons and ended with a passageway. It was what she was looking for but guarding the hallway was a menacing looking creature with red, glowing eyes. That was the real bouncer. She knew she could deal with him, but she'd rather not make a scene.

Scanning the crowd her eyes quickly landed back on the bar and its keeper. The man was tall and well-structured, with dark hair that he wore long. It looked good on him. He was attractive and she had no doubt he was using it to his advantage. It was a working club after all.

This should be pretty easy, she thought as she made her way past the writhing bodies and grabbing hands and slid into a recently vacated seat. She raised a hand to get the tender's attention. It didn't take long before he spotted her and sauntered over.

"Hello beautiful," he said with a lazy, sexy grin, "what can I get for you?"

Her first thought was to bare her teeth and see his reaction. It would be amusing, but Cady's voice flittered through her mind. Instead she leaned forward a little and touched one of his hands. He briefly looked down and then back at her, his smile widening.

"Something unique. What do you recommend?" she asked as she started tracing circles against his soft flesh.

He shivered and completely ignored another raised hand from nearby. "Really depends on what you prefer," he said, lowering his voice.

A distinctive perfume wafted off him and tickled her nose. The scent was unmistakably Unidahia, a lovely and hypnotic aroma that was a common but expensive tool of the courtesan occupation. Though immune to it she decided it fit her purposes nicely. She rose from her seat and nuzzled her face in his neck.

"Where?" she asked in a husky voice.

The tender leaned back a little, his eyes heavy and nostrils flared. He gave a brief wave to someone at the other end of the bar and motioned her to follow. They stepped into the hallway without so much as a look from the Bouncer. Once away from the music, the tender pushed her against a wall and tried to kiss her. She gave him her neck. She wasn't ready for him to feel her teeth just yet.

"You want to do this here?" she purred, letting her hands roam a little to keep him interested, "or is there a room we can use?"

He growled a little at the interruption but grabbed her hand and pulled her along after him. Down and in they went until they came abruptly to a door. He pushed her against it, pinning her there.

"Close enough," he mumbled, attacking her neck once again.

"Oh my dear little man," she murmured close to his ear, causing him to shiver again, "if only you really had the skill to handle me."

The words were not what he expected and caused him to start to pull away. She never allowed him the chance as she grabbed him by the head and bit down on his neck. He jerked once but then relaxed as she sucked softly and carefully. Too much and he'd die, too little and the aphrodisiac slipping from her teeth into his system would wear off too soon. Before she over-indulged, she pushed him back. His eyes were glazed but he smiled as he dropped to the ground and passed out.

Sniffing the air she wasted no time stepping over him to proceed further into the underground of the club. Various scents drifted through the corridors, some old and some exceedingly recent. None were terribly offensive, but they were not what she was looking for. Finally she found it. The distinctive smell that only belonged to one man, Ryce Rathers. Wrinkling her nose, she followed the scent until she hit the source. Standing in front of a door, she knew he lay just beyond it and as unhappy as she was about seeing him again, she was fairly certain he was going to be more upset to see her. She shrugged. Hope he's at least clothed this time, she thought as she turned the handle and entered the room. A wave of dust and must sprang up as she crossed the threshold, nearly gagging her. The space was completely dark, but that was to her advantage. She looked around the squalid quarters. A crumpled form lay in the corner mostly covered by a ratty blanket. His mouth was wide open in sleep, his fingers clutching a bottle of some alcohol. Pieces of straw and muck were stuck in his unkempt beard and he smelled filthy. Never before had she seen the only heir of Vigo in such a condition. Disgusting, she thought but stayed where she was when she called his name.

Getting no response she called out to him again in a higher voice. Still he didn't stir. With a sigh she moved to the bed and reached down to nudge him. That was the moment he chose to attack. Before she could move, he smashed the bottle against the wall and held the broken, jagged edge against her throat. His bright blue eyes bore into hers with a hostility that was at once familiar and expected. Glancing down she noted he was naked.

"I see being a slovenly drunk hasn't impaired you much," she commented dryly as she looked back up at him.

His eyes narrowed dangerously. The desire to use the jagged edge toward its intended end was evident. Despite the weapon and the man behind it, she wasn't concerned for her health however.

"Who says I've been drinking?" he growled.

"You're breath for one."

"Why are you here Jaq?" he queried, no trace of inebriation in his words as the glass bit further into her skin.

"Put that away before you hurt yourself."

"You do know if it weren't for Cady, I'd kill you right now?"

"Likewise Rathers."

A heavy exchange of animosity passed between them. Finally, he pulled the broken bottle away and curled back to his former position.

"Next time you try to sneak up on me, walk a little softer," he mumbled.

"I wasn't sneaking. I've come to collect you."

"Unless you have news of Cady, we have nothing to talk about."

"I do."

He stiffened and for the briefest of moments she felt a small ping of remorse. She smothered it quickly and hoped he hadn't sensed it. A harsh laugh escaped him, wrought with more pain than humor.

"You don't have anything, do you?"

"Not exactly," she said, irritated she'd let emotion for him leak in.

"Your nuances don't interest me. Go away."

"Go away?" Jaq scoffed derisively. "That's the best the son of Vigo can come up with? How disappointing."

He stiffened at the sound of his father's name but said nothing in reply.

"How the mighty have fallen. I wonder what Cady would say if she were to see you like this."

"Well that's the point isn't it? She's not here. I mean it. Leave now. I have no desire to be involved in any of your or Fae's political games any longer."

"You ranshani, I am not here on behalf of anyone."

A cold, heartless laugh escaped Ryce. "Really? And how do explain how you found me?"

"It is not as hard as you might think. With the way you've been whoring yourself out, it's a wonder you believe you're hidden at all."

"At least I'm getting some, or did you finally figure out those teeth of yours are for mating, not killing?"

"They have many uses. Now get up. We don't have a lot of time."

"There is no 'we' Jaq," Ryce gritted out, "we're not friends."

"No," Jaq replied and there was almost a note of regret in her voice, "We'll never be friends but we stopped being enemies a long time ago. Now grab what you need and let's go."

"No."

He was starting to get on her nerves but she knew she had to show some restraint. She needed him and it was a bitter pill to swallow.

"Poor Ryce," she chided softly as she withdrew, "still feeling sorry for yourself. You know, it's not really so surprising that she left. Look at you. What has she lost? You're a mockery. If this were the fortitude of my Qui, I'd have abandoned him too. I'd -"

With blinding anger he bolted straight from his floor and pounced on her like a lion. She was ready for him this time though, rolling with his weight and clipping him soundly across the cheek with her elbow. He staggered and fell, showing for the first time just how drunk he actually was.

"You're pathetic," she said as she rolled to her feet and dusted herself off.

He laid where he was, spitting out the blood pooling in his mouth. They were both quiet for several moments.

"What did you find Jaq?" he finally asked.

"A way," was all she said.

His bright blue eyes drilled into her. She had to be very careful not to reveal too much to that gaze. He studied her at length until he finally nodded and started to get to his feet. Before Jaq knew what was happening, a cloth was thrown over her head and a fist hammered into her face. The bastard had tricked her. As consciousness start to fade she chided herself on being so stupid as to trust him.

CHAPTER 5

Lazarus stood on the threshold to the mechanical room and took a moment to look around. The two technicians sat, braced against an energy that they couldn't comprehend, but could only perceive. He noted that the dark haired man seemed more tense than the blond one. He was by far the smarter of the two technicians, something Lazarus usually found useful, but in this case was becoming increasing displeased with.

That was fine, he thought. He was close to accomplishing what he wanted at this facility and would soon have no more need of either man. Dismissing them, he turned a pair of pale blue eyes to survey the rest of the scene. Everything was neat, clean and exactly the way he left it. Turning at last to the Guard, Lazarus took a step toward the creature and stroked its face lovingly.

A near imperceptible purr came from the belly of the beast, lifting the corners of Lazarus's mouth into a faint smile before he pulled his hand back and turned away. The dark silk of his garments shimmered and swayed with the movement, but everything else in the room was utterly still. Without wasting any more time Lazarus went to the Room. The door swished open just in time for him not to miss a step.

Precision. That was Lazarus's watchword. Everything from the perfect cut of his short hair to the crisp movements of his long body screamed of his meticulousness. It was what he demanded of everyone and everything around him. Within moments he'd crossed the long corridor that lead to the Room. As before, the door opened just before he arrived, ensuring he didn't break stride. The ground clanked as he stepped in and two figures stopped what they were doing to look over at him. Only one interested him.

"What is the update Doctor?" Lazarus asked in his evenly modulated voice.

Two of the Doctor's eight limbs extended behind him and propped him up while another arm hit a button on the nearby wall. A screen dropped down in front of Lazarus.

"See for yourself," the Doctor replied.

Lazarus wasted no time in further discussion as he began to scan over the readings.

"There is little here to suggest you've made any progress," Lazarus commented.

"On the contrary," the Doctor replied, taking the tablet, "Come look at this."

Slightly put out at the lack of concern the Doctor showed toward his dissatisfaction, Lazarus chose to put aside his irritation for the moment and walked to the opposite side of the chair. The chair's current occupant was squirming and looking at him with wide, fearful eyes. A more appropriate emotion to be sure, but the creature was little more than a humanoid and hardly worth his attention.

"What?" Lazarus asked, still keeping his voice moderate.

"Look at the eyes," the Doctor replied, his gravelly voice slightly more animated.

Lazarus flicked his gaze from the ugly, squid-like Doctor to the subject. Chestnut colored hair was plastered against her pale face, and were it not for the hallowed out cheeks and various cuts marring her naked body, she would have been considered quite fair, even though she was of a species he considered of little more value than ants.

The frail female gurgled something but Lazarus paid no attention as he fixed his attention on her eyes. At first he saw nothing out of the ordinary and was about to thrash the good doctor for wasting his time. Then he saw it. As he moved closer he confirmed it.

"You requested my presence to tell me that you could effectively blind a mouse? Doctor, I don't believe this is why I have you here."

The subtle shift in Lazarus's voice caused the Doctor to pick up on the gravity of his current situation. All seven of his large beady eyes blinked in rapid succession.

"She is not blind," the Doctor said in a rush, "she is not able to control the movement of her eyes."

"The technicality does not interest me," Lazarus stated.

The Doctor held up four hands in protest, "Look again. I have something else to show you."

For a moment Lazarus considered killing the bottom feeding jelly. Since that would only momentarily appease his current frustration he dismissed it and looked again at the female.

This time a sharp scream ripped through the room as the woman's hands shot up from her sides and started clawing viciously at her eyes. Jagged nails, presumably bit up in a lame attempt to stop the pain, dug and gouged spastically. She was being forced by something. A minor tremor of excitement rolled through Lazarus, quickly quashed by the recognition that this sorry excuse for a species was still somehow fighting the control being imposed upon it.

Nettled but still mildly interested, Lazarus watched with amusement as the woman continued until she'd ripped through most of the skin and was hard at work at the muscles. After a few minutes he held up a hand and at once the woman stopped. Whimpers of tears and pain continued to emanate from her, but Lazarus ignored them.

"That is what you should have started with," he said, his pleasure evident.

The Doctor gave a hesitant smile in return, "I wanted you to see that it was not in control first."

Lazarus waved off the mistake and went back to the screen. He rescanned the data.

"This is better but this is not what I asked for."

"I - I know," the Doctor stuttered.

"She is fighting your control still, which means that you haven't gotten the compound right yet."

"Yes but I will, very soon."

Lazarus smiled for the first time. On such a face as his, almost angelic in design, it should have looked beautiful. Instead it solidified his cold expression into something resembling ice. The doctor trembled and Lazarus chuckled mentally as he retracted his six perfectly serrated teeth and closed his mouth. If the Doctor was the scum of the ocean, Lazarus was the shark.

"As always Doctor, I enjoy my visits here. I'll see you again within the week. You'll have it finished by then I presume."

"Yes, yes of course," the Doctor stuttered.

Lazarus barely heard him before the door slammed shut behind him.

CHAPTER 6

Jaq woke to a pounding in her head that was only compounded by a heavy whirring sound nearby. It took a moment for her to collect her thoughts and remember what had transpired. When she opened her eyes she tried to look around, but everything was bathed in light and nearly blinded her. Shutting her lids she tried to focus on the sounds.

"You're in your ship," said a voice through the din.

It was Rathers. Anger bubbled inside and she tried to move but found herself bound.

"I figured that would be your first reaction," he explained softly.

If it were said by anyone else she'd take the low tone as sympathy for her aching head, but it was Ryce and his words were devoid of compassion.

"You can release me you know."

"And have you eject me like you did last time? I'd rather not."

"You've disabled my controls by now. I'm no threat."

"I always assume you're a threat. I also don't consider you that stupid to leave only one way to control your ship."

Ryce leaned forward and hit a button turning off the lights shining directly in her face. After a moment she opened her eyes to find herself in the passenger seat of her small ship. Her arms and legs were tied down as was the middle of her waist. Stars passed by them as they sped through space, as well as a few planets that she didn't immediately recognize.

"Where are we going?"

"We're not going anywhere. I'm dropping you in Kiversain."

Jaq felt a small measure of dread lick through her. "Planning on drowning me?"

"If only I could," he muttered more to himself than her.

She looked at him, ready to lash out, when she noticed his bent form. He looked as though a hundred planets were sitting on each shoulder. Long ago she'd questioned Cady's attraction to him. Not only because he was of the Masdon race, something that made him revolting, but because he didn't align with Cady's usual tastes. Over time Jaq had gained an uneasy respect for him and though she never held Ryce in the same regard as her friend, she began to see what Cady had known all along. He possessed a pure heart.

"Stop that," he said abruptly.

His voice was rough and his knuckles white on the controls of the plane. Jaq looked away and reigned in her sentiments.

"It's true Ryce."

The muscles in his jaw tightened in agitation.

"It may have been once, but not now."

"If that were so, you wouldn't be able to read me anymore," she replied.

"People change."

"The coat of paint on a ship may change but the ship does not," Jaq quipped, the words falling from her lips before she realized it.

Ryce stiffened. It was an old saying of Cady's and an endearing one. No doubt it brought back many memories.

"You still don't believe that I have news do you?"

"You can talk but you're still going to Kiversain."

Biting back a sigh Jaq replied, "Two months ago I came upon a compound, a chemical. It was present in the bloodstream of a man who died suddenly after he convulsed for nearly an hour straight. The man who examined him said that there was a foreign substance that attempted to worm its way into the base of the motor controls in his brain. The examiner suspected it was some kind of crude mind control."

Ryce said nothing though Jaq knew he was listening, albeit unwillingly.

"I've been tracking this compound to find its purpose and who's making it."

"Let me guess," he cut in with some scorn, "Lazarus."

"Yes," she cut back, "whatever your blind stupidity allows you to believe, he's not the innocent you suppose him to be."

"I hardly consider him innocent, but he may not be not the villain you paint him as."

"Go to the Yard. You'll see why I dragged your sorry ass out of that filthy establishment."

Ryce shook his head, "I don't care about Lazarus-"

"It's not the weapon. It is who he's experimenting on."

"I don't understand."

"You will."

CHAPTER 7

Out in space there are many docking stations. Some are reputable, and some not. As with everything else it was all about location. In the middle of the Vigo quadrant there was a particularly opulent station called Verdana. It was composed of seven docking rings that circled a large, staff like tower. The tower had rooms to rent and multiple recreational spaces for all manner of things, and everything was staffed by robotic servants that held no memory. It was both posh and exceedingly private.

Occupying the top floor of the tower, the dining deck was ovular in shape and lined floor to ceiling with windows all the way around, affording guests the most gorgeous of views. Normally the restaurant would be bustling with people, but this day there were no parties present save for two men. One was already seated near the windows. He was hunched forward, but with thick hands and a mean looking scar down the center of his cheek, he didn't look particularly cowed. The other man was fair and lighter in structure, but held himself with confidence as he carried himself across the room. The bulkier man flicked his gaze from the windows upon seeing the man's reflection in the glass.

"Hello, Lazarus."

"Herlitch, what a pleasant surprise," Lazarus replied as took up a seat at the man's table. He noted that his companion had not risen upon seeing him.

"Surprised? I called you for the meeting."

"Yes, but you are the most uncouth of the Queen's advisors," Lazarus replied as he unfolded the linen nearby and placed it on his lap. "Am I to glean a certain message from the selection of her emissary?

"No," Herlitch stated, "and you don't need a napkin. I won't be staying for dinner."

"But I will."

That got the bigger man's attention and his eyes narrowed as he carefully observed his companion.

"Shall we proceed Herlitch, or would you like to stare at me as I order?"

Just as he finished his question, a servant appeared. Herlitch's gaze returned to the windows and the abyss that lay beyond. Several minutes of silence ensued while food was brought to the table.

"Herlitch, you've been quiet for too long," Lazarus commented as he started dicing his food.

"I have no use or time for the small talk Lazarus. I'll wait till you're done."

"But then I'll be bored and you'll be rude and neither condition is good for business."

Herlitch cleared his throat, "What would you like to talk about?"

"How did you hear of me?" Lazarus asked before popping a bite into his mouth.

His tone was nonchalant, but Herlitch knew the kind of beast that lay beneath. The bigger man shrugged.

"Who doesn't know of you by now?"

A small smile appeared on Lazarus's face, "Flattery? An interesting choice, but unnecessary. Let me be more specific. How did you hear of my product?"

"Word travels fast, particularly when it is good."

"Odd. I specifically didn't inform your Queen or any of her allies of this project."

Herlitch bristled, "You excluded us? Why?"

The men stared at each other. Herlitch's gaze quickly descended to a glare. Lazarus continued to eat and after several moments of this, the smaller man burst into a cackle. It held joy, but not for

Herlitch. Lazarus twirled the fork in his hand, a sparkle of delight in his eyes just before he raised the utensil and plunged the tines straight through Herlitch's hand and into the table.

Pain ripped through Herlitch but he bit his lip against the scream that wanted to escape. The heart of his nervous system was in his hands and with that one fell blow he'd been effectively crippled.

"Hurts doesn't it," Lazarus said, snapping his fingers. A moment later a new fork appeared. "But that was punishment for asking the wrong question."

It took longer than Herlitch wanted but he managed to compartment some of the pain, allowing him to think a little. Lazarus didn't seem to mind the wait as he continued to eat.

"What's the right question then?" Herlitch hissed.

"Tsk, tsk. Always so impatient," Lazarus said as he put down his tableware and took a sip of tea, "but you're in pain and I'm in a hurry so I'll make this quick. I already know that you're not here on the Queen's request, but Jaq's."

Herlitch opened his mouth to protest but Lazarus waved him off.

"Your leader may be lacking in any real money or influence these days but at least she is not as dull as you. Now, given the who and my statement about not wanting your species to have my latest compound, the right question would've been why did I take this meeting."

Herlitch just stared at Lazarus. He'd already recognized where this was headed and silently scrambled for a way out. The fact that the big man was little more than a worm on a hook only excited Lazarus.

Getting up from his seat, Lazarus walked around the table, his hand never leaving the fork as he gyrated it around with him. Herlitch held out as long as he could but was finally reduced to trembling mass, unable to block the pain any longer. He didn't cry out and that angered Lazarus, who took the fork out with a vicious tug.

"The reason I took this meeting Herlitch, is because I need to send Jaq a message and you seemed like a good way to do it."

With that Lazarus tipped the man back in his chair and shoved the fork through the thick layers of his belly, hitting the heart and killing him instantly. Lazarus let the man fall forward as he withdrew the fork and wiped it off.

"And just to answer your first question my dear man, the reason I excluded your race is because you are the ones I intend to wipe out with it."

CHAPTER 8

"You don't honestly think this will hold me for long do you?" Jaq queried as she watched Ryce bend over her and fasten another knot.

"It'll keep you long enough for me to disappear."

"I'll only find you again."

Ryce shook his head. "You only found me because Fae told you where to look. She may have thought herself clever leaving bread crumbs for you to follow but I always knew who was dropping them. I won't be so clumsy anymore."

"I know your scent Masdan."

"And I know how your mind works Vadan," he replied quietly as he secured the last knot and stood to leave. "And you can tell Fae I will never be speaking to my father again, no matter how she presents the offer."

"This has nothing to do with either of them you muler," she said angrily.

He gave her a skeptical look.

"Yes, Fae told me where to find you but she doesn't know why."

"You lie. Fae always knows."

"Search me," Jaq demanded.

For a second Ryce paused and she knew he was considering it, but he abruptly settled the matter by pulling away. Silently Jaq cursed him.

"You're grief is understandable but it is blinding you."

Ryce grabbed her by the chin and forced her face level with his.

"Look at me," he demanded.

Even with the sun he was too close for her not to see his gaunt cheeks and the dark circles under his eyes. Even more disturbing was what Jaq didn't see. His esch, his fire, had simmered to nothing more that dying embers and his expression was hallow.

"Do you wish for me to pity you? Because I don't," she said harshly.

He pulled back from her. "I don't want to be contacted again. That is all that I wish for."

"Is that what I should tell Cady then, when I find her? That you aren't there because you just didn't want to be contacted?"

"If you find her, you can tell her whatever you like. I doubt she'll let you get one sentence out before she rips your throat out."

Jaq stiffened. It was a low blow from him.

"We all did things that led up to the events of that day," she said quietly.

Ryce didn't respond. He didn't have to.

Just go to the Yard, she said silently as she watched him walk away. By the slight stiffening of his shoulders she knew he heard her but was stubbornly refusing to listen.

CHAPTER 9

He was a dead man. The Doctor knew it. From the moment he had seen the Room, two things had been perfectly clear to him. The first was that Lazarus was a determined and dangerous man. The second was that this was an opportunity he could not refuse as it was a chance to work uninhibited. Uninterrupted by prying ears or spying eyes, the Doctor would have every means at his disposal to prove his theories. He'd been awed by such a prospect, causing the first consideration to fade while the second came into sharp focus. With a giddy squeal he'd signed on. Now, after months, it was done. A full two days ahead of schedule. The Doctor was about to send Lazarus a comm burst requesting his presence when it suddenly occurred to him that his time of usefulness was probably at an end. Even reproduction of the compound would be incredibly simple now that it had been discovered, leaving no need to keep him around. Considering how Lazarus viewed useless things, the Doctor knew his days were numbered.

The Doctor shivered at the very thought of that cold, calculating monster having utter dominance over anything. The fact that Lazarus already did, in effect, dictate his every moment somehow escaped the Doctor's reasoning as he paced back and forth and considered how he was going to save his slimy hide and walk away with the compound. He'd stopped dead in his tracks. His latest subject was still whimpering in the chair. The Doctor turned to the testee with a gleeful laugh and hit her with a sharp rap.

"That's it. There is no reason he should get it at all is there?" the

Doctor muttered to the nearly dead woman on the slab, "It is mine after all. I developed it. We'll just have to mix something up before he gets here, won't we?"

The subject said nothing of course, but the Doctor didn't care as he started humming and going about preparing his final concoction.

CHAPTER 10

Ryce was halfway out of the atmosphere when a series of thumps sounded from somewhere in the ship. He knew the ship was Jaq's own personal transpo and knew she'd never let even a bolt get out of place. The noise sounded again, indicating whatever it was it was in the floor below. A few minutes later Ryce pulled out a disfigured creature from the rear compartment. The beast dropped to one knee and bowed.

"Get up," Ryce commanded with irritation.

The creature did so.

"Who are you?" he queried.

"Manut."

"What are you doing on this ship?"

"Waiting for the Vadan."

"Jaq? Why? How did you get aboard?"

Manut held out the device he'd been given and Ryce took it with some amazement. Jaq had let this creature on willingly? Looking up from the key, Ryce eyed the beast critically.

"What did you want with Jaq? With the Vadan," he clarified when Manut looked confused.

Manut's eyes cast to his feet, "I asked her to kill me. She told me to wait here."

"Did you attack her?" Ryce queried, still mystified as to what was going on.

Manut shook his head.

"Then she was not going to kill you."

"She said as much," Manut said sadly, "but she said she would help fulfill my request if I helped her."

"Your request, huh?" Ryce remarked derisively. The beast tensed.

The wave of hopelessness and anger that flowed from the miserable creature was so pure and overwhelming that Ryce cleared his throat and changed his tune. Something was amiss. Jaq couldn't read like he could, but she was even more cautious. Why in the universe would she offer to help this mongrel?

"Where did you find Jaq?" Ryce finally asked.

"At the Yard."

The Yard. That couldn't be a coincidence. When Jaq demanded he search her, despite his rejection, he had done a quick probe. She hadn't been lying about not telling Fae. It didn't mean that wily woman didn't know, but Jaq hadn't been scheming with her. She had found something at the Yard she wanted no one but Ryce to see. It didn't mean it had anything to do with Cady, but it was significant enough that she made the decision to come to him. Something he knew she hated. Ryce sighed mentally and looked at Manut.

"Show me exactly where you found the Vadan."

CHAPTER 11

Another day had passed for Rapht. As he lay in bed he thought of all the things he could be doing instead. It was driving him nuts and today it seemed worse. He didn't know why but something had changed. An anxious mood permeated the facility and even the stoic Guard was on edge. When Rapht had made a slight calculation error, the Guard had growled at him, something he'd never done before. It scared Rapht more than he cared to contemplate. Sitting up, Rapht rubbed his face and flicked on his light. The glow disrupted the monotony, but not the unease.

"Jime," Rapht called out in a whisper.

When the other man did not reply, Rapt got out of bed and went over to his roommate's space. To his surprise he found the bed made and no sign of his co-worker. He checked the bathroom next, but found nothing. His nervousness trebled. He went to the door and he reached out to open it but hesitated. Should he go looking for Jime? Would it get him killed?

The questions raced but they all boiled down to one thought, Rapht would rather be dead with someone than alone and scared. With a sigh, he stepped out into the maintenance room. The Guard was nowhere to be seen.

"What is going on?" he murmured before moving to the door the furry beast normally stood at.

He had a sudden and wholehearted desire to get out of there. He tried unlocking the door with his personal code but the lock buzzed and the door stood still. Damn, he thought, no easy escape for me. Rapht turned and looked around. There was only one other way besides the one that led to the dining area and that door had never opened while he was around. Rapht went to the panels that Jime handled. He hit every button but nothing moved or even responded.

"Okay think, think," Rapht muttered to himself. "Maybe Jime controls that door. But you'd need his code. Oh, what was it."

The seconds seemed to drag out as Rapht went through every memory he had of this place. At some point he must've seen Jime punch in his numbers. At last he remembered and wasted no time pulling up the access panel. Sweat slicked his skin but he managed to type in the code.

"Welcome back Jime," the computer said and Rapht slapped his hands together with a triumphant yelp.

"Okay, let's find out how to get you open now."

Rapht tried several buttons and combinations of buttons before he finally found one that sent the door open with a distinctive swish.

"Jime you sneaky bastard, you knew how to get out of here the whole time."

Wiping his brow, Rapht stepped through. Something caught his foot and sent him sprawling. Unable to catch himself his head smacked against the ground. The pain was immediate but quickly pushed aside when he heard a sound from nearby. It was a faint pop. He was not alone.

Untangling himself from whatever held his feet, he nearly swallowed his tongue. Jime's broken body was jammed up against the frame. Rapht scanned rapidly for a way out when he saw the Guard. He was supine on the floor, neck snapped.

"What the hell?" he murmured, sweat pouring off him.

He started to get to his feet when he heard the sound again and froze. His heart started to beat so fast it nearly hurt. Two large tentacles suctioned against the floor came into view. When he looked up he caught sight of the ugliest thing he'd ever seen.

"Wha - What are you?"

"I'm the Doctor," the creature replied.

"The Doctor?" Rapht asked in disbelief. "How ... How-"

The creature waved one tentacle, "That is not really important is

The Ink Slingers Guild

it? The important thing is whether or not you want to live."

"I really, really do," Rapht said, nearly tripping over his tongue to get the words out.

"Good," the Doctor replied and some kind of smile formed on its face.

Another tentacle appeared. This one held a syringe and it moved rapidly toward him.

"What is that?"

"A way for you to keep breathing," the Doctor said. "Well, sort of."

The syringe pierced his skin, sending an odd tingly sensation over him. The next moment, Rapht found himself being held up in the air by the Doctor but he could neither feel his own body, nor move it at all. The grotesque smile on that inhuman face was the last thing that he saw.

CHAPTER 12

Ryce had not only taken Jaq to the horrid planet of Kiversain but he'd dumped her on the most remote island he could find. Really it was just a spit of land. It barely fit the two of them, let alone anything so big as her ship. He had tied her to a tree and left her to rot.

Aside from the never-ending water surrounding her she had another problem. The sun was out in full force, which weakened her strength considerably. Rather than waste time cursing Ryce or working against the bonds he cleverly put on her, she relaxed against the tree, gathered her energy and started to send out telepathic messages. Distance was not a problem but availability was. The ones she could call on were few and far between. Most would either extort or kill her if they found her in such a predicament.

There was one that Jaq trusted though and it was only a matter of time before she arrived. Within a couple of hours Jaq heard a familiar whirr and smiled. The bonds slackened, releasing her as a pair of hands helped her to her feet and shielded her eyes as she was taken onto the ship and directed to a passenger seat.

"Strap yourself in and I'll turn out the lights," the woman said.

"Thanks," Jaq replied, doing as she was told.

A moment later the overheads blinked out and they were

airborne. The darkened space was a blessing and finally she opened her eyes. Her rescuer's form was the first to come into focus. An ethereally beautiful woman with soft features and an inviting presence. To the uninformed she could appear delicate. She was, however, anything but.

"What kind of mess have you gotten yourself into this time Jaq?" the woman asked.

"It's good to see you too Fae."

Fae smiled and the warmth was soothing. It reminded Jaq at once of Cady, which was no surprise considering they were sisters. Both were endowed with a sort of magnetic power that had served to guide Jaq at different, turbulent, points in her life, but beyond that they were very different. Fae was more subtle and diplomatic, while Cady possessed a raw fire that tended to sweep even the most antipathetic along with her. It was something Jaq severely missed. Realizing what she was thinking, Jaq looked over at Fae with a contrite smile.

"It's okay," Fae said, her smile falling a little into sadness, "I miss her too. Do you have any news?"

"Possibly, but I'm not sure yet. I have a contact who was meeting someone at the Verdana but he hasn't checked in. Can you take me there?"

"Yes, but I can't stay."

"That's fine, I'll figure something out."

Fae punched in the needed coordinates and then set the ship on auto before turning to Jaq. She gave her a long look before speaking.

"You're hiding something from me. What is it?"

Jaq hesitated, "I found Ryce. He's not in good shape."

"I know, but he'll be fine and that isn't what your holding back."

"I don't want to share until I've confirmed. I don't want to get anyone's hopes up."

"Especially yours," she said, quickly discerning Jaq's real concern.

Just like Cady, Jaq thought and nodded.

"Fine," Fae continued, "but I want to know whatever it is soon. I can get it from you another way if you don't, but I'd prefer not to."

"I understand and I will."

Fae smiled again, settling the matter. "Good and by the way, the answer is yes, I'll keep your meeting with Ryce from Vigo."

Jaq smiled faintly at Fae answering her unasked request. She didn't know how good of an idea it was to keep Vigo in the dark about his son but for now she needed him far out of the picture. With the speed of Fae's ship and her unrestricted progression through the various checkpoints, it wasn't long before they arrived.

Knowing time wasn't on her side, Jaq moved quickly through the halls of the tower and straight up to restaurant. There were a host of people surrounding the entryway as well as a few authorities trying to push them back. At once she knew Herlitch was dead, but she still needed to see his body. Slipping through the crowd, she saw a couple of officers huddled together. She sidled up behind them and bumped one, lifting his ident chip off his belt. He turned to give her a stern look but she mustered up a sheepish smile and walked off. Approaching the posted guard, she flashed the chip at his scanner and he waved her on through.

Whatever had happened must've been recent because the body hadn't been moved yet. Jaq went over to Herlitch and hunched down so she could inspect without being noticed. Lazarus's smell was all over him. So he had at least made the meeting she concluded. She was about to leave when something about his tattered shirt caught her eye. She grabbed an imaging device from one of the pockets of her pants. It was small and cubed until she took one corner and pulled it out. The material stretched until it was the size of a small window. She then pressed the corner to hold it in place. Next she pushed Herlitch back a little so his chest was flush and straightened out his shirt. There was a message there, coordinates. Going back the screen, she tapped a button along one side and snapped a photo. Grabbing the corner again, she retracted it until it was back to its original size. As she headed back out the door she handed one of the guards the chip she'd taken.

"One of your men will want this," she said and disappeared back into the crowd.

CHAPTER 13

Ryce entered the airspace and angled the ship vertical, turning the vessel into a knife that sliced through the irradiated, bumpy smoke of the upper atmosphere. As he descended, he thought about Jaq's words. Though he'd told her he didn't care it was the ever-present possibility of finding Cady that drove him, and kept the worst of his fears at bay.

Several minutes later he came through the haze and nearly plowed into a mountain face. He grimaced as he maneuvered away and took the ship just under the cloud cover. Pulling up Jaq's flight manifest, he found her coordinates for the dome and plugged them into the auto function.

The ship soared through the sky like a bird and soon found a suitable place to land. Taking off his harness, Ryce made his way to the storage room. Opening the door, he found Manut squished but alive. He grabbed the beast and dragged him top soil. Before he let him go, Ryce bound them together with an electric leash.

"I do not intend to run away," Manut said.

Ryce looked him over. He was the reason Ryce gave any credence to Jaq's story. He had never believed Jaq's theories about Lazarus, but Lazarus was wily and if he was involved at all, there was no way Manut had just happened on Jaq.

"Show me where the Vadan was when you found her," Ryce said.

The creature nodded and led the way. Soon enough they came to the spot, a pit at least a mile in diameter and possibly just as deep, piled high with bodies. They were in various states of decomp and the smell was almost overwhelming, but that wasn't what caught Ryce's attention.

"Give me your other hand," Ryce instructed his escort.

Manut did as he was told and Ryce secured him with the leash. As Ryce walked up to the edge of the pit, he pulled out a small scanning device and pointed it at the front of the pile. Seconds later his suspicions were confirmed; they were all the same species. A second beep from his device surprised him and he looked at the screen in confusion. Race: unknown. The words sent his mind spinning. With everything in the known realms already catalogued, the ramifications of that were immense. Jaq would've known instantly. An almost giddy bubble formed in his belly, but then he looked back at the bodies and his smile fell.

Ryce put away the device and dropped to a knee next to the closest form. With only four limbs and the simplest of features, the design of the creature was understated yet elegant. It was clear not only was she a woman, but that she'd been heavily abused. With a heavy heart and a trembling hand, he reached out and pulled away the long strands of hair that were plastered to her head before moving to the scratches along her face.

"What did this to you?" he murmured softly as he stroked her cheek, rubbing away some of the dirt that had collected there.

Her skin was soft and pale, the body still warm. Ryce got up and turned to Manut. His rage caused the beast to tremble.

"Where did she come from?" he asked.

Unable to find his tongue Manut merely shook his head. He had no idea.

"Where was this done to her?" Ryce demanded.

Manut hesitated for only a second.

"I will show you."

CHAPTER 14

Lazarus walked into the facility and instantly knew something was wrong. His Guard was in place and the two technicians were seated, but he felt nothing from any of them. The dark haired tech turned his seat around to face him.

"The Doctor is ready for you sir," the man said.

Never before had the tech the nerve to face him, let alone talk to him. Something was definitely amiss. With a frown he ignored the man and went to the door. It swished open, but he'd had to pause a moment so as not to run into it. Lazarus's irritation quickly rose. Taking the hallway with hurried steps he arrived to the room in seconds.

At first glance everything looked exactly as he left it. The Doctor looked up from a screen with an almost jubilant smile.

"You're here. Excellent. I have good news sir," the Doctor said, immediately pushing a button to lower a second screen for his boss.

The Doctor's tone was not only confident, but also arrogant. Lazarus was done with him, but he did want to see the results first. Stepping up to the screen, Lazarus made sure to keep his senses on alert as he started to read the data.

"Did you figure it out?" Lazarus asked abruptly, not really caring what the readings said.

"Yes, I did."

"Excellent, let's see."

The Doctor's rotund body quivered in excitement as he went up to the table holding the latest testee. Pushing a button along the side, a clear blue liquid filled the tubes. After it finished injecting her there was complete silence. It lasted for only a few moments. The girl on the slab raised a hand and pulled out all of the tubes. Next she sat up and got off the chair, standing completely still, eyes glazed and body limp, like a puppet on marionette strings.

"Is that all?" Lazarus asked, not impressed.

"No, there is more," the Doctor replied his excitement amping up.

The girl started moving in a circle and then dancing before stopping abruptly and walking over to the counter. She took a knife from the tabletop and shoved it into her arm. She did not move nor flinch, and waited there for further instruction. This was curious to Lazarus. He walked over to inspect her further, turning his back to the Doctor. As he peered closer, he felt a stabbing prick in the left side of his arm and a tingling sensation spread over his body.

The Doctor stood a few feet away, watching the Boss standing utterly still. A sense of triumph ran amok through him. He hadn't known if he would have the courage to go through with it, but seeing the look of disdain on Lazarus's face the moment he'd walked in had decided him.

He knew it worked too, because he'd more than doubled the dose he'd given to the Guard. After the shock of having accomplished his aim wore off, the Doctor went about exercising his control, wanting the Boss to go over to the counter and find something to kill himself with.

Lazarus righted himself, infuriated at the nerve of the insignificant squid attempting to dominate him. Pivoting, he saw the Doctor's look of elation die almost immediately and his rage turned to satisfaction.

"I don't understand," the Doctor stammered.

"Of course you don't, you imbecilic fish!" Lazarus roared, shaking the very ground they were standing on. "Did you honestly think something as silly as chemicals can control me?"

The Doctor quivered under the malevolent waves coming off Lazarus and tried to run for the door. Half way across the room, he froze. He tried to move but found himself grounded and unable to do anything more than blink. Two of his arms moved of their own accord and wrapped themselves around his throat and started to constrict. True terror started to set in when he realized he had absolutely no control over his body.

"How are you doing this?" the Doctor gasped, trying in vain to find air.

"I have no need for a compound," Lazarus replied, almost bored. "It was developed for someone else's use."

Life started to drain from the Doctor, but still he fought against the iron control.

"Please," he tried, "please let me live."

Lazarus laughed and a second later the Doctor squeezed his own neck so hard that he crushed his throat. Finally gratified, Lazarus released his control on the squid. Walking over to the counter, he stopped and pulled up a sleeve, revealing his wrist. Tapping it twice, a small section of skin retracted to reveal a chip. After moving the chip directly over the center of the screen, he hit a button to download all of the Doctor's research. As it processed, he started to turn his attention to the woman still standing off in the corner when a new sensation hit him.

He looked towards the door and sniffed the air. Jaq had arrived. He smiled.

CHAPTER 15

Jaq touched down outside the compound a few minutes later. Ever since she had punched in the coordinates on the new ship she acquired and saw where they led, a slow burn had begun inside her. Entering the atmosphere of her dead home world, the burn turned to a molten fire.

Jaq stepped out of her ship and sank into the ground. With nothing but ash as she walked along, she could almost hear the cries of the dead.

Of all the places you had to pick here, didn't you Lazarus she thought with fury.

Without bothering to scout around first, Jaq walked up to the front door of the facility and found it open.

"Cocky snake," she muttered as she entered.

Stepping in from the daylight, she found herself in a long hallway that was utterly dark. That was perfect and she absently wondered if Lazarus had done it just for her. He had a twisted sense of humor that way.

It wasn't long before she found the control room and as with the front, all doors were open. She sniffed the air and found where his scent was the strongest. Following it she quickly came into the Room. There was some light, but it was dimmed and it took a moment for her to adjust.

"Sorry. If I had more time to prepare, I would've had them all out by now," Lazarus said from somewhere in the room.

Jaq smiled but hate was in her eyes.

"In whichever lighting you choose, you're still an evil bastard," she replied.

"Tsk, tsk. Always so impolite Sasjaq," he replied and shot the entire room into brilliance. "Didn't Cady ever teach you to be respectful to your superiors?"

Hearing her name from his lips made her bristle more than she'd liked. Lazarus seemed to find that amusing, as he laughed. If she could have seen properly, she would have lunged at him.

"Come now, my little Vadan. You do not have possession of her name and stop contemplating killing me. You won't get what you want if you do."

"I'll find Cady another way," she replied as her eyesight returned slightly.

He was right in front of her. His silk garments shimmered as he laughed again. Jaq reached behind her and took out the small knife she always kept at her back. It was thin and sharp, and would easily pierce through his chest. She lunged but just as the tip reached his skin, he grabbed her by the wrist.

"And you call me evil, trying to kill me without even a fair fight."

"Fair is not in your wheelhouse," Jaq replied as she tried again to plunge the knife into him.

He held her at bay easily, despite her immense strength.

"I only need one of you to find Cady," he said, his voice now hard, "and you're making it easy for me to decide which one."

Jaq tried relaxing to lure him in to a false sense of victory but when she tried driving again he pushed her to the side. She stumbled from the force and hit the ground hard. Lazarus scooted her knife away and walked towards her.

"It really is a pity. You're almost too beautiful to kill, but a lover is better than a best friend, especially considering the betrayal by said friend," he said kneeling beside her.

He grabbed her hair and pulled back her head, revealing her neck. Opening his mouth, his incisors flashed and his eyes gleamed.

"Yum. It has been a while since I've tasted a Vadan. So few of you left," he said as he lowered his face towards her.

As he was about to bite down a long blade ripped through his chest and nicked her. For a second he was motionless, a shocked expression on his face. Jaq shoved him off and he fell to the ground.

"Didn't see that one coming did you, you ass?" she said with satisfaction.

Looking away, she glanced up to see Ryce's face. A worried expression knitted his brow when he saw the slice on her chest.

I thought you weren't going to come, she said silently.

I thought you were going to leave me alone, he replied and some of the tension between them eased.

"Cutting it a little close, aren't you?" she goaded.

He frowned and held out his hand. "You know, you could just say thank you for a change."

Jaq smiled as he hauled her up to her feet, "And miss giving you a hard time? I'd rather not."

He gave her a brief smile before turning his attention back to Lazarus.

"He wiped the data and killed the technicians, so whatever he knew is gone," Ryce said.

"You were fiddling with the computers while I was in here being manhandled?!"

Ryce shrugged, "You were a good distraction."

Jaq shook her head. "Well, there is something he left behind."

Ryce looked as she pointed toward the corner. The woman was still standing there, unaware of anything that had just transpired. Ryce gently took her by the arm and started walking out of the compound.

"Flush whatever is in her system and use her to find Cady," Jaq said.

Ryce snapped his gaze back to her, "There is no guarantee that is where Cady is and besides, I'm not the tracker of the two of us."

"Lazarus all but confirmed that's where Cady will be and you're better with the female species than I am."

Ryce observed her for a bit and she held his gaze.

"Jaq you're not afraid to find her are you? She will want to see you."

She sighed, "I'm not afraid but Lazarus is right about one thing, it'll be better if she sees you first."

By this time they stepped outside and approached both of their ships.

"Ah, I see you haven't crashed it like you did the last one," Jaq said, hoping to dispel the slightly awkward moment as she held out her hand for her key.

"And you've stolen yet another ship," he replied, giving her the device, "How many is that now?"

Jaq shrugged but smiled.

"Where is Manut?" she asked.

"I fulfilled his request," he said simply.

That stunned her. "You really have changed, haven't you?"

He gave her a long look but said nothing. Hopefully you haven't changed too much to get her back, she thought but kept that tightly hidden. There was too much at stake for Ryce to have any doubts.

"What're you going to do?" Ryce asked.

"As we both know, Lazarus is not dead. I need to find out what his plans are for the compound before he finds a new form."

His brows rose, "Assassin turned investigator? Are you going soft on me Jaq?"

She smiled. "Oh, so you do have a sense of humor left. Good. I almost thought you left it back there in that meat house."

Ryce stiffened a little at the name. "I wasn't sleeping with anyone there by the way."

By the lack of certain scents, Jaq had already guessed as much. "If you weren't there for the obvious purpose, then why?"

"Looking for answers," was all he would say.

They were silent for a moment, each lost in their own thoughts, knowing they were at a cross roads and they may never see each other again. While they didn't hold love for each other, they shared something that bonded them tighter than most.

"Will you tell me if you find her Ryce?" Jaq asked quietly.

"Of course."

"Well then, I think you'd best be on your way."

If they had been friends that would have been the moment to hug or maybe shake hands. They weren't though, so they didn't. Ryce gave her a small smile.

"Good luck Jaq."

She smiled back and gave him a little nod. Ryce lead the zoned out woman onto his new ship. Things were about to change. For better or for worse, she didn't know, but either way pandemonium was about to hit. Jaq could only hope that they all survived it.

About Rhiannon Matlock

Born in 1981 before YouTube, Twitter or Twilight, Rhiannon Matlock remembers when you played your songs on Walkmans and actually had to tell your mother where you were going before you went out to play.

Now a well-seasoned traveler who still considers herself a child at heart Rhiannon enjoys such diverse activities as bungee jumping, white water rafting and volunteering in third world countries, but dislikes slow drivers and people who malign their friends.

Rhiannon doesn't like to talk about herself much, insisting that everyone else has a much more interesting story to tell. She especially likes to spin a good yarn, particularly ones where the white hat wins.

Connect with Rhiannon:
facebook.com/rhiannonmatlock

Other books by Rhiannon Matlock:
Beyond the Threshold (Anthology)

Beginnings

By Lisa Barry

As the sun continued to its peak, vendors set up on the outer edge of the oval courtyard to sell their wares and trinkets. The common ground was normally used for addressing the citizens' or to present a comedy or drama, but today's show was a well-built tower of wood and iron bars. He was on display and scheduled for the gallows the next morning.

Occasionally a daring child would run by and throw rocks or mud into the cage. The dark skinned man never reacted, just crouched quietly on the barren floor. He was huge, at least six hands taller than Meela, which didn't say much really, considering her small size. She had been watching the stranger since her arrival in Daushtra the day before.

She watched him lift a powerful arm and brush something from his chest, probably a mozzie. They had stripped him down and left him in only plain linen breeches. Earlier someone brought the man bread and water, shoving it between the iron bars. He had nodded his thanks and then ate slowly, as if savoring it.

Meela took another sip of ale and picked at a bowl of venison stew while she watched through a window of the inn. Earlier when she asked the innkeeper about the stranger he had shaken his head.

"Sad really," she replayed his words in her mind. "He had one too many ales and when Goff came along and accused him of bedding his wife, he didn't budge, just ignored him. Goff kept picking a fight and getting real ugly. Sir Raj...Rajer finally broke and backhanded him." Meela raised an eyebrow at that point.

"Yea, you wouldn't think much of that, now would you?" the innkeeper who had the same Daushtran dark skin had asked, and when Meela shook her head he had nodded in agreement. "Well, in this case, Rajer mind as well have tossed a century old oak onto Goff. His neck broke instantly." At that Meela had raised both eyebrows.

"I know," the innkeeper said as he shook his head, "Rajer tried to heal him, but it was too late. I don't think that healing stuff works on the dead."

After that, Meela started watching Rajer. With his skills, he could be a good companion on her journey and that was exactly what brought her to Daushtra in the first place. A plan started to formulate and she spent her afternoon gathering the supplies they would need.

~~~

When night finally fell, the inn was crowded with patrons. Some spoke of the trials of their workday, others of money-making schemes, but most spoke of the event on the morrow. Avoiding attention, Meela swept out through the back entry.

The light from the inn cast eerie shadows and she pulled her hooded cloak closer to shield against the chilly breeze coming off the nearby ocean. When Meela stepped up to the cage she could barely make out the man called Rajer in the darkness. Only the eyes that watched her were clear.

"Sir Rajer," she addressed him quietly. He chuckled softly and deeply.

"I don't think that applies anymore." She saw his teeth wrapped in a smile of darkness.

"That's relative," Meela answered. She passed a blanket through the cold metal bars.

"I have need of your services," Meela started, "and I'm not talking about back handing my enemies to death." Again she heard a deep chuckle void of mirth.

"If you wish to continue this life further," she continued, "then you must trust me on the morrow." Rajer was silent for so long Meela started to think maybe she had misjudged.

"Whatever is to be shall be and I will follow my destiny," he finally said.

"Then I shall see if your destiny bends my way," Meela commented and turned to leave. As an afterthought she turned back and whispered 'goodnight' before heading back to the inn.

The next morning Meela was up just as the sun started to stretch over the nearby ocean. Dressing quickly in plain tan trousers and a brown tunic, she pulled on her soft leather boots and pulled back her hair, tying it with a thin strip of leather. Her loose brown curls fell down her back just below her shoulder blades. She braided it and used a second strip to keep it bound.

As the sun finished stretching over the ocean and began making its way over Daushtra, Meela added to her dry stock and purchased fresh fruit and bread for the journey. She packed two saddlebags and readied her horse Sym, as well as a new Daushtran horse she had obtained the day before.

The common area had already turned into a bustle of activity. Merchants had lined up, one after another, with all manner of folk bartering for a meal or trinket. Many just stood and waited for the procession to the gallows. Meela bought dark trousers and a white tunic she thought would be large enough. She then waited with the throng.

When the sun settled directly above, six council members wearing colorful robes, garnished with gold and silver thread and precious stones, congregated about twenty hands from the cage.

Meela was startled when a Woman of God from Bausc stepped in to stand with them. She knew that Bausc Women sometimes consulted churches and town councils on their beliefs, frequently in attempt to convert, but Meela never thought she would see one in such a superstitious society as Daushtra, and certainly not standing with their council.

The head councilman stood tall in his bright red and orange robe. His skin was black as night and slick with oil, his hair in a long braid and partially gray. He motioned with a wave of his hand and a drummer beat out a quick rhythm that effectively silenced the crowd.

Moving up to stand between the council and the dead man's cage, her skin prickled slightly when the Woman's gaze fell upon her. Meela met her gaze with a bored look.

"Sir Marshele," Meela addressed the head councilman, going down on one knee. It made her appear but a child compared to the crowd around her. She lifted her bowed head and continued, "I would ask that I may legally buy this man's life for my own purposes."

The crowd burst out in whispers before quieting with a hush. Sir Marshele motioned for Meela to stand, which she did quickly.

"Small lady," he addressed her and smiled, appearing to be amused by her request, "How is it that you wish the company of a man killer?"

Meela stepped closer. "It is my belief that the man acted to protect himself," Meela said. She glanced at Rajer, who watched, his face blank. Meela continued, "A man who is as cold as you suggest would not stay to see the gallows, but would leave in the night for his own neck."

"And how do you propose such a man would manage that feat from an iron cage?" another councilman asked.

"No bars hold this man, sir," Meela answered as she bowed her head slightly to the councilman, "May I demonstrate?" When Marshele nodded, she turned to Rajer and merely gestured. Rajer looked at her for a long moment and then at Marshele. He put his hands around two of the thick bars and pulled them apart as though they were wax. He stopped before they were wide enough for him to step through, and then bent them back into place.

The Bausc Woman stepped forward and said to Marshele. "Surely you don't believe this is evidence of his character? The trial is done and he is condemned to death!"

Marshele turned to the woman, a flash of anger crossed his face. "Madam, when I need your advice, I shall ask." He glanced at Rajer before turning back to Meela.

"Now small lady, you bring something to my attention that I should have seen for myself. How is it that you will control a man of such strength – even if we agree to a price on his head?"

It was Meela's turn to smile. "May I again demonstrate? I will need him from the cage."

"Why certainly," Marshele smiled, "this is nothing if not entertaining."

Meela was glad to know that Daushtra's lead councilman was easily entertained. In Bausc, she would have been dismissed after her first address. In fact, in Bausc, she would have probably stolen the man from the cage in the night and prayed they wouldn't find her too quickly.

As the cage was being unlocked, she watched the other council members. It appeared they were waiting to see what Marshele decided before entering their own thoughts. All but the Bausc Woman, who looked like her head might burst into fire at any moment.

When Rajer was led over to Meela, she looked up at him. Her head reached to just below his chest. She motioned him down and whispered instructions. He raised an eyebrow but nodded.

He straightened to his full height and slowly curled his hand into a fist half the size of Meela's head. Then he raised his arm into the air. Rajer's eyes bore into hers and she winked at him. His fist came down toward her head. Cries and shouts of alarm took over the crowds. Just before he crushed the life from her body she lifted her hand, palm down, and flicked her fingers as though brushing aside a mozzie. Rajer's eyes widened as his feet left the ground and his huge form hurtled toward the cage. The crowds gasped. Before Rajer crashed, Meela straightened her fingers. He hung suspended for a moment before her fingers bent down slightly and he was gently lowered to the ground.

The startled look on Rajer's face made Meela smile. The crowd stood in quiet awe. Meela turned to Marshele, who was clapping enthusiastically.

"You see, Sir, I can handle myself quite well," she said, ignoring the growing roar of the crowd behind her. Before he could answer, the Bausc Woman stepped forward and burst.

"What God gives you the right to save a killer?" she demanded. Meela could practically see the steam wisp off her skin. She rolled her eyes. Some Bausc Women were aware that there existed beliefs other than their own, but some, like this one, insisted that anything other than the Bausc was abomination and blasphemy.

"What God gives you the right to judge what you do not understand?" Meela's voice was stone.

"Tribula!" Marshele calling the Bausc Woman by name, "Remember your place here." His face softened and he chuckled. Meela was really starting to like this place. Tribula couldn't take it. She closed her eyes, made a motion in the shape of a cross at her abdomen, glared at Meela and took her leave.

Marshele ignored her. Obviously her preaching and consulting had not affected his beliefs and superstitions. Meela smiled inside, knowing her gut was right. These were not a hateful people and they did not wish to kill where it was not warranted. It was the exact opposite of some places she had visited, one of those being Bausc.

The innkeeper stepped up and bowed. "Sir Marshele?"

"Yes, Augey?"

"I saw the...er...incident, sir. It was indeed an accident." He glanced into the crowd and then back to Marshele. Meela followed his gaze to a handsome, proud looking woman draped in a black robe, a still healing gash across her chin. Meela suspected she was the one free of the now innocuous Goff and started to put two and two together on who was actually cheating and who wasn't.

"I will not ask why you were not present at the trial Augey," Marshele's eye sparkled, "but I will allow this lady to take Rajer in banishment from Daushtra in exchange for a favor."

Marshele looked at Meela. She began to feel nervous for the first time that day.

"All be well," Marshele said flourish of his hand. A different drumbeat sounded, dismissing the crowd. Rajer went back into the cage to wait as Marshele gestured Meela to his side. He put his arm around her and led her to his home, not far from the common area. A very beautiful Daushtran woman, dressed in a robe of bright purples and greens, greeted him at the door.

After introductions, he gestured them inside.

"Now, my favor…"he said as he closed the door behind them.

~~~

After leaving Marshele's home, unscathed and chuckling, Meela bid farewell to Augey, the innkeeper. She promised to come back and visit again someday.

After leading the horses from the stables, Meela mounted Sym and led the mammoth Daushtran horse to the cage. Rajer stood and a single guard, almost Rajer's size, unlocked the door. Stopping Sym, Meela reached over into one of the bags that hung from the other horse and pulled out the trousers and tunic she had picked up earlier. She tossed them to Rajer as he exited the cage. He smiled and quickly pulled them on. Meela motioned to the new horse and Rajer mounted without hesitation.

"I'm Meela," she said as they set off.

"I am very glad to meet you this day, Meela." Rajer's voice was deep and sad.

They rode in silence through the town toward the surrounding forest. At the village edge, Rajer stopped. He turned to gaze upon his home for the last time. His long face bowed, his lips moved in silent prayer. Pulling in a deep breath, he raised his head, nodded, and kicked his horse forward. His silence didn't bother Meela. She understood all too well what it was like to lose a home.

Meela's task for Sir Marshele and his wife had taken most of the afternoon, and it was nearing dark by the time they hit the outside of Daushtra's borders. They reached a clearing about halfway to her first destination, Hrana Lake, and stopped for the night. The clearing had a smattering of trees with names Meela did not know. Two streams came down from the mountains and met there, one of which wound its way down to Daushtra.

Choosing a large tree near one of the streams, Meela pulled out dried meats, cheese and bread. Rajer gathered wood for a fire. Once the fire was blazing, they sat down across from each other and Meela handed him most of what she had taken from the bags. She poured water from a skin she had filled at the stream into wooden cups and passed one to Rajer.

"Cheers!" she said and Rajer chuckled deeply.

"Cheers," he said smiling and the 'clunk' of their cups filled the forest.

They studied each other for a moment in the firelight. The shadows cast on Rajer made him appear bull-like.

"I suppose you may be curious as to my intentions," her voice carried easily over the crackling of the fire. Rajer's now familiar chuckle filled the darkness.

"I must admit, I am wondering if the gallows would have been an easier choice." It was Meela's turn to laugh softly.

"Well, I'm afraid that remains to be seen. I am accustomed to working alone, but I find myself on a quest that requires a companion. I have no desire for a servant, nor a slave," she looked at him thoughtfully, "just a companion who might find a perilous quest as interesting as I."

"I see," Rajer said while rubbing his chest, "before I hear your quest, what can I do for the favor of my life?"

Meela made a noise similar to the tsking of a child as she considered him. She pushed extra sticks into the fire before answering.

"The price of the horse and clothes seems fair. The task exchanged for your life was simple," she shrugged, "I received satisfaction in helping you escape unearned death."

"What was the task might I inquire?" Rajer asked carefully. Meela laughed, the sound soft and musical.

"Apparently Sir Marshele is most appreciative of mating rituals. He and his mate wished to try theirs without the restrictions of gravity."

Rajer's initial surprise was replaced with laughter.

"I was a bit concerned…" he said, "about what was asked of you.

I'm pleased that was its extent."

"Indeed," Meela said, "I, too, was a worried about the 'favor' and once I understood, I was only too pleased to help!" They laughed comfortably together.

"I am sorry that you were forced to leave your home," Meela said. "Especially in those circumstances." Rajer nodded in answer.

"We are a peaceful people," he said, "thus discipline is swift to keep that peace."

"I can understand that," Meela answered. "What was your life like before?"

"I built things; hut homes, worship rooms, carts, anything. I had my own small hut home that will now be taken by the next grown to manhood," he said wistfully. "I had wanted to do some traveling before settling down but had been too busy. I guess the Gods have chosen now to be my time for travel."

"Maybe so," Meela murmured.

"And what has led you to this quest you're on?" Rajer asked. Meela looked at him a moment before beginning. He seemed like a good companion thus far. His size and demeanor couldn't have been better suited to her needs.

"My mother was a trader. Silks, trinkets, elixirs and the like. I travelled with her throughout Bausc until she took fever several years ago. Then I continued on my own, but trading my skill instead." She paused and Rajer nodded for her to continue.

"I'm searching for something. I follow threads in stories, knowing that they will lead me to my destiny. Threads of truth. I find them interesting and until I run across a reason to settle or I run out of stories to follow," she laughed, "I will keep following them. This is what leads me to my current quest."

Rajer leaned forward when she spoke again.

"There are rumors about the south hills of Bausc. They say there is an evil, high in the mountains that sends destruction down to the hill villages. Apparently it only occurs during the new moon. In order to avoid death and destruction, the villagers must hide carefully, leave or deliver sacrifices." Rajer raised an eyebrow but stayed silent.

"Two towns, two stories. Those in the north tell the story but they consider them just tales. I want to find out for myself."

"And where do I fit in?" Rajer asked quietly.

"I was in Stolidus, by request, helping to build a small fort when I realized that I had not travelled alone to the south. I was always with my mother and we usually travelled with a caravan of sorts. It's been years since then and it may not be smart to travel alone despite my abilities. I have been lucky thus far but have been in familiar territory." Rajer acknowledged her with an 'ah".

"I had never been to Daushtra but had heard of the size and compassion of your people. I felt drawn there with the possibility of finding my companion. Then I found you."

"Hmm…" Rajer's hand went to his chest again.

"Now, as I said," Meela continued, "if you wish to take your leave, I would prefer it to an unwilling companion."

Rajer nodded and sat thoughtfully. Meela poked at the fire and then retrieved a thin, but warm blanket from her saddle bag while she waited for his answer.

"Here's the way I see it," Rajer said as Meela settled down again by the fire with her blanket. "Destiny has brought you to me, or perhaps me to you." He paused and smiled. "Either way, life has taken a sharp turn for me. I have no family, no home and no direction yet to find my place in this world." Meela felt her heart twitch and waited quietly for him to continue.

"I dare say I have one friend," he started again and Meela gave him a half smile, "and it would seem that I shall accompany her until such time that I pay my debt and find my place."

"Thank you," Meela said softly and her smile broadened. Rajer gave her a distant smile, unsuccessful in hiding his sadness. Meela lay down on the ground, her head on her folded cloak and pulled the blanket over her. She heard Rajer settle down as well.

"There's a blanket in your saddle bag," she murmured as she drifted off to sleep.

~~~

Rajer lay awake long after Meela fell asleep. In just a matter of days he had gone from being a simple builder with a simple life to being the protector of an elfin girl, for surely that is what she was. His people had circulated elfin stories for longer than his age, but he didn't think anyone had ever actually seen one, let alone talked to one until now. He imagined the town gossip was now to the tune of how much good fortune had been bestowed on them by her strange appearance. And now he was her protector.

As he finally drifted off into a light and wary sleep, Rajer wondered how much truth there was to her story.

~~~

Meela could hear the music before she could see the encampment. It was mesmerizing and drew her in with a magnetic pull. A lone flutist filled the air around her with beautiful, soulful notes. She found herself caught in a whirl of emotion, feelings of warmth and pleasure filling her. Eyes closed, she found herself swaying and moving uncontrollably with no thought of anything else.

The song ended slowly and Meela found herself slowly awakening from its grasp. She opened her eyes and gazed upon the one who could capture and seduce her. She looked into his eyes and found they were bright blue and sparkling with life, a half smile of amusement rested on his face. Meela's heart quivered and she became suddenly self-conscious as she looked down at her simple white cotton dress. The man sat resting his hand with the flute on his knee. He admired her openly.

"I've been waiting for you," he said softly, just before his eyes widened and his smile faltered. She heard a hissing and rattling sound at her side…

Meela's eyes flew open. Rajer's bulk was lunging over her and grabbing something at her side. She froze in place and glanced to her right to see a serpentine creature caught and struggling in Rajer's fist. Reaching to her hip, she pulled out a small knife and handed it to Rajer. He stepped over her, pushed the serpent to the ground and, with one foot on the snake, sliced off its head.

Meela let out a breath and sat up. Rajer held up the snake. It was roughly twelve hands long. He turned and smiled at Meela.

"Breakfast."

Meela returned the smile as she shook her head. "I haven't slept that soundly in a long time. Apparently too soundly. I thank you for your help."

Rajer bowed his head to her briefly before walking over to the fire pit to prepare their meal. A snap echoed through the forest followed by a soft mutter from Rajer. He looked down at his feet and then at Meela who questioned him with raised eyebrows.

"At the next town, I think I would like to get some boots," he commented. Meela laughed, the tinkle of her voice echoing in the forest. She found herself unexpectedly looking forward to their first quest together.

About Lisa Barry

Growing up in Florida was not a good enough reason for author, Lisa Barry, to avoid wearing black. A daily color choice, Lisa constantly pines for cool enough weather to wear boots.

Living with her supportive (and hot) husband and amazingly awesome kidlets, Lisa counts it a blessing that they still love her despite the deafening sound of her music muse throughout the house.

Writing and reading every minute she can, Lisa counts on the cats to keep her keyboard warm and on the countless gargoyles who listen carefully when she reads to them aloud.

Connect with Lisa:
www.lisa-barry.com

Email: authorlisabarry@gmail.com

twitter.com/authorlisabarry

facebook.com/authorlisabarry

Other books by Lisa Barry:
The Guardians (Book One of the Gargoyles Den Series)
Beyond the Threshold (Anthology)

Revelation
Part two of the Foo Fighters Series

By Robert Broughton

WALTER REED MILITARY HOSPITAL 2012

First Lieutenant David Eagles woke from his nightmare in a cold sweat. Looking around the hospital room, he groaned. The nightmare was real. The previous twenty-four hours came flooding back in disjointed pieces, a kaleidoscope of images that needed to be brought into focus. Asleep or awake the disjointed mosaic of his mind sought to fit the pieces into some recognizable pattern. A blinding white light dissolved into images of a desert, a sign: *Government Property - Restricted Area -Violators Will Be Shot*, a fire, explosions, voices shouting, someone in a uniform saluting him, again the blinding white light. The confusion was bad enough, but the images carried emotions and those feelings were a rollercoaster, sometimes plunging him down, and then twisting him around in gut wrenching turns.

Groaning, David threw the sheets to one side and placed his legs over the edge of the bed, waiting until the dizziness passed. He turned on the bedside light and crossed to the sink and splashed cold water on his face. The image in the mirror looked drawn but vaguely familiar, handsome, definitely Native American, Sioux. He screwed up his eyes as the pain stabbed once more, then just as suddenly it passed. More images: the interrogation from Colonel Grant USAF, and Rice Knightly NSA – what was he doing wandering in the restricted area called 51, how he had gained access, and why was he wearing a USAAC (United States Army Air Corps) uniform. Staggeringly Grant had revealed that it was no longer 1944; it was now 2012. Sixty eight years had passed in the blink of an eye.

Once again the pain stabbed behind his eyes and he hung his head in his hands. The images shifted around, balls of white light moving in the sky over a tree lined lake, the name Foo Fighters. The scene shifted and he was looking through the plexidome of a B-17 and there again were the Foo Fighters dodging erratically between squadrons of bombers. He shook his head in an effort to get all the pictures to align.

Checking his reflection once more in the mirror, he smiled and shook his head "*Great Spirit*, what have you done to me?" The image in the mirror lied; it said that nothing had changed and apart from the headaches he felt just the same. But beyond the threshold of the hospital room waited a world that he could not imagine. Once again he shook his head as if to clear it, the conundrum as far as he could evaluate had no solution. Time heals all wounds, but for David time was the problem. He had no choice but to live in 2012 and try to find out why the *Great Spirit* had taken the only life he knew.

The gravity of his situation began to sink in. The visit from the USAF Colonel and the NSA agent was hardly innocuous. David had once been part of the military and knew the military mind. Glancing toward the door he could not see the armed guards through the opaque glass, but he knew they were there. Quietly he searched the room and in the cabinet beside the bed he found his uniform pressed and neatly folded. Relieved, he quickly dressed, throwing the gown on the bed. He pulled the medical tag from his wrist. He badly needed a cigarette; it had been a long time since he had had one. His Zippo and Lucky Strikes had been confiscated, but David had persuaded Rice to return them.

David memorized the room then turned out the light. Soundlessly he pulled the chair out from the corner, stood on it and lifted a ceiling tile. Finding a ceiling joist within reach, he pulled himself up. Moving by touch from joist to joist as quietly as he could he lifted the occasional tile to see what was below.

The storage room provided everything he needed: a surgical gown, a disposable hat, and a biohazard bag for his own clothes. Wearing his own shoes in case he needed to run, he then opened the door and looked out. The corridor was deserted. To his right he could see a nurse's station and figuring that direction to be the way out, he left the security of the storage room. The night nurse had her back to him, her finger on a dark screen as she typed with her other hand. As David approached he realized that her typewriter was silent. Glancing at the desk he spotted an identification tag and clipboard, which he lifted. The end of the corridor gave him two choices, left and right, both empty corridors. As he pondered which way to go a bell startled him. The silver doors slid open and two uniformed men stepped out. Deep in conversation they barely glanced at David as they carried on down the corridor to his right. David hesitated. When the silver doors started to close he jumped inside and looked around unsure of what to do; a mechanical sound preceded the dropping of the elevator. Seconds later the doors opened again and an orderly stepped in David nodded at him. The orderly examined the buttons and finding none alight he asked "Which floor?"

David pretended to study the clipboard, "What? Oh, the lowest". The orderly smiled and pressed "P" and glanced at David whose eyes were still on the clipboard. As the doors opened once more, the orderly stepped out onto his floor and David started to follow.

"You did want Underground Parking?" the orderly asked. David looked around and gave the orderly a thumbs up as he stepped back into the elevator. The doors closed and he descended. When the doors opened again a burly armed guard stood facing him.

The guard scanned David from head to toe and something must have registered as not being quite right. As the guard reached for his side arm, David dropped the clipboard and swung an uppercut to his jaw before the gun could clear the holster. The guard fell like an oak in the forest, down and hard, unmoving. David removed the gun and holding it against the guard's temple, he checked his pulse. Relieved that the guard was still breathing he dragged him between nearby cars and changed into the guard's uniform pocketing his wallet. Unfamiliar with the design of the cars parked around him, David wisely decided to escape on foot.

The alien world outside the hospital threw him once more into confusion. Dwarfed by the sheer size of the buildings, he wandered the early morning streets. Everything from the garbage trucks to street crossing signs challenged his lack of knowledge. Finding a park he sat down on a bench. He needed a plan beyond escape from the hospital. Knowing that he was in Washington D.C., he decided to travel towards familiar territory and wondered if they still had trains. Enquires provided the direction to the rail yards. There he found a train travelling West, but even the rail yard challenged him. The wooden box cars of his recollection had been replaced with metal containers painted with strange symbols, the old steam trains now multiple electric engines. He managed to find a flat car and hitched a ride, wanting to keep what little money he had stolen for food.

NSA

Colonel Grant swaggered into the NSA Operations room at the Pentagon and found Rice Knightly, "What's up?"

"Eagle One is on the move."

"Well it's about time. Which direction?"

"As you predicted west, moving slowly, so probably on a train. We will have eyes on him in a second. There." Rice pointed to one of several screens.

David was clearly visible lying back on a flatbed between two boxcars.

"He's wearing the guard's uniform. Be ready in case he uses the credit cards."

"He won't have any idea what they are.

"David Eagles is one smart boy. Did you make sure there was enough cash in the wallet?"

"Four hundred should keep him on the run a while, if he's careful."

"This may not be Eagles' world, but I don't want to rely too much on all our technology and underestimate his abilities. Have a chopper on standby and give me one of those GPS phones with a hotline here."

"Strange don't you think? The guy's a war hero and one of us, yet here we are tracking him. Do you think that he suspects that we arranged his escape?"

"I try not to."

"What?"

"Think. I just do as I am ordered. Anyway it doesn't matter whether he knows or not. Don't go sympathizing with the quarry or you're no good to me and I will have you replaced. Understood?"

Rice kept a straight face. "Understood Sir."

Grant pushed his face into Rice's "Eagle One represents a viable threat to the security of this nation, that's all you need to think about. Remember he penetrated security in *Area 51* as easily as I walked through that door back there. Given the top secret projects we have going on there, especially *Project X*, you don't find that an amazing coincidence?"

Rice felt uncomfortable with Grant in his face but he refused to show it. Grant reminded him of a drill sergeant he once knew, pushy and uncompromising, the type who would wave the flag from his grave. He had seen too many of them over the last few years, fanatics on some personal Jihad. The cause did not matter, nor the flag they waved; they unstabilized society as a whole. Rice stepped back and pushed against Grant's uniformed chest "Get off your high horse and back off. I don't believe in coincidence any more than you do, not in this business."

"Then you don't buy Eagles' amnesia story. He's playing us and I want to be the one to nail his ass!"

"That's your problem right there. You're so blinded by patriotic fervor that you miss the details - his memory loss is real all right.

Eagles is a pawn in a larger game just like the rest of us; but if you think I don't intend to win this game, then you're wrong. I will help you hunt him down no matter the cost. Let's just keep the bloodbath to a minimum; it's not good for business!"

Grant smirked, "Then we're on the same side, I just needed to check your level of commitment."

He straightened his jacket, brushed away an imaginary speck and marched from the room followed by his armed escort.

Rice turned back to his screen and studied the perfect image of David Eagles lying on the flatbed of a railroad car. "Where are you going David? What's your game plan?"

~~~

David removed his Lucky Strikes, shook out a cigarette and flashed the Zippo under the tip, inhaling deeply he closed his eyes and relaxed. The cigarette still tasted the same, which was amazing considering how old it was. The lighter felt heavy in his hand, a reminder of the past. He drew deeply and held the smoke in his lungs. The kaleidoscope in his mind shifted, images aligning - that first meeting on the airstrip in front of the line of B17's where he had spoken to First Lieutenant Paul Strong. The images shifted again – him standing in the woods, the huge hairless bear, *Gici Awas* of Sioux legend, the shape shifter who tested his courage on his quest to prove his manhood at the age of ten. The memories mirrored his current situation. They too were out of time, out of sequence. Relaxing he finished the cigarette and flicked the butt out onto the rails. Exhausted, he fell asleep.

"Lieutenant? Lieutenant David Eagles can you hear me?"

His escape had seemed so real. His eyes seemed to be glued together, tiredness weighed him down. The slap across the face stung, but it had the desired effect and he forced his eyes open. He was back in the hospital room. The face that looked down on him showed only irritation. The white hair gave the impression that the chiseled face had been carved out of marble, it was cold and hard. The brown eyes were accusative, as if their owner had run out of patience a long time ago. The uniform of a Colonel in the U.S. Air Force was immaculately pressed, row upon row of colorful ribbons across the chest.

"Finally. Look at me, focus. I am Colonel Mel Grant United States Air Force! This is Rice Knightly from the National Security Agency." Grant indicated the other man in the room. Rice looked of Italian descent, his dark features handsome and clean shaven. His black suit, white shirt and black tie looked expensive. The dark eyes were filled with compassion, as if Rice empathized with him.

"Can you understand me? Can you speak?"

David nodded and tried to answer, but his throat felt scratchy and his words were unintelligible. Rice handed him a glass of water. As he drank he experienced a feeling of déjà vu. This all seemed familiar as if it had happened before. "What am I doing back here?"

Grant looked across at Rice, who shrugged.

Rice asked, "What do you mean back here?"

"Look I have had enough of this crap, what do you know about 51?" Grant demanded.

David looked confused "I don't know anything about 51, what is it?"

"Area 51 is classified Top Secret, yet we found you wandering around there just over a week ago. We want to know how you gained access?"

David looked around the hospital room his confusion deepening. It occurred to him that he had been drugged and his mind was being manipulated. If that were the case he certainly wasn't going to tell these goons anything. "How did I get here?"

Grant began to boil over, "This only works one way. I ask the questions and you answer."

"If this is the same America that I fought for, then I have

inalienable rights, so I am not saying anymore until I get a lawyer."

Grant grabbed David by his hospital gown and shook him "If you don't tell me what I want to know right now, you will disappear into a drug induced stupor that you will never come out of."

The train shook from side to side waking David from his nightmare. He jerked upright and looked around. The train repeatedly blew its horn as it snaked its way through a small town. David took out another cigarette and torched the end with his Zippo. Once more the weight of the lighter confirmed this reality to be true. David had refused to accept the unlikelihood that this was now 2012, after all time travel was impossible. But the nightmare had served a purpose, allowing his mind to at last come to terms with his situation.

His thoughts turned to the *Retribution* and that fateful night over Germany in 1944. He wondered what had happened to Paul Strong and the rest of his crew? Was he the only survivor? Why was his last memory of an aircraft carrier? All questions to which he needed answers but he wasn't sure where to find them. Officially he no longer existed. He had little money and no knowledge of the world in which he found himself. He had enemies who would be pursuing him. He needed allies to help him survive, but where would he find such people? Not his tribe, if they still existed. Government security forces would expect him to go there first, and he had no wish to bring further suppression down on his people. In order to outfox the hunters he would have to abandon the identity of David Eagles and become Twin Eagles once again.

The train crossed the Appalachian Mountains and continued on through Indianapolis to St Louis, where Twin Eagles jumped off. Eagles needed a change of identity. The uniform was far too conspicuous and a secondhand clothing store filled all his needs. The clothes seemed enormously expensive, still he was relieved to change out of the guard's uniform. The four hundred dollars he had taken from the guard had seemed like a lot of money. He had exchanged the biobag for something a little less obvious, a canvas tote bag slung over his shoulder was far easier to carry.

His next stop was a secondhand book store where he spent an hour before hunger drove him to a roadside diner. While eating he started his research from one of a half dozen books he had purchased. Eagles had a lifetime of catching up to do and the sooner he started the better.

As Eagles read his attention was drawn to a handicapped man who entered the diner. His speech was slow and deliberate and he used his hands to try to get his meaning across. It occurred to Eagles that if he mimicked this method of speaking it would attract far less attention to him than his own outmoded manner of communicating.

One of the books entitled *UFO'S and Area 51* gave him an author in Independence that he should contact. Eagles needed to find the easiest way to get there.

Leaving the dinner, he tested his new theory on communicating. People were more than willing to assist him and he learned that the best way to Independence was to take a bus via Kansas City.

~~~

Gary "Gaza" Spicer lived in the attic of a two story weatherboard with his mother on South Nolan Rd, between Walnut and Truman across from the park. At twenty four Gaza had few friends and spent most of his time on-line. There Gaza felt on equal terms. His main achievement to date was an eBook he had published on Amazon with ten additional printed copies. The subject of the book was his real passion - *Area 51*, a government research and testing facility out in the Nevada desert which had until recently been kept a closely guarded secret. Gaza's room was filled with books on conspiracy theories, unexplained phenomena and ancient aliens. Photographs of strange objects were pinned to the walls along with a slogan: "The Truth Shall Set You Free". He firmly believed that aliens had visited Earth and the videos on YouTube proved it beyond a doubt. From pyramids on Mars to *Atlantis*, Gaza was fascinated by all of it.

Mary, his Mother, called from the kitchen "Gary get off that computer and put out the garbage for me dear."

"Sure Mom, get off the computer and put out the garbage, got it." Gaza pulled on a black UFO Magazine sweatshirt and bounded down the stairs. As he wheeled the big green plastic bin to the pavement a stranger approached him.

"Gary Spicer?" The man asked as he held up a copy of a book he was carrying *UFO'S and Area 51*, Gaza's book.

Gaza eyed him suspiciously "Wow, I can't believe you've found one of the ten copies I had printed of that."

"I would like to talk to you about it. I found it very interesting."

"Yeah, are you for real?"

"For real yes. Could you spare a few minutes to walk in the park?"

"Mom, I am just taking a walk, back soon," he yelled. Behind him he could hear his mother's acknowledgement. "So you have an interest in UFO's Mr...?"

"Pardon me. My name is Eagles, Twin Eagles."

"That some kind of Native American name?"

"Yes it is Sioux. I'm from your neck of the woods. Gary, I have a strange story to tell you, to be honest I can hardly believe it myself."

One hour later Gaza shook his head. "You must think that I am simple or something, that has to be the biggest load of bull anyone has ever tried to pile on me."

"Eagles held up the book "In the back of your book you cite the sources of your research."

"Yeah, so?"

"Look." Eagles handed him the book and pointed. *"Foo Fighters: Real or Fiction? By David Eagles."*

"You said your name was Twin Eagles."

"That's my tribal name."

Gaza tried to absorb the enormity of the statement.

Eagles lit another cigarette and watched him struggle to fit the almost impossible data into a frame of reference that would not allow for it.

"I ... have you got some proof?"

Eagles dug into the canvas tote bag and pulled out a crumpled uniform and an ID card.

Gaza eyed them suspiciously, examining the items.

The ID looked primitive but the name matched. He shook his head "It could be fake. Tell you what, you wait here and I'll be back soon."

Eagles glanced around nervously.

"Look you want me to trust you, well you are just going to have to trust me first. I won't be long."

Home, Gaza jumped straight on his computer. A website run by the Mormons gave him all the data he needed, including a black and white photo of David Eagles. Gaza was stunned. The old black and white photo could have been taken that day, Eagles had not aged at all. He sat staring at the screen, his mind in turmoil. He loved sci-fi but knew it wasn't real, just a possibility of what could be. Still, the evidence was staring him in the face. More data, that's what he needed he thought. His fingers flew across the keyboard. After twenty minutes, he rushed downstairs. Excited he returned to the park across the street.

"Ok, let's say that I believe you. What do you want from me?"

"Gary I need help. I know nothing of this world. I have no friends and the government is chasing me." Eagles dug out the wallet he had taken from the guard and then he showed Gaza the credit cards. "I have no idea what these are. The way people talk is even strange to me, especially when they speak into little boxes."

"Call me Gaza, and welcome to the twenty-first century. I can't wait to tell Spider this story."

"Who is Spider?"

"Spider's cool, my friend; she lives in Sioux City a couple of hundred miles away." Gaza jumped up excitedly. "Man have you got a lot to learn. Come on. I'll show you. This will blow Spider's mind." Gaza took Eagles back to his house and gave him a brief rundown on how a computer worked. Eagles watched, fascinated, as Gaza sat before a black flat screen and started typing. Once Gaza had explained the situation to Spider he sat back and said "This should be good."

Gaza read Spider's reply: *"Keep him there, you got me. I am getting in my car now. Don't let him out of your sight and record everything he tells you."*

Gaza typed, *"But he already told me a bunch of stuff."*

"I mean everything else; this is the biggest thing that will ever happen to us. God, I have prayed for something like this. I feel as if I'm in some Spielberg movie! Remember don't let him out of your sight."

"She says she's coming right over. It'll be a while so make yourself at home." Gaza told Eagles.

"May I ask, is Spider your girlfriend?" Eagles asked.

Gaza became flustered "What no, she doesn't have boyfriends. I mean we're just friends, we like the same stuff that's all. She's what you call my homegirl."

Two hours later a battered red mustang screeched to a halt outside.

Spider burst into Gaza's room, a speeding ticket in her hand. She fixed her sights on Eagles sitting in a chair and crossed the room, handing the ticket to Gaza.

Eagles found himself shocked by Spider's appearance. Obviously Asian, with short bright red hair under a porkpie hat, she wore denim bib and brace overalls covering a Spiderman t-shirt. The legs were rolled up showing a pair of black lace up boots. On her right hand between the thumb and forefinger was a small tattoo of a red spider. In the same position on the opposite hand was a black one. Her lipstick was black and each ear had eight piercings each with small gold rings.

Spider obviously had a fascination with arachnids, and just as obviously went to great lengths to make herself unattractive.

Eagles found her confusing since if one took away the horrible fashion and placed her in a dress she would be pretty.

Spider beamed from ear to ear as she held out a hand "You must be David. I'm Spider and you are a very interesting man."

Gaza inspected the speeding ticket, "Man that's gonna cost you."

Spider waved away the ticket as if it hadn't existed.

Eagles held out his hand, "Hello Spider, I am Twin Eagles. It's a pleasure to meet you. Can I ask why do they call you Spider?"

Spider turned to Gaza while shaking Eagle's hand "I really thought you were joking, this is so awesome." Turning back she answered, "Because I'm always on the web of course, and I have a fascination for spiders."

"Well, I see. That's very unusual. Won't you take a seat and join us? Gaza has been trying to bring me up to date. I fear that I have a great deal to learn."

Spider laughed, "I live for days like this but you never expect them to happen. Hang onto your seat belt Mr. Eagles, your education begins here."

Gaza went downstairs to raid his mother's fridge. When he returned Spider was in full flow mode. "Gaza and I went to the same school. We started a club for UFO enthusiasts, modern mysteries and ancient riddles that sort of thing. Most people live in their own little world, heads in the sand, but we're different. We want to know the truth."

"What truth?"

"Everything from Big Foot to Big Brother, we try to solve the mysteries and bring some truth into the world."

Gaza listened as he set the food down "Spider's right, we're fringe dwellers, we exist on the outskirts of society. Some call us whackos, no one really takes us seriously. We provide indisputable scientific evidence that aliens have been here before, and are probably still here, and they call us conspiracy nuts."

Spider took over "It's the government dudes with their disinformation, they don't want anyone knowing the real truth, supposedly for our own good. This ain't the fifties anymore and it's not *Orson Wells* reading *War of the Worlds*. Thanks to the internet and TV people are educated; there would be no mass hysteria if people found out what was really going on." Taking a breath she slammed down a soda and wiped her mouth.

"Sorry, who is *Orson Wells*?"

Spider slapped her forehead, "Sorry ! Of course you couldn't know it happened in the fifties in America. This actor dude *Orson Wells* read a story over the radio. He was so convincing that everyone panicked, grabbed their guns and ran away in terror. They thought it was a real alien invasion. Can you believe that, Martians invading Earth?"

"At this point in time I could believe almost anything."

Gaza watched Eagles' reaction and put down his own drink. "Spider forget that. Eagles came to us for help. We have to do whatever we can."

Spider stopped eating and laid the chicken back in the bowl.

"Eagles you have had longer to think about this than us. What do you want to do?"

"Yeah dude, you can count on us. Just tell us what you want."

Eagles smiled "Seems to me my biggest problem is that I have very little knowledge of your world, that's why I came to you. I'm, what did you call it? A fringe dweller as well. We're part of the same tribe you and I. I am just as curious as you are to find out the answers, and I am the key to that knowledge. What I do know is that the Great Spirit has some plan and he's using me to execute it for him. In order to do that, I have to remain free."

"That is so cool dude. I never thought of myself as Sioux, even though I live in Sioux City. But you're right, we are the same tribe and we do have to keep you free." Spider turned to Gaza, "We have to go public. It's the only way to keep Eagles safe. Plaster his story all over the net, that way the government won't be able to touch him."

"Think Spider, if we do that the media will be all over us. It will be a circus especially when it goes national, hell it will be international. Eagles won't be able to move anywhere without a microphone stuck in his face. Every bimbo anchorwoman will be asking stupid questions, the paparazzi will photograph everything he does. Every real wacko on the planet will be drawn to us like a magnet; they'll be looking for *Elvis* for god's sake, and trampling down my mother's fence to do it. You seen the movies man, remember *First Contact* from *Sagan's* book? It will get crazier than *Orson Wells* believe me!"

Spider shook her head to throw off the image, "I guess you're right Gaza, I just didn't think it through. So what do we do?"

The silence lasted some time. Gaza paced his room restlessly and Spider scribbled down ideas then screwed up the paper and threw it in the trash.

"51."

"What???"

"Think about it, it's the only solution."

"Gaza are you completely INSANE? There is no way, I repeat no way that anyone is even getting close to *Area 51*. The NSA, Homeland Security, you name it, if they don't shoot us on sight we'll get first class accommodations at Guantanamo Bay for the rest of our lives!"

"Eagles got in."

Spider looked at Eagles "How did you do that man? That's truly awesome."

"Some force snatched Eagles from the jaws of death in '44, dropped him not in Central Park or by the Golden Gate Bridge, but in *Area 51*."

"I see where you're going, there has to be a reason, something which connects the Foo Fighters to 51. Love it! Let's do it."

"I really hate to interrupt, but I have no idea of what *Area 51* is?"

Gaza turned to Spider with a big smile "Let's show Eagles what we do."

Spider sat at the computer, her fingers flying over the key board, and official looking documents flashed across the screen. Gaza kept up a running commentary as she worked.

~~~

Across the street in the park a man and woman embraced. Between them they held the laser steady. The beam reached across the street to the attic window picking up the sound vibrations inside the house. The entire conversation could be clearly heard and then transmitted to operations and other agents stationed around the target area. The information was relayed straight to Rice Knightly in the NSA Operations Centre at the Pentagon.

Rice already had profiles of both Spider and Gaza on separate screens while watching a live satellite feed of the house on S. Nolan Road. Rice took notes as he coordinated the surveillance. He couldn't help smiling as he shook his head. Eagles had really found himself a couple of whackos. They had no idea what they were up against. If they had decided to go public, they would already have been incarcerated. Rice wanted Eagles free believing that it was the only way to really get to the bottom of the mystery. Even while Eagles had been in a coma at the hospital Rice had argued that the best way to get results was to set Eagles free with a tracking device implanted in his leg. Still, he had to grudgingly admit that Grant had been right, Eagles was smart. Finding the UFO buffs had been a stroke of genius. Rice and Grant were on the same team, they both needed to find out how Eagles had been able to penetrate the strict security of *Area 51* without being detected. However inter-agency rivalry aside, Rice doubted that he and Grant had the same agenda.

While Eagles had been in a coma, an investigation had been launched into his background. According to one of Eagles' own books, at the age of ten he had first encountered the Foo Fighters and the experience left a lasting impression. Devoting his life to the study of the subject, Eagles had earned a Native American scholarship and majored in Engineering and Propulsion, graduating from a prestigious university with honors. During the Second World War the Allies had deemed the Foo Fighters an Axis threat and brought Eagles in to head up an investigation team. After joining the Air Force, Eagles became part of *Project X*.

When Rice started to dig deeper into the specifics of the project his enquiries had been blocked and flagged. Despite his high- level clearance the Pentagon's computer had stonewalled him. Within an hour Grant had been sent to warn him off, and Rice had complied, but his curiosity had been aroused. Grant had alluded to the fact that

Project X now came under USAF jurisdiction and its development was still ongoing at 51. Rice wondered and not for the first time, if this could be the same Project X as the one from 1944. Realizing he could not solve this mystery without more data, he turned his attention back to the computer screens and the profiles of the new players. He printed out files on Spider, her family and contacts, and Gaza, his family and contacts.

~~~

Eagles had watched in fascination as Spider dazzled him with information. To Eagles, a computer and the internet were nothing short of a miracle. In 1944, there was radio but television hadn't yet been invented. Now one could access information from almost anywhere on any subject, even talk live with someone across the world. How incredible, he thought, technology had advanced beyond his wildest dreams.

Spider downloaded information on *Area 51*, UFO's, aliens, secret projects, reverse engineering of downed spacecraft, and examinations of alien bodies, perhaps even live ones. They watched a video on YouTube from Google Earth of the mysterious *Area 51*. As Spider zoomed in, Eagles could make out several runways, buildings and hangers, multiple mounds and circles, all in a desolate setting. Eagles was fascinated by the videos of Foo Fighters, allegedly taken by ufologists, over *Area 51*. The information seemed endless and it took them hours to sift through it all.

Finally Eagles stood and paced the room. He had so many pieces of the puzzle now, but had yet to analyze them to form a true picture. One piece stood out - there seemed to be a connection between 51 and the Foo Fighters, he just didn't know yet what it was. Gaza had been right when he said they had to go there. Even though Eagles had materialized at 51, he had no idea how that had come about. It seemed that the Foo Fighters had somehow moved him through time and space, a seemingly impossible feat. Reason dictated that if he could somehow locate the Foo Fighters and communicate with them, then he could persuade them to transport him again. That was a big IF. He turned to his new friends "I believe that I may have a plan. It's risky, so I know you will appreciate it." Eagles explained his plan while Gaza and Spider listened attentively. When he had finished his audience were nodding their heads.

Spider turned to Gaza "Game on, give me five."

"That's what I'm talking about dude."

They decided to rent a four wheel drive. Spider paid cash for the white Range Rover and pulled up in front of a fast food store. Gaza turned to Eagles "Would you like a gut grenade?"

Spider laughed at the look on Eagles face, "He wants to know if you would like a burger?"

Eagles Laughed "Sounds like I'm taking my life in my hands?"

"You probably are, but have one anyway."

Now after 300 miles, Spider argued that there was no Spirit Lake on the GPS. Eagles explained that Long Lake near Bismarck, North Dakota had been known to his people for generations as Spirit Lake.

Arriving at their final destination, Spider parked and they removed the camping gear. Eagles took point and they set off to find a suitable campsite. "This will do nicely we're close to water. Pitch the tents and set up camp while I find some wood."

In the forest Eagles bent down to pick up some wood for a campfire. When he stood up, a hand wrapped around his mouth and held him firm. "Make no sound. I have been following you for some time Twin Eagles. You have forgotten who you are. Your eyes no longer see and your ears no longer hear. I have come to help you brother, and you are sorely in need of help. Follow me and try to remember that you are a Sioux warrior." Eagles nodded and the hand disappeared. He dropped his bundle of wood one stick at a time as he followed the stranger, using a pine broom to sweep the trail behind him.

The mysterious figure stopped behind a huge, flat rock and crawled out to the edge. Eagles joined him. From the higher ground, he could easily see Gaza and Spider noisily setting up camp.

Several minutes passed in silence as Eagles regained his true self. He was able to see what at first had been invisible to him: Gaza and Spider were being watched by several camouflaged soldiers positioned at various points around the campsite.

"Do your eyes see now?"

"They do, I count at least five. They are well concealed."

"Ha, they are like buffalo, noisy and unaware. I have counted fifteen and they have been in position for some time. You were expected."

"That is very interesting." Eagles tried to look at the figure next to him; he appeared to be a Sioux brave about sixteen years of age.

"I must help them, they are my friends."

"Very well. Do you remember the twin oaks halfway down the ravine about a mile from here?"

"I do."

"Good. You will find three horses there. I will create a distraction so that you and your friends may escape."

"I don't understand. I have told no one of this place. I have written of my experience here, but never have I named it. The protection of the Foo Fighters has been paramount to me. I did not even tell my companions where we were going until we were almost here."

"There is much about this time which is unknown to you. The ones who hunt you have an eye in the sky and watch us even now."

"How can this be?"

"While you were in the hospital they placed an electronic tracking device in your leg. They have been watching you ever since they allowed you to escape."

Eagles was taken aback at his own naivety.

"Calm yourself brother. Deceit is not in your nature and the hunters fear you."

"But why? I am no threat to them."

"I disagree. You can be, and your beloved Foo Fighters certainly are."

"They have never harmed anyone to my knowledge."

"But they cannot be controlled and they demonstrate great power. That makes the authorities fearful. It challenges them and so they seek to use you to defeat them."

Eagles digested this information. It burned him to know that he had not fully understood the game he played, and his own part in it.

"Then they leave me little choice, I will protect the Foo Fighters at any cost."

"So be it. Roll up your right trouser leg."

Eagles did as instructed and the young warrior passed a hand over his leg. Turning it over he showed Eagles a tiny capsule. "I will carry this and they will follow. Lead your friends away and may the Great Spirit be with you."

"Wait, who are you?"

"We are old friends you and I. I am *Gici Awas*, the shape shifter. Do you remember the gift I gave you? Well you will make good use of it soon." The young warrior disappeared into the brush.

Eagles smiled. He had been right, the *Great Spirit* needed him.

Pentagon

"Sir, he's moving away from the lake quite fast, shall I order the unit to pursue?"

Rice spun around "What of the other two?"

"They are still at the campsite."

"Have six men stay. The rest follow Eagles, and notify Colonel Grant to keep pace in the chopper. Stress that there is to be no interception until I have a chance to evaluate the situation." Rice moved to the screen. He could just make out a rider through the trees and watched as the rider stayed undercover as much as possible. "He knows!"

Quickly he called Grant on a secure line. "Rice here, Eagles knows that we are watching him, he may try to evade you." Rice could barely hear the reply over the noise of the chopper.

Turning to another agent he barked, "I need four more choppers in that area. Bring in the other units to cut him off and get me a map up on that screen, with a position plot so we can track him. Get me a closer view. Now! Have local police and the National Guard block off every road in the area, search every vehicle and make sure they use rubber bullets. I don't want some untrained hot head shooting anyone. And have Gaza and Spider brought in."

With the map now visible, Rice studied it carefully "East, he will go east. That's where the river and the airport are."

"Sir, Eagles is riding mainly south."

"Yes, that's a decoy to shake off the hunters. I want dogs and patrols on the river and I want that airport buttoned up tight, no flights in or out."

~~~

Grant watched the GPS locator as he directed the pilot of the UH-72A Lakota Helicopter to drop lower over the trees. "He should be ahead about a quarter mile on this heading." Looking up he scanned the treetops ahead through the tinted bubble of the canopy. The trees whipped by at a rapid rate, but he stayed focused, glancing occasionally at the GPS tracker. "He must have heard us coming, he's changed course, now heading west."

The pilot banked the Lakota into a new heading as the trees thinned ahead.

"There!" Grant pointed, and the pilot nodded. They watched as the rider looked up at the chopper laughing, before abruptly swinging the horse onto a new course. Then they lost him. For several minutes the rider played hide and seek between the trees, and Grant began to curse.

Four more Lakota's joined them buzzing the trees like angry wasps. Frequent changes of direction broke up the formation and they had to be alert not to fly into one another.

Grant's frustration increased; the rider seemed to be taunting them. "Snipers - bring him down with tranquilizers. Repeat, bring him down!" Grant grabbed his own rifle and opening the side door, stuck the weapon out of the chopper.

The rider seemed to have a sixth sense; just as a sniper fired he turned the horse on a dime and ducked back under cover.

~~~

Eagles stealthily made his way back to the campsite, leaving unconscious soldiers in his wake, but by the time he arrived at the camp Gaza and Spider were on their knees, hands strapped together above their heads. Two armed men in camouflage stood guard over them. Alerted by the lack of communication from the rest of their squad, the guards were ready for trouble.

Eagles circled behind them and picking up a rock he gauged its weight. The pitch was perfect. It struck one guard on the back of the neck and he fell forward almost landing on Spider. The second guard spun and aimed low, rubber bullets kicking up dirt and ricocheting off the rocks in front of Eagles.

Gaza threw himself at the guard's back knocking him to the ground and Spider jumped on top of him. By the time the guard had untangled himself, Eagles was rearmed and scored a second strike. Using the guard's knife he cut his friends loose. "We have to go. Now."

"Thanks dude, that was some awesome pitching. Who are these guys?"

"Trouble. Follow me fast as you can." Eagles started toward the horses and abruptly stopped. Something warned him not to go there and he followed his instinct. "Back to our transport, let's go."

Spider grabbed his arm "Won't that be guarded?"

"Probably."

At the car Gaza and Spider created a diversion and Eagles continued his winning pitching streak, dispatching two more guards. Spider gunned the Range Rover for all it was worth along the dirt track; the tail of the vehicle fish-tailing back and forth as Spider fought the wheel. At last, the tires bit into the tarmac. Gaza turned to Spider, "How on earth did they know where we were going?"

"That's my fault. They implanted a tracking device into my leg while I was in the hospital."

"Dude, cell phones, they can track us too!"

"Throw them out the window now." Two cell phones hit the road and shattered on impact.

"Which way do you want me to drive?"

"Left. We have to try to make it to the river or the airport" Eagles said.

Almost immediately Spider spotted the roadblock "Sorry no can do," Spider said and swung away in the opposite direction gunning the V8 engine. Sirens wailed and lights flashed as the chase got underway. Spider looked across at Eagles "If I were them I would be setting up another roadblock about a mile ahead."

Gaza watching the chase out of the back window spotted a light plane closing in on them fast. Eagles wound down his window and stuck his head out, just as the aircraft passed low over the Range Rover "By the *Great Spirit*, I don't believe it!"

Eagles grabbed the steering wheel to hold it steady. "Follow the plane and when he lands get out of the car and enter the aircraft as fast as you can." The Cherokee lifted off only seconds after touching down, its three passengers breathless in the rear. Eagles pulled himself forward and sat in the copilot's seat buckling himself in. He turned to the pilot grinning, "You're late."

Paul Strong smiled back, "It's good to see you too.
Which way?"

"Anywhere but here," Eagles gripped his friend's shoulder laughing. "Gaza, Spider, this is an old friend – First Lieutenant Paul Strong."

"Welcome aboard, you better strap in."

Spider recovered first "Old friend? Well if he's as old as you are, better tell him to fly as low as possible or they will pick us up. The authorities will expect us to head for *Area 51*, so I would head North first, then circle East."

"I always did like the scenic route. So how have you been Eagles?"

"Can't complain, how about you?"

"Here and there, you know."

"I do, I do." Laughter filled the plane.

~~~

Again and again the rider disappeared under cover of the trees. The Lakota followed and had to veer sharply to avoid hitting another chopper, throwing off Grant's aim.

"Hell, this is turning into a farce. Instruct the others to back off and hold a half mile perimeter before we have a collision." He lifted his tracker, but where there should have been one moving red dot there were now four. "What the...!" he shook the GPS with no change and banged it against the cockpit in frustration. "Grant to Rice, my tracker is now showing four different positions. Do you have a location? Over."

"We do Grant. It seems the bird has flown the coop. We had a report of three people escaping in a light plane off the highway, north of your position. Over."

"That can't be Eagles. I have a positive ID. Over."

"What can I say? Our ID is positive also. We need to regroup. Return to base. Over."

Grant threw the GPS out of the door and slammed the door closed in frustration.

Below him the shape shifter dismounted, walked a short distance, morphed into an owl and flew out from under the trees winging its way between the cordon of helicopters.

NSA Pentagon

Rice rubbed his eyes, the lack of sleep and stress making them feel gritty. Eagles had escaped his carefully laid plan, and Grant was on the warpath. Eagles must have had outside help, it was the only explanation. But who were these new players? Rice needed more data before he could formulate a new strategy. Where had the light plane come from? And who was flying it? And how could there have been two positive ID sightings of Eagles in two different locations? Rice brought up the two satellite images on his screen to compare them. Grant was right - Eagles must have a clone.

~~~

Eagles watched the countryside slip past below. He too felt confused. "Don't take this the wrong way Paul but I thought you were dead?"

"And I thought you were dead. The last time we saw one another we were in a burning B17 over Germany in 1944 and the last thing I remember was this blinding white light which enveloped both of us. When I came out of the light, I was by a country road, standing amongst some trees. I heard shouting and walked towards the commotion. I could see a roadblock, police and troops. Three occupants were dragged out of a white vehicle and arrested. One of them was you! I couldn't believe it, or understand it. I watched the troops drive you away and then I hightailed it back into the woods. Next thing I know the white light returns and drops me right here in this plane. I look down and see the same white car driving along being chased by police. I descended to find out what was going on, and I saw you stick your head out of the window, so I landed."

"No way dude that's incredible."

Gaza grabbed Spider in amazement "Holy crap. I researched this!"

Eagles turned in his seat "Would you mind explaining please."

Gaza laughed, "It's in my book man, aircraft and pilots mysteriously disappearing; reports from all over the world of UFOs and these white lights. Just like you, only in your case the B17 was probably too badly damaged to save. It's rare, but it has been reported that some abductees have reappeared, and even aircraft and ships have turned up after being missing for years."

Spider held up her hand "So you're saying that the Foo Fighters snatched Lieutenant Strong from the *Retribution* in 1944 and put him in an aircraft then dropped him here in 2012 to save us? That's more than incredible."

"It's more than that. They also dropped him ahead in time so he could see what would happen to us and then put him in this aircraft to fix it!"

"Shut the door, no way that could happen! Could it???"

Gaza gave Spider a smile, "Beam me up Scotty."

Excited laughter filled the Cherokee.

Paul looked across at Eagles, "Who are the two characters in the back? I can't understand a word they're saying."

Eagles laughed, "It's a long story."

"I have all the time in the world, fill me in."

"All right, but I warn you *H G Wells* has nothing on us. Let's start with the year - its 2012!"

"Impossible!"

Spider reached across and held his hand in front of Strong, "This is the part where I would show you a phone the size of my hand with the date. Oh, and with this phone, I can call anywhere in the world and see who I am talking to, only we had to throw them out of the car window."

"That, my friend, is only the half of it; but Gaza can explain it much better than I can."

Paul wondered what kind of a warped reality he had woken to and then the thought crossed his mind that perhaps he was dreaming or dead.

"Don't feel bad Lieutenant, if it's any consolation this whole thing isn't any easier for us to wrap our wits around and we believe in this stuff but never expected to actually be living it."

Paul nodded, but he really didn't understand what the hell was going on.

~~~

Grant slammed his fist on Rice's desk "Do not give me that crap! I don't believe in clones or aircraft materializing again after disappearing for ten years any more than I believe in Santa and the tooth fairy. You have got to get a grip on reality Rice, or I will be forced to replace you with someone more stable."

Rice inspected his desk to see if anything was broken, "If you are going to argue with me you need to define your terms. Let's start with reality, what is your definition?

"What! Don't argue semantics with me, everyone knows what's real."

"Do they? Then how do you explain Eagles?"

"He's simply an anomaly for which we have not yet found an explanation. When we clear this mess up, and we will, then I guarantee you will find some hoax at the bottom of it all."

Rice realized that he was getting nowhere "Then let's examine the evidence. Did the search for Eagles find any tracks? Have you located the mysterious light aircraft yet?"

"Don't try to put this back on me! I am not going to tell my superiors that this nation's security is compromised by clones, Whackos and phantoms are you? This is a damn circus and we're all starting to look like clowns. I am going to *Area 51* and I am going to shoot anything that does not belong there. You are going to sort out this debacle and then report to me, understand?"

Rice matched Grants cold stare "Yes sir, I understand perfectly. Manure rolls down hill."

"Exactly, and you're in it up to your eyes."

~~~

Lieutenant Paul Strong was having the limits of his reality tested. Unlike Grant he could accept the necessity to redraw the borders, given all he had experienced. Still it was not easy and the back of his head throbbed as he tried to assimilate the data. Somehow it kind of made sense if one believed in mysterious energy forces and time travel. "To recap, you want me to fly you to this highly classified *Area 51*, where in all probability we will be shot on sight, and we are doing this to help the Foo Fighters. But I'm not sure why they need our help?"

Eagles turned to Spider "I believe that it would help if you could tell us more about *Area 51.*"

Spider smiled "One of my favorite subjects, *Groom Lake, Dreamland, Home Base, Paradise Ranch, Area 51,* call it what you will, is located in southern Nevada, about a 100 miles north-northeast of Las Vegas. It's essentially a military station, a testing ground for experimental aircraft and weapons both for the military and private arms merchants. All top secret, the government denied its very existence until July of 2003. This is the place conspiracy theorists love to talk about - you name it - secret weapons, UFO's... the biggest cover up was a spacecraft which crashed near Roswell in New Mexico. The remains and wreckage were taken to *Area 51.*

Former employees at 51 who have come forward say that many of the components of that craft were reverse engineered. Some even claimed to have film of live aliens taken from the ship. Since then there have been rumors that the government was able to contact other aliens in space, that UFO's have been seen to land at the base and that we trade them people to experiment on, in exchange for technology."

Gaza could see that Spider was getting off the track and jumped in, "Point is the base is heavily involved in weapons research and testing. Spider and I have been talking, you know, and wondering what is the connection to the Foo Fighters? And this is what we have come up with..."

Spider took over the narration, "To understand where we're coming from we have to return to your time, October 28th 1943 and the Philadelphia Naval Shipyard, specifically the Navy destroyer escort *USS Eldridge* and *Project Rainbow*. *Project Rainbow* dealt with electromagnetic energy; we are talking Einstein's Unified Field Theory combined with Tesla's experiments. Special equipment had been set up aboard the escort to make the ship invisible to enemy radar and she vanished in a flash of blue light. Now here's where it gets really weird. Two hundred miles away in Norfolk, Virginia, Carlos Allende aboard the *SS Andrew Furuseth*, witnessed the *Eldridge* appear for a brief time and then totally disappear. For the observers in Philadelphia, the *Eldridge* re-appeared in its original position so experiment was thought to be a success until bizarre things were discovered with the crew.

Some had disappeared, some were reported actually fused to the ship, and others had just gone mad. The Project was said to be cancelled but if you look at the dates here, it was around the same time that *Project X* came into being. Eagles was recruited to head up *Project X* and research Foo Fighters as they were deemed a threat to national security and Eagles was the world's foremost expert on Foo Fighters."

Paul turned to Eagles "So that's what you were doing on board the *Retribution* the night we disappeared?"

"Yes. I reported directly to the Commanding General of the Eighth Air Force, who believed the Foo Fighters were some sort of German secret weapon, contrary to the evidence I provided."

Spider continued, "Now we come to the really interesting part - what if the two Projects were combined, and the Air Force took over control from the Navy and moved the project to *Area 51* where it continues to this day. That alien technology we spoke of earlier could have been used to perfect electromagnetism both as a power source and possibly as a weapon." Spider paused allowing speculation to fill the void.

Gaza watched Eagles "Is it possible that the government had an ulterior motive for *Project X*, one of which you were unaware?"

"Possible I suppose, but we have no evidence."

"Don't we? Then why are we being hunted? There's also the interesting question - why are both you and Paul here at the same time? We have already deduced that the Foo Fighters could have dropped you off almost anywhere in time or not dropped you at all. There can be little doubt that we are dealing with highly advanced, highly intelligent entities with peaceful intention. What could they possibly have to fear from us? Unless we have some sort of a weapon which could be used to destroy or capture them." Gaza held Eagles eye, "I am no scientist, but I am willing to bet that in *Area 51* there is an electromagnetic weapon which can capture a Foo Fighter and hold it in stasis for experimentation. Think of what could be learned far beyond *Project Rainbow* - dimensional travel, unlimited power, even time travel. Any nation who possessed such power would literally rule the world and possibly beyond."

Spider shook her head "That is really scary dude, I don't know about you but I would never sleep again knowing any government had that kind of control. Year Zero man, you could enslave the universe. Makes Darth Vader look like a boy scout."

"It also proves that your Foo Fighters are peaceful and benevolent."

Paul looked across at his friend Eagles and shook his head in disbelief. "This is a little over the top for me, I need time to think this over."

Eagles nodded, "It does solve one problem for me. I had been wondering what the *Great Spirit* had brought me here for."

"This is crazy, anyway how do we know that we're not being tracked by the government right now? They could dispatch fighters of their own to bring us down."

Spider chipped in "Well for one thing Paul, I don't believe that the Foo Fighters would give you a craft which can be tracked, and for another if the Air Force knew where we were, they would already have taken us down."

"I hate to play the devil's advocate, but we don't even have a plan" stated Gaza.

"Eagles does. That's why we went to Spirit Lake, we just didn't know we were being tracked."

"They have to know we're coming, they have 51 connected with Eagles."

"Hey, I never said it was going to be easy, just that someone has to do it, and fate has selected us" replied Spider.

"The whole thing sounds perilous in the extreme."

Heavy silence filled the cockpit, as each grappled with a reality so strange that not one of them could ever have imagined it.

Gaza looked around at their despondent faces. "We need time to think and plan, this is all a little overwhelming. I suggest we land near Vegas on some deserted road where we can hide the plane. We may need it later. Then we find a place to lie low, get some food and sleep, and formulate a plan." He looked from face to face, receiving affirmative nods.

~~~

That evening Paul sat on the wooden steps of the rented cabin. Eagles crossed the porch and sat beside him handing over a cup of coffee.

"Thanks I need this. I have a few questions."

"Join the club Paul, that's all I've had since I awoke in the hospital."

"Funny, you are now my oldest friend, yet we have hardly spoken, and I know almost nothing about you."

"True, but there is nothing normal about our situation, If you remember, I promised you an explanation over a drink."

"I thought you would at least buy me a beer, considering."

"Sorry but alcohol doesn't agree with my Native American blood. What you do know is that I am an expert in Foo Fighters, and that the Government brought me in to head up *Project X* when they became paranoid about the UFO's. Back then we were strictly gathering information for the Generals to evaluate. They believed, against my protestations, that the Germans had developed some sort of secret weapon."

"Yeah, I heard some of the wild theories, bit like *Area 51* if you ask me."

"Exactly, I realize now the reason they were so paranoid was that they themselves were engaged in secret weapons research. I feel I must apologize to the crew of the *Retribution*. If I hadn't been aboard, the Foo Fighters would never have taken us."

"No need to apologize, we would probably be dead now if not for you. I'm curious when the light surrounded the *Retribution*, what happened to you then?"

"I found myself on the aircraft carrier *Enterprise* in the middle of the Pacific, standing right in the path of a landing Corsair."

"Strange. Why would the Foo Fighters send you there?"

"I have often asked myself the same question."

"But how did Grant and Rice know that you had materialized on the *Enterprise*?"

"Rice told me there had been a film crew of war correspondents from British Pathe onboard. They were doing a documentary on the war in the Pacific, and they happened to film me as I appeared and disappeared. That's how Rice knew."

"Eagles, do you remember anything of being in the light?"

"No, do you?"

Paul shook his head, "No."

They drank in silence for awhile.

"So, we are still fighting the war then, only this time we have a different enemy."

Eagles smiled "Seems that way. Remember we are pledged to fight all enemies, foreign and domestic."

"Difference is we are trying to stop our own country from enslaving or destroying aliens."

Both men sat in silence for awhile. Eagles then asked "Have you thought about your future?"

Paul smiled and shook his head "You mean if we get out of this alive? Things have happened so fast since we were reunited, so no I haven't. Have you?"

"My fate was decided before my birth. The *Great Spirit* has a purpose for me, the mountain directs the flow of water, as the wind directs the cloud."

"I prefer to be above the clouds that way I can see what's happening."

NSA

Rice too had been following a plan - just not his own. Grant had ordered both Gaza and Spider's parents to be detained under the Anti-terrorism Act. If either of the whackos called home, the call would be immediately transferred to the NSA. Rice disagreed with the strategy but made the arrangements.

Area 51

Rodney T Hopwood could buy almost anyone he wanted. The billions he had made from Allied Armaments bought him a unique place in society – right on top with the biggest stick. Hopwood had dirt on most of the Congressman and Senators in Washington. Those he couldn't bribe, he buried. His dark cold eyes bore holes through Colonel Grant. "I have paid you an enormous amount of money to maintain the security of my various projects. Hell, I put your kids through college, paid for your wife's operations, cars, vacations - you get the picture? I own you, lock, stock, and barrel. This project to which I have devoted much time, effort and resources is now in jeopardy. Not from the Russians, the Chinese or even the North Korean's, but from two whackos and two dead men whom you can't even locate. The project is finally ready to launch and I want a flawless demonstration of its potential. When Eagles lures the Foo Fighters here, you will be ready with helicopter gunships, Predators, F15s, missiles – whatever it takes. Put the entire Navy on alert. Do I make myself clear?"

Grant tried to mask his fear. Hopwood was a ruthless man and ruination would be the least of his worries. "Sir, David Eagles is still the key to our success."

"Then make sure he stays alive until I have my prize. He's your responsibility. Now get out."

Two armed guards stood to attention as Grant exited the conference room. He looked visibly shaken, but pulled himself together as he walked to a waiting electric cart. Without looking at the driver he ordered him to take him to Research and Development.

The Area 51 base above ground covered roughly 36 square miles, but that was nothing compared to the maze of multilevel underground tunnels and hangers. Even though the electric cart had been modified to travel at fifty miles an hour it still took them a quarter of an hour to reach the hanger housing the R&D section, one of nine built under the nearby mountains for extra security. Grant cast a trained eye over the defense preparations as they sped past armed guards, stopping only at checkpoints. Cameras and sensors recorded their every move. These in turn were linked to automated kill zones - 100 feet of tunnel lined with lasers designed to incinerate everything - spaced every half mile throughout the tunnels.

Finally they came to flashing red lights and warning signs as they entered R&D. Once through the elaborate security, armed guards escorted Colonel Grant to the test firing range.

Grant entered a massive dome shaped hanger with white painted walls so bright that the illumination seemed to emanate from the very walls themselves. Then Grant noticed random burn marks scattered over the walls and the ceiling.

Several scientists stood around a small table, their excited voices annoyed him as he strode towards them. One of the scientists, a bald man of about fifty, spotted Grant and his escort and warned the others of his arrival. The group parted, falling silent.

Grant smiled. He loved to intimidate people. "I am Colonel Grant, USAF. Mr. Hopwood has informed me that you are about to give the weapon a final test." The bald scientist stepped forward, hand out. The man's neck and wrists were covered with tattoos and Grant instantly took a dislike to him and refused the handshake. The scientist awkwardly dropped his hand and mumbled "Indeed, you came at an opportune moment Colonel. I am …"

Grant immediately cut him off. "Let's dispense with the introductions. I am not here to make friends. I want to know if the damn thing works."

The scientist smiled "Indeed it does," he replied looking at the weapons on the table. Grant stared at the innocent looking black boxes. They reminded him of old Kodak box brownie cameras. He felt disappointed he had expected at least a *Buck Rodgers* type space gun.

The scientist picked up one of the boxes, slipped his hand through a leather strap and flipped down the back panel to check the settings inside. Satisfied he turned his back and walked forward "Max release the targets."

Grant watched as several pre-programmed small white balls were released at the end of the cavernous test range. They flew in a random pattern, though Grant could discern no method of propulsion.

"They operate off the same technology as the weapon. Electromagnetic energy forming around the balls generates antigravity. Einstein was right." The explanation had come from the woman in the white coat next to him; he could hear the pride of achievement in her voice.

The remaining scientists were now donning welders' goggles and ear protection and Grant wondered why. He watched the bald scientist move to the center of the room and wondered how he could possibly aim such a harmless looking box.

Suddenly electromagnetic energy emanated from the front of the box. Four blue jagged lightning bolts streamed out and then intertwined as they reached out toward the targets.

Grant felt the hairs on his arms stand up. The noise was deafening. He took an involuntary step backward while bringing his arm up to protect his face from the harsh glare.

Grant could understand now that the device was easily aimed by simply directing the energy beams toward the target. The deadly electromagnetic energy simply surrounded its target in a blue glow. The bald scientist operating the weapon slowly turned sideways, the ball following the source of the emissions. The scientist lowered the ball towards a boxlike container of Kevlar composite which had been welded to the floor. Another field of blue energy generated from inside the box on the floor, now surrounded the ball. The scientist switched off his weapon and the field inside the box took over as the heavy lid closed with the ball captured inside.

The other scientists removed their protection, and all smiles, congratulated one another.

Grant stared dumfounded at the innocent looking chest on the floor. His ears rang and he could smell ozone in the air.

"Professor Metzler had to shave his head; his hair would stand on end for days after one of these tests. We have only to increase the output to disintegrate the balls completely. Impressive don't you think?"

Grant was very impressed; this harmless looking group of eggheads had produced the most awesome weapon he had ever seen, one worthy of *Buck Rodgers* himself. He felt his confidence return.

His brief was simple, capture at least two Foo Fighters and destroy the rest if necessary. Grant was sure that it would indeed be necessary. He would place the entire base on high alert ensuring not even an ant would get through without being incinerated. Grant breathed a sigh of relief. His future was secure, nothing could possibly go wrong. All he had to do now was wait.

<<<<>>>>

Robert Broughton
with a Foo Fighter

Robert was born in Yorkshire England, then immigrated to Australia in 1970 after living for one year in New Zealand. After marrying a New Yorker he moved to Florida. Robert's greatest pleasure is to create and as an artisan he specializes in making dreams reality. Working a wide variety of jobs in his life he has, to name a few: promoted Hovercraft, spent two years as an outback photographer and made wedding videos. Currently a member of the Ink Slingers Guild he writes for fun and is working on the third novel of his epic trilogy, MAGI.

Connect with Robert:
www.facebook.com/robert.broughton.1848?fref=ts

Other books by Robert Broughton:
Beyond the Threshold (Anthology)

The Quarter

By Anne Cargile

Going to the beach was always fun and in the summer of 1979 we went every week. Four of us crammed into a blue Mustang convertible, my mom and I, her friend Betty and Betty's son, Ronny. Ronny and I were opposites, he fair-haired and blue eyed and always laughing, me dark and always too serious for a ten year old. Ronny was my best friend.

Our favorite beach was Pacific Beach with its long stretches of clean white sand and waves that were always big enough to catch a ride with a boogie board. Riding a boogie board was like defying gravity, and which unlike stunt biking or roller-skating, when you fell you didn't break any bones. Sometimes we'd go to other beaches, but Pacific Beach, or P.B. as we called it, was our favorite because of Tuggs.

Tuggs was a motorcycle bar. Why our mothers thought this was an appropriate place to take a pair of ten year olds I have no clue, but we loved the place. The first thing you saw when you got near were the bikes, mostly Harleys, parked all around the bar in neat lines. The black paint and chrome would gleam in the sun and the bikes would take on an air of menace, like metallic animals ready to bite if you got too close. The salty smell of the ocean drifted through it all; curling through the smells of hot asphalt and motor oil. Tuggs itself wasn't much to look at from the outside. The building's walls were covered in bawdy murals; usually of bikini clad women and garish palm trees. They were obviously done by different artists, and none of them were very good.

When I would step inside the combined smells of pine shavings, fried food and beer would always hit me first. It was like the doorway of Tuggs formed a divider between the brilliant world outside, and the dark, cool world within. The sound of the jukebox and men talking would come in to focus with the first step inside. Another two steps forward and I could hear the best sound on earth: the ding-ding, beep-beep, smacking sound of pinball machines. Pinball was the reason Ronny and I loved Tuggs so much. It was a special thing, just for beach days.

One particular day Ronny and I were each given two quarters to play, a veritable fortune of goodwill from our moms. The mounting anticipation of sending the small silver balls flying and banging and beeping had us bouncing and with a laugh and a wave from our moms we ran, dodging waitresses with trays of beer and bikers lumbering to their tables. We raced to those pinball machines, eager to get our scores up there at the top, slamming our quarters in and banging the buttons while happily belting out "My my my my Sharona!" to the jukebox.

My quarters didn't last long that day. Disappointed at the short-lived entertainment of losing twice so quickly, I poked Ronny on the shoulder to let him know I was going back to our table. I wanted to see if I couldn't beg just one more quarter. Not taking his eyes off his own game, which I jealously saw was already at a higher score than I had been able to get to, he nodded and kept playing. As I started shuffling back to the table I heard someone call out to me.

"Hey kid. You like the pinball, huh?"

I glanced around to see who had spoken to me. It was one of the bikers, fresh in from the look of him, still wearing his riding chaps, dirt on his neck and face. He was leaning forward, his massive arms on the table. A half drained mug of beer sat next to him, drops of it still sticking to his mustache. It made him look a little bit like an angry sea lion.

I nodded a yes, trying not to laugh at the image of an angry sea lion in biker clothes.

"Come here then. Come on, I don't bite," he said.

The thing was, I wasn't scared at all; Tuggs was perfectly safe for me, there was nothing perilous in the place. That was just something I knew instinctively. The people who sat around in Tuggs wouldn't always be very nice to grown-ups, but we kids who managed to make it in were always treated well as long as we minded our manners. Glancing back to see that Ronny was still playing his game, and curious that this man felt the need to reassure me, I walked over and sat down at his table, keeping my face pleasant and innocuous.

He looked at me, his eyes dark and very direct, and leaned forward a bit more. I heard the table groan from the weight and noticed again how huge his arms were, easily twice the size of my thigh. I looked right back at him.

"Do you know what inflation is kid?" he asked.

"No, Sir," I said a little confused.

"Inflation is how something costs more and more over time. Let me ask you this. What can you buy with a quarter?"

I thought about it. "A game of pin ball or two packs of gum, or a ride on the bus," I answered.

He nodded and took another drink from his mug. "OK then, what do you think you'll be able to buy in three years with the same quarter?"

My face must have shown my disgust with being asked such a silly question because he started to glare at me. Oops. I needed to take him seriously. I thought about it for a minute longer and finally said, "I don't know."

"That was an honest answer kid. Good for you. I'll make you a deal. Interested?" The biker man smiled at me, white teeth peeping out from under his bushy mustache.

Obviously this man didn't know me. Straightening up in my chair, I felt my sass starting to slip out as I said to him, "Tell me the deal and I'll tell you if I'm interested."

He laughed a big laugh, showing a belly that had a good amount of bounce to it. The Iron Maiden skull on his t-shirt took on an even wider death grin as it attempted to stretch across his gut. I leaned back a little alarmed.

Smacking his hand down on the table loudly enough to make me jump he said, "I'll give you two dollars in quarters to play your pinball machines. But!" and here he slid a shiny quarter across the table in front of me, "you have to save this one quarter for three years. You can't spend it. You can't give it away. In three years you have to look at this quarter and think about what you can buy with it." He leaned back and watched me, his dark eyes missing nothing.

I couldn't believe my ears. This was easy money! He was going to give me two whole dollars for the pinball machines just to save one quarter? My mind raced ahead to showing Ronny the bounty, and then leapt to having to explain this to my mom. Shrugging all those thoughts off, I stuck out my hand and said, "Deal!"

This massive dirty biker took my hand, engulfing it in his own huge paw. He put a little pressure in to it and held on firmly. I could not take my hand away and I was forced to look at him directly.

"You will save this quarter, and you will keep your promise kid. Understood?" he said quietly, his dark eyes pinning me to my chair.

I gulped and nodded, suddenly very committed to protecting this quarter. When he finally let go of my hand, I asked him if he would wait a minute. I went up to the bar and asked Jim the bartender for some tape and a piece of paper and a pencil. Going back to the biker man's table I carefully wrote down the date three years ahead. I taped the paper all around the quarter and held it up to him for his approval.

He just nodded and slid over a stack of quarters. "Take care kid. Good luck on that pin ball."

"Thanks."

I watched him walk out of Tuggs and I never saw him there again.

I never did make a high score on the pinball at Tuggs, or anywhere else. I have also never spent that quarter. Every few years I take it out of my memento box and I think about what I can buy with it, and what I can't. Certainly not two packs of gum now, or even a game of pinball.

I think about that man and why he picked me. I wish that I could tell him how much I learned from him, and how when I hold that quarter in my hand I realize that sometimes it's the small things that have the highest value. The quarter I will never spend has been worth every penny.

About Anne Cargile

After decades of trying to ignore the voices in her head and appear normal Anne Cargile finally sat down one day and let them take over. She habitually only shared her mental adventures with her garden plants, but they steadily worked to convince her to share with humans too. She finally gave in to their incessant nagging and has been working on writing and publishing her stories to "real" people. Squeezing in time to tap out a few pages a day between the demands of her family, her chickens and her half acre garden Anne currently resides in New Hampshire.

Connect with Anne:
www.facebook.com/pages/Anne-Cargile/228517673925252

www.goodreads.com/author/show/6571171.Anne_Cargile

www.amazon.com/author/annecargile

Email: Anne.Cargile@gmail.com

Other books by Anne Cargile:
Beyond the Threshold (Anthology)

Complications

By Dinah Shatter

Prologue

The streets were silent, cold and empty save for the drifts of autumn leaves buried by mounds of snow. Not long after 2:30 am, a tall figure walked past the flickering streetlights toward the local swamp. The silhouette moved silently down the slope leading to the water's edge. He sniffed once, twice and then sneezed.

"I'm glad you came." A woman's voice sounded from the dark. "These humans would be hard to finish all by myself."

The figure growled low in his throat and stepped closer to the water, to which the woman responded with a sinister laugh, "Don't kid yourself fool. To fight with me would be to seal your sad fate. Perhaps…that's what you want?"

"All I want is for you to leave the humans alone," the figure finally said. The woman laughed again as she swirled into view. The moonlight shone queerly on her wet gown and the two soaked bodies she held in her grip. Whether the dampness was from the water or from their blood, the man couldn't tell.

"Allan," the woman called. The figure looked away from the bodies and up at her, fuming.

The woman raised her hands, the nails gleaming innocuously. "They are dying. It's no use." Body rigid, his fists clenched, he began to walk into the water.

Chapter 1

Three months before…

Tory, also known as the Asian kid, walked into the dim office. He slid off his large green headphones and scanned the backs of the strangers at the tables. Four people sat at computers, and one guy was outside on a balcony. It seemed none of them were the person he was looking for.

"Hey, it's the new kid!" he heard from his left. A lean black guy walked in from the balcony. His glasses were a little fogged, and he took them off and wiped them on a handkerchief that he pulled from his back pocket. "It's freezing out there huh? Did you just get here?"

Tory nodded. "Yeah, uh, I'm not late, am I?"

The guy put his glasses back on and held out his hand. "No! Not at all. I'm Raisin Falsh, but you can call me Ray. You are?"

"Tory Hae...I'm kind of new in town... but Mr. Konko told me that you would help me out a bit and show me around?"

"Yeah that's fine! You want to get started? I'll show you how to open up the program." Raisin, he asked to be called Ray, walked over to the desks and turned on a monitor.

Ray double clicked a funny icon on the computer screen and after a moment's pause a program popped up. "This thing takes a bit to load up but once it does, it runs okay." Tory scoffed in amusement and Ray smiled at him.

"By the way," Ray said, turning to Tory. "Addy, Jace," Ray pointed to a few guys over at the tables, "and a few other guys and I are going to a bar to watch the game tonight. You want to come?"

Tory smiled, "Sure! Is the bar nearby?"

"Yeah, it's not too far of a walk. Us office guys could stand for a little exercise anyways," Ray replied. "That will give you a chance to check out the city too." He glanced at the screen. "Halleluiah! It's running. Okay, let me show you how this works."

~~~

That night as Tory walked out with Ray he asked, "Do you want to stop by Starbucks? I need my coffee."

Ray laughed. "Sure," he said as he pulled a pack of cigarettes, "I know how that feels."

They dropped by the coffee shop quickly and Ray invited Tory to check out his place. When they got there, Tory was introduced to Ray's cat, Eileen, a fat black, longhaired mix. Ray grabbed a scarf and his warmer jacket and they headed back outside.

They arrived at the bar, lit up by a bright sign on it that said Benny's Bar. The lights were fluorescent and happy; a welcoming sight that implied inside was warmth and merry voices.

Tory saw all the crowds inside and got nervous. He turned to Ray and said, "I'm sorry. I'm not a people person. I get awkward around others." Ray smiled at him as Tory looked at his shoes.

Ray shook his head, butting out the cigarette he held. "No worries. My friends are all honest and great guys. You'll like them soon enough."

Tory smiled and argued, "I don't really like football either though. I'm more into Dungeons and Dragons." Ray let out a long peal of laughter at this and Tory punched him in the shoulder as they walked into the bar.

The first thing Tory saw were the tables, old wooden ones that sat on legs that wobbled perilously whenever someone leaned on them. They were big enough that seven or eight friends could sit comfortably at one of them. Addy and Jace were waiting at one of them, along with three other men.

Ray moved through the crowd smoothly and Tory tried to follow along.

The room was warm and lit by old-fashioned chandeliers that glowed a homey yellow light down onto the men and women in the bar. The T.V's were all playing some sort of sport, and Tory tried to pick out a game that he could understand. "Touchdooowwn!!" Came a shout from the far right side of the room. A cheer rose up and Tory could hear mugs clinking together. He felt comfortable suddenly. He liked the smell of yeast, ale and harder whiskey. It reminded him of something, but he couldn't quite catch what the memory was.

Someone bumped him hard in the shoulder. He looked around and saw a small woman make her way through the crowd like a fish going with the current. "Hey!"

Tory looked back around. Ray was standing with the other guys. "Did you see someone you know?" he asked.

Tory screwed his mouth up and frowned, shaking his head. He stood still for a moment longer, wondering why he suddenly felt so cold. His spine was stiff, and his neck felt tense. He shook his head in wonder. What the hell was that?

He shook it off and walked over to greet everyone at the table with a nod. Ray turned to the men at the table that Tory didn't know. All of them were tall and all of them were covered with muscles. One man seemed to be a stereotypical lumberjack, while another had a big fashionable coat on, his hair gelled back; the last man was sunburned, wearing only a wife beater and some jeans. How he had survived in the cold outside was beyond Tory's imagination.

"Guys, this is Tory Hae. Tory this is Gus," (the lumberjack) "Jason," (the guy in the nice coat) "and this here is Rex" (the guy with no temperature receptors). "You already know Jace and Addy." Tory attempted to give a bright smile, but they were an intimidating group of men, especially all grouped together staring at him. No-Temperature-Receptor guy smiled a toothy grin and held his freckled hand out to shake Tory's. "Nice ta meetcha keed! Yew new er sumthin'?" Tory tried not to look too shocked at the man's thick accent. It sounded like someone who had popped right out of a country CD.

"Yeah I'm new. I just moved here last week. Where are you from?" Rex dropped his head back and cackled like a witch. He was about to answer when Gus patted Tory on the back, potentially breaking a few bones, and said, "You're kind of small, kid. You over nineteen?"

Tory nodded, smiling. "Don't worry though. I'm the designated driver." That cracked them up.

"Keed," Rex said, "Thur ain't no such thing round here." Jason, who had been watching the game suddenly slammed his fist on the table and shouted, "Touchdooowwn!" Tory turned to the T.V to see the replay.

Later, a very sober Tory shouldered a very drunk Raisin down the quiet streets. Quiet except for the howling wind that rushed along the pavement as if late for an appointment with the frigid rain, perhaps. Ray mumbled something like, "I'm going to hurl man, I have to stop and rest..." but Tory kept on. He knew if he put Ray down the guy would conk out like a light. Looking down a dark alleyway he thought he saw a figure lurking in the shadows. He shivered and trudged on.

Finally back at Ray's house, which was closer than Tory's, Tory tugged Ray over to the weathered couch. Eileen meowed loudly at Tory, and wouldn't move her fat behind off of the seat. "Move it fatty," he murmured to her. Ray began to snore and Eileen meowed again. Tory gave a few more aggressive tugs to get Ray up on the couch, but to no avail. Sighing, he set the body down on the floor, giving up. He sat on the couch, which was surprisingly comfortable.

Leaning back, he fell asleep soon after to the sound of the wind outside.

A third person stood in the room. The intruder sniffed loudly and held in a sneeze, making Eileen stand and hiss. The sniffer walked over to Tory, sleeping soundly now, and sniffed his shoulder. Outside the wind howled like a beast as the stranger stood as still as stone. He pulled out a tissue and blew his nose, then sniffed Tory's shoulder again. This time the sniffer seemed satisfied with the smell he received and murmured, "Imelda..." Then, as if the howling wind pulled him along and away, he was gone.

Chapter 2

Cold water flooded Tory's nose and eyes like an invasive alien. He spluttered and gagged, waking up instantly. Sitting up, he waved his hands about him. "What the hell man?" he croaked. Laughter was the reply and he wiped his eyes to see who his attacker was. A tall black guy stood over him, looking suspiciously like Ray.

"Morning sleeping beauty. You have ten minutes to get off my couch," he said and walked off into another room as Tory felt at his soaked shirt. Ray walked back in holding a spatula. "I'm the only one with a hangover and I wake up an hour before you do. Did you enjoy sleeping on my couch?"

"Yeah. Sorry about leaving you on the floor. You were kind of like a corpse and I couldn't get you onto the couch."

"So you slept there instead," Ray smirked.

"Yeah." A popping noise came from a different room, and Ray turned saying, "You like bacon I hope?"

"It's okay."

Ray walked out of view. "You had better start loving it because that's what I mainly live off of."

Tory smiled. "Will I be here often?"

"If you want. You did a good job getting me home, designated driver."

Tory stood up on wobbly legs. "Is that my new nickname?" Following Ray in to the kitchen he saw a plate comically piled with bacon.

"Sure." Ray swung about, topping the bacon tower with yet another piece. Tory was astonished that it didn't fall over.

"Okay. Then you'll be Bacon King."

~~~

After a greasy breakfast Tory was introduced to Ray's younger brother Crazy, a lazy college student. "His name is actually Craisin," Ray told Tory. Crazy threw a pillow at Ray, which he caught and whacked him with. Later, Tory found out his name was actually Crashing And Scary.

"What kind of a name is that?" Tory asked incredulously.

"What kind of a name is Raisin? My parents were high when they named us. So we shortened his name and called him Crazy."

Tory laughed himself into a fit over that. "What a weird family you have."

"Don't rub it in," Ray grumbled.

Over the next few weeks Tory got into the groove of driving home members of his big-muscled group of friends. Ray was a constant. Sometimes Crazy came along as well. The funniest nights were when Rex-No-Temperature-Receptors came along, singing old folk songs in some sort of Irish language. "Is he Irish or Country?" Tory asked one night over Rex's garbled tunes. Gus-The-Lumberjack and Jason-Rich-Guy laughed for a minute straight about that, but Tory never got his question answered.

One night at the bar he bumped into someone who seemed strangely familiar. She glanced at him as she strutted by, slipping through the crowd as he carried a few drinks to his friends. He nearly dropped them, she bumped him so hard. Tory felt a weird shiver flow quickly down his spine as he watched her fade into the ocean of stranger's faces.

She's so beautiful he couldn't help but think to himself. He didn't even realize he turned towards her and had followed her through the crowd. She sat at a table in a corner of the bar, waiting for him. "Hey there handsome," the woman said.

Tory smiled, not sure why he had followed her. "Hi… um" he started to say.

She stood and slipped a hand over his shoulder. "Guys like you always play the innocent card, huh?" she murmured, her breath smelling sweet and strange. "Wanna party?"

Tory thought that sounded great, but as she leaned forward quickly to kiss him Tory acted on instinct, whipped his hand out and punched her in the jaw. She gasped as she fell backwards, knocking over a mug of beer on the counter behind her.

"Oh my God. I'm so sorry," Tory choked out as he backed away. "Oh man, I'm so sorry." Her nose was bleeding slightly and Tory's eyes got wider. She glowered at him. He wanted to stay and help her, but he just kept backing away.

He got back to his table feeling oddly out of place and stiff. Ray noticed his expression and said, "Did you see the last play? It was hardcore." Tory looked up the T.V screen, now fully accustomed to the terms in football.

"No," he said after a long pause, "I didn't see it. I guess I wasn't watching. What happened?" Tory tried unsuccessfully for twenty minutes, but he couldn't slip back into the usual feel of the evening. Finally he stood up and said quietly to Crazy, who never got drunk, "I'm going to go outside for a minute, okay?" Crazy nodded, watching an about-to-happen-bar fight over on the left side of the room.

Walking out into the cold, Tory began to shiver. "Oh man. Why did I come outside?" he asked himself quietly. It felt good to be away from the laughter and the loud cheers. He closed his eyes and listened to the howling wind. Minutes passed. His nose began to run slightly and his hands shook, but the moon was so big and the darkness was so quiet and beautiful.

"Go back inside."

Tory jumped at the angry order that shook him from his meditation. He looked over and saw a man with a black eye and a crazy hair-do staring at him from the darkness next to the bar's dumpster. Tory looked around. Is he talking to me? He saw no one else outside. The guy walked a bit closer and Tory frowned. The stranger was shivering like a wet puppy and his build was small, but he had the strangest feeling of power surrounding him.

"Now."

"Are you talking to me?" Tory asked, embarrassed.

"Who else you idiot? Go inside. Now. Don't come out here alone."

Tory frowned deeper. "I think you're drunk," Tory said quietly and turned to walk away.

Cold fingers gripped his arm like a vice. "Do what I tell you to do," the man growled in his ear. Tory thought he saw someone else in the shadows of the back alleyway.

Tory held up his hands. "Okay, wait up. Chill out alright? I'm going inside, okay?"

Tory let Mr. Cold-fingers lead him back toward the door. The stranger opened the door for Tory and shoved him inside.

"Stay inside," the man said again and slammed the door behind him. Tory rubbed his arms, feeling far colder than he should have. The strange man's grip had left a frosty needle-y feeling where his finger's had been. Looking around, the familiar bar scene seemed surreal and strange.

Finally getting to the table, he sat down and smiled at Ray, who smiled back and offered a soda. "Got this for you."

Tory grabbed it. "Thanks."

"You okay?" Crazy asked.

"Yeah keed. Yew lookin' kinda eel."

Tory gave Rex a quirky smile and shook his head. "No Rex I'm fine. It's just a little cold outside."

Rex giggled, "Kinda cold? Keed it's colder than uh polar bear's ass!"

Jason felt Tory's head with his wrist. "Tory, you're worrying me. Are you alright? You look really pale."

Tory felt ill, but he lied pretty well. "Are you kidding me? Listen mom. I'm fine, okay? Just because I'm short doesn't mean you get to baby me. Besides, it was just really cold outside." Jason looked unconvinced but turned back to the game.

The night went on and Ray got pretty drunk, so Tory patted him on the shoulder and said, "Time to go kid."

Ray giggled, and leaned his full weight on Tory. "Take me home officer, I'm drunk." Then he giggled himself practically into a fit.

Tory looked around the table. "Do you guys have rides home?" They all said yes, they did, so Crazy and Tory lugged Ray to the car and they drove off, Ray humming one of Rex's weird folk songs.

"Why do the guys and Ray like to drink so much?" Tory asked Crazy.

Crazy shrugged and laughed softly. "Who knows? A lot of people like to get drunk, don't they? It's a way to get away from reality, that's what I think. Or a way to open up to people, maybe? I don't know. I've never asked them myself."

"Yeah but, they do it like two to three times a week. Is that normal?"

Crazy leaned his head to one side, watching the lights flash by the window. "Maybe they became alcoholics without knowing it," he said softly, "I know it's not right to get drunk that often, but I don't know how to help them. I want to," he looked at Tory with piercing eyes, "I really want to help them stop this bad habit but..." Ray had fallen asleep, and his snoring audible.

"How did it begin, do you know?" Tory asked, feeling a bit like a secret detective.

"Ray was going to get married to this chick named Madeline, but on the day of the wedding she ran off with some guy who could play the guitar." Tory glanced at Ray through the rearview mirror. Crazy continued, "So he started buying beer on the weekends, and he would just sit there and watch T.V. Sometimes... sometimes he would cry, really hard too. I think he loved her. I mean I think he really loved her. And then- where are we going?"

"I'm just going to get some food at Checkers if that's okay with you."

"Yeah no problem. Anyways, he started buying two packs of beer and would finish it all in one sitting. I told him that he shouldn't, but he just ignored me. He's not an angry drunk he's just a big crybaby. Because one night I went and turned the T.V. off, right? And I said, 'you can't drink your feelings for her away' or something like that, and he was so hammered that he just sits there for a second saying, 'Turn that back on.' But I just kept saying things like, 'You need to handle your life' and 'She's not coming back.' Real harsh shit, you know?"

Tory was shocked that Crazy had cursed, but he stayed silent and watched him with weary eyes.

"So I keep saying these horrible things to him and he tries to throw a pillow at me but he misses by like, five feet, even though I was right in front of him. And he just stares at the pillow, you know? Just stares at it. Then these huge tears, the biggest tears I've ever seen, start pouring down his face." Crazy looked about ready to cry himself. "'I can't stop' he says, and just keeps crying, his whole body shaking he was crying so hard, you know? I didn't know what to do. He says, 'Help me. God, help me.' And he just keeps saying that. Over and over. What was I supposed to do?" Tory turned into the parking lot of Checkers. "So I just bring him a blanket and take the rest of his beer away from him, right? He just won't stop with the whole, 'God help me thing.' So I just tell him, 'God's going to help us, okay? He's going to send help.'" Tory parked, but left the car running as they sat in the dark, Ray snoring away in the back.

"Then he starts going to the bar. It just went downhill from there. I used to have to get up at three in the morning, to answer my phone and he'd be on the line saying, 'I don't know where I am.' Crying and all, right? He'd be begging me to come get him and I'd have to go find him curled up in some back alley, sobbing. Begging God to send help."

There was silence in the car as Crazy wiped his eyes. Tory thought he saw the streetlight glint off of a tear, but he couldn't be sure. "And then…?" Tory asked softly.

Crazy laughed, "Then you came along and started driving Ray home. You know, he used to go out drinking every day, right?" Tory shook his head, shocked. Crazy nodded and leaned back, exhaling loudly. A minute passed by in peaceful quiet.

"Thanks for listening."

"Of course Crazy, any time. I'm here for you and your brother."

Crazy laughed and turned back to look at Ray. "Dumbass doesn't even deserve you," he said.

"What am I, his wife? Oh, no wait. I didn't mean…"

Crazy laughed, relaxed. "Let's get some food."

~~~

After Crazy got home and put Ray into bed he sat down on the couch and thought about what he'd told Tory. Possibly an hour went by, when he heard a noise like the ticking of a clock on the living room window. As the sound got louder, it rose out of the silence and penetrated his thoughts. Crazy frowned. There were no trees outside of the window, so there should have been no disturbance. His body felt leaden as he got up and a trickle of fear slid down his spine. Their apartment house was on the seventh floor, there could be no one at the window. Walking over to the curtains he stood in front of them and watched them hang motionless on the hanger. But the tapping, ticking noise continued. He forced a tight smile. He was merely scaring himself, that was all and he pushed back the curtains.

Chapter 3

Six o'clock the next morning Tory woke to his phone ringing incessantly. He answered and heard Ray babbling, "-and I can't find him anywhere! I checked all over, and the window was open and I think I saw some blood on the floor! I don't think it was, but what if he-"

"Calm down!" Tory shouted as he stood out of bed. "Explain what's going on, slowly. I didn't hear the first part, okay?"

Ray began to sob, "Should I call the police? Ohh god Tory... He's gone! He was in the apartment when we got home, but then when I woke up he wasn't, and the window was shattered and the curtain was ripped to shreds and- [hiccup] and he- he's gone!"

Tory was confused and very tired, but he aimed at sounding calm and alert, "Did you check outside?" The thought of Crazy jumping out of their apartment window seemed comically unreal, but Tory felt that he needed to ask.

"Yes! Nothing was there except for some broken glass!"

Tory paused for a moment and then restrained a laugh. "Then he's alive, you idiot. Stop crying." Ray didn't answer. "Listen. If the window was broken, and he wasn't lying on the ground outside, dead, then he's alive. He probably just left the house angrily after punching the window...or something."

"Why would he do that though?" Ray inquired, apathetic.

Tory scoffed, "I don't know, but last night we talked about some crap, and maybe he was stewing over it and got pissed off or something, alright?"

Ray sounded calmer when he finally said, "Oh..."

"You are such a crybaby, man," Tory stated, and went to get his coffee started. It wasn't like he was going back to sleep. "What are you going to do?"

"Wait for Crazy to come back, I guess. I'll see you later." Ray hung up and Tory began making eggs thinking, it will be okay. But he had a strange foreboding deep inside his stomach.

When he got to work, the foreboding feeling had morphed into full-fledged, nauseous terror. There was something wrong. Crazy wasn't okay, as he had assured Ray that he was.

He waited nervously for Ray to arrive at work, but by two-thirty he still wasn't there. Getting out of his chair, Tory asked Jace if he knew where Ray was. "He might have a real bad hangover dude, give him another hour," Jace said and laughed.

At the end of the day, Tory rushed out of the building, a cold sweat gluing his shirt to his back. He had called Ray twice, but his friend had not answered, and Tory's worries hadn't lessened any.

He called again, every ring making him feel more and more

wooden. After the fourth ring, the voice-mail blared into his ears and he hung up. Sighing, Tory put his hands against his heart. It was beating too quickly.

Looking around into the night, Tory Hae suddenly felt hunted. With no rhyme or reason to his fear, he broke out in a cold sweat when an ambulance siren began to wail far off. He glanced both ways down the road, his hands shivering. Running across the street, and feeling dumb for running, he couldn't help himself. Rushing to get in his car, his heart danced franticly in his chest. On his way to Ray's house he kept glancing in his rearview mirror, but not for a car. He wasn't sure what he was looking for, but he felt something was after him.

~~~

Tory knocked on Ray's door. The hallway was dim and smelled of laundry lint. He had already knocked twice. There was no noise that he could hear coming from inside. That was unusual, and it made him more nervous. Even though it was warm inside Tory's fingers were still cold from the frost of outside. He blew on them softly. I wish Ray would just call me so that I- His phone vibrated in his pocket, and broke the silence with a bashing of drums. The song Holland 1945 filled the hall.

Heart in his throat, he flipped open his phone, not even checking to see who it was. "Ray?!" he nearly shouted, "Are you alright? Where are you? Where's Crazy?!"

There was a long silence, and then some static as Ray sighed. "Hey... yeah, I'm at the Mortin Pot's hospital. Do you wanna come over? I won't be coming home tonight."

Tory nodded, even though Ray couldn't see him, "Yeah! Yeah I'm coming right now." And he was. He booked down the stairs towards the exit, bursting through the doors to sprint back to his car, the phone still glued to his ear, "What happened?"

"Just...just get here and you'll see."

~~~

Tory walked into the hospital room, sweating and breathing heavily. Ray sat in a visitor's seat, looking tired. "What happened?" Tory asked him.

Ray looked over at the hospital bed and sighed. "Crazy's ribs are broken."

"What, all of them?!"

"No, only a few. Three, I think the doctor said. I wasn't really listening."

Tory looked at Crazy lying on the hospital bed. Most of him was covered by a blanket, but a dark hand could be seen clutching the white covers. Tory walked closer to the bed, "Where did they find him?"

"I found him," Ray corrected aggressively.

"Okay. You did. Where did you find him?"

Ray pointed out the window toward a large field to the left of the hospital. "You see that lake?"

"Yeah."

"He was halfway in the water, near the road."

Tory shook his head, confused, "What? I don't get it. What happened to him?"

Ray looked down, bags hanging low under his eyes, like heavy purses that business women carry. "I don't know. The doctor asked if he was in some sort of street gang. He said it looked like someone had taken a hammer to his bones." Tory winced and Ray nodded. "I know. They said he wouldn't be able to walk around for a while." Then he scoffed, "A while."

Tory pulled up another visitor's chair. He felt horrible. "How long was he there? Do they know?"

"They said it seemed like he had been there all day." Ray had been looking at his hands, but now looked over at Tory. "It's okay man. It's not your fault."

A nurse walked in, her dark blonde hair in a thick braid. She carried a few pills and a shot on a tray. "Hello gentlemen," she said quietly, smiling. "Visiting hours ended at 10:00." She sounded apologetic. They thanked her, stood, said goodbye to Crazy, Ray promising to come the next day, and left.

Tory drove Ray home, and then he went back to his place. Walking into his dark house, he felt scared. Was someone in his house? Was there a dark figure over there, by the couch; rank breath, yellow eyes, waiting to jump on him and slit his throat? Or did he hold a hammer, with which to break bones? Like Crazy's. He turned on the light, and breathed a silent sigh of relief when the shape turned into his coat hanger. So he went to bed, still completely unnerved, feeling like a rabbit in wolf territory.

A few nights later it happened. Snow covered the ground, a

sheet of grey-white. The wind bit at faces like angry bugs and those who didn't have to work stayed inside. Tory was in Wal-Mart, buying some coffee for Ray. He hadn't been drinking, and had a major headache. Tory was searching through the aisles when he looked over and saw a woman who was familiar. She stood in the dairy section staring at him, giving him a strange, knowing smile. Tory frowned and gave a small wave as he continued walking when he stopped dead in his tracks. Looking back the woman was still staring at him and a cold shiver ran down his spine. She beckoned him, turned, and walked towards the front of the store.

Tory followed, cautious and frightened. He had seen this woman before, he was sure of it. Her long hair flowed down past her waist and her black dress dragged a bit on the shiny store linoleum. She walked outside and Tory followed.

"Do I know you?" he asked as soon as he got outside. His car was parked near the front door and out of the corner of his eye he saw Ray staring at him from the passenger seat.

"You could say that," the woman said. "My name is Draculara and there are some things I would address with you."

Tory tried not to laugh. Draculara? What kind of a weird name was that?

"You see, your friend, he looked a lot like his brother, and I was wrong to mistake one for the other."

"Do you get what I'm saying?" she asked. Tory glanced at the car where Ray sat making a 'get-it-on' motion with his hands. Tory shook his head. "Well," Draculara said, "I'm saying that the person who broke Crashing And Scary's bones was me."

Tory slowly took a step back. His head began to spin. "Go away from me," he said, but she continued speaking.

"I made a mistake, but I will fix it now. I meant to come after you two."

Tory heard the car door open. He wanted to laugh, but it didn't seem like the correct time to do so.

"I don't understand," he said as Ray walked over, "Why would you want to kill us?" She leaned her head back and laughed. It was deep and beautiful, but Tory didn't really think so. It just gave him goose bumps.

"Because you punched me in the face!" she yelled, her face twisting, looking masculine and demonic. Ray had come to stand beside Tory, looking mostly angry because Tory didn't have any coffee.

"Hey, what the hell is going on?" Ray asked.

"Um, this girl, I punched her in the face one night when she was hitting on me."

Ray raised an eyebrow, "Okay, so apologize."

"Well that's not the problem. She says that she's going to kill us, and that she was the one who hurt Crazy."

Ray looked unnerved. "Then she's insane and you shouldn't talk to her," he stated and began walking to the car. But the car wasn't there.

Chapter 4

How Tory would explain this later, he didn't know. The car was there, then with a sudden gust of wind, it was gone. He felt as if he were looking at picture frames, one was a picture that was taken when the car was there, and then suddenly the frame switched to a picture of the car not there. Out of the darkness of the night came the sound of something falling and crashing to the ground. Ray shouted in surprise and fell backwards onto the pavement. Draculara stood where the car had been, her laugh frighteningly similar to a hyenas. "I was going to spare your friend until that stupid tree sucker Allan barged in and started protecting you two. When someone challenges me like that, it gets my blood pumping."

"I'm sorry, who? Who's Allan? And what's a tree sucker?!" Ray yelled as he stood, "And mostly, WHERE IS THE CAR?!" Tory didn't say a word, just looked into the darkness, his head pounding.

"Allan is a vegetarian vampire," she sneered. "He has a stuffy nose and a stupid soft spot for minorities."

"What?!" Ray said, getting into the woman's face. "Tory, I can see why you wanted to punch this woman. You're messing with the wrong black guy, girl."

Tory shook his head, finally looking over at Draculara. "Where is my car?"

"Don't be rude. I threw it over there," she waved a hand vaguely and shrugged. "It's probably broken, ruined, smashed, destroyed…but that doesn't really matter. You won't need it, because I'm going to kill you."

What happened next would be a memory that the two men would never forget. Draculara moved at Tory with an inhuman speed. Right before she hit him, a figure came into view, blocking Draculara from his sight. A wave of air pressed against Tory and pushed him back. A tall redheaded guy in a long black trench coat and a long red scarf stood in front of him.

Ray was shouting profanities and yelling at Tory to "Run idiot, run!" He stayed where he was, unable to move, and watched a line of blood spray from the tall figure's arm. He heard the woman growl like a dog, and she pounced ten or twenty feet back.

"You again!" she said, almost in a scream.

The man turned to face him. Tory stared into a pale, freckled face with a black eye. The guy sniffed and said, "You should go to your friend."

Tory looked over at Ray, who had stumbled backwards, reluctant to leave Tory behind. "Let's go man!" Ray shouted. Tory looked back at the man's arm. A long gash ran from the elbow to the wrist. A wave of nausea rammed against his vision.

"Who are you?" he asked as he backed away.

The man took out a gun and cocked it, "The name's Allan, human. Now get out of here." Tory flinched as Draculara came zipping around Allan and rushed at him.

A shot rang out and Draculara tripped and fell. Her face wore a mask of shock as blood spurted from her mouth.

"Run!" Allan yelled again, and Tory ran. He sprinted away, pushing Ray on the back. "Go go go!" he urged frantically. They ran down the dark street, pelting past stores whose 'open' signs had been turned off hours before. A loud boom thundered from behind them and Ray began cussing again.

They reached a subway station and paid the woman in the booth for two tickets. She slid them under the fogged and scratched glass with an unaware expression. "Have a nice ride," she said.

The subway arrived and they got on board, slipping into the back seats and catching their breath.

"What the hell just happened?" breathed Ray as he slipped off his glasses and wiped them with his shirt.

"I don't know. I just don't want it to ever happen again."

"Was it even real?"

Tory shook his head, unsure. "How about this, we'll find out tomorrow. If we're dreaming, my car will be in the driveway. If not, we'll know that this was real." Ray agreed with this, and the rest of the ride they rode in silence.

The next morning Tory got up and walked to the kitchen, his head heavy and his legs shaky, to start some coffee. Scratching his stomach, he turned to get some milk from the fridge. A tall man stood in the front of the fridge, blocking his path.

"Gravity is a strange thing," Tory mentioned to Ray later. "One minute you're standing, and the next minute you're on the ground." And this was indeed how it had happened. "What?! How did you get inside?!" Tory yelled, his eyes round and blood-shot.

"Contrary to popular belief, vampires can enter any house they please, without being invited in," Allan said and helped Tory to his feet.

"That's not what I meant," Tory stated. For a moment he just stood, staring at the tall man, but then he resumed his quest for milk.

"Then what did you mean?" Allan inquired as he walked to the small table and sat on one of the chairs.

"I… I don't know honestly. I was hoping you and that lady weren't real."

Allan tilted his head to the side, "What do you mean?"

"I was hoping that I was dreaming. Or that someone had slipped a drug into my water."

Allan nodded in understanding and looked around the kitchen. When he looked back at Tory he simply said, "Well, I'm real."

Allan looked quite out of place. His black eveningwear contrasted badly with the bright room.

"How are you able to be in here? I thought vampires couldn't be in the sun or else they would burst into flames or something. Wait, do you sparkle?"

Allan barked a laugh and said, "No, not quite. We have just found ways around burning and melting in the sun. You could say we've become more advanced."

Tory laughed. "You're not actually a vampire."

For a moment Allan stayed where he was, looking placid and almost doll-like, his face serene.

Then he dissolved.

His feet went first, black smoke pouring off his body like dry ice, but when the smoke rose, his feet were gone. So went the rest of his body, disappearing quickly within the dark smoke. Tory gaped. Allan was gone and the only noise was the soft whisper of air as the smoke traveled about the room. "What?" Tory murmured, and an echoing laugh answered him.

"You see?" the smoke said. When it spoke, the air vibrated. "Can any mortal do this? No they can't," he said, answering his own question.

Tory shook his head, "No way…"

"Yes way. I am a vampire." The smoke swirled down like a tornado and formed into a human shape. Then the shape paled, and the hair turned red again, as if a shadow had passed over. Allan's skin formed freckles, and his eyes became glossy and normal. He smiled, "I don't mean to scare you, but there are some things you have to know so that you can try to win against Imelda."

"Who the hell is Imelda?"

"She calls herself Draculara, but that name is fake of course."

Tory nodded, his eyes as wide as a deer in headlights. "I should call Ray."

"Yes you should. He needs to know these things as well."

"Is he safe to go around by himself?"

"Yes. Imelda prefers not to go out during the day. Ever."

~~~

"Listen," Tory said to Ray quietly outside of the apartment, "There's something inside that, uh, might kind of freak you out."

Ray glared at him, "What is it? There's no one naked up there, is there?"

Tory shook his head, "No. It's just weird."

They turned and went upstairs, Ray looking suspicious and Tory feeling slightly giddy, or nauseous. At the apartment door he turned to Ray and said, "Try to keep an open mind."

They walked in and found Allan bent over, and speaking quietly to a large black cat that sat on the stove. When they entered, he straightened out and offered his hand to Ray, "Hello Ray. My name is Allan. I'm sorry about your brother." Ray didn't shake his hand. He just stared at Allan's bright hair and frowned.

"Hey Allan? What's up with the cat?" Tory asked.

"Ah yes. Sorry. This is Foreman, my senior, master and the man who sired me."

"What does that mean?" Tory questioned, "And why is a cat

your senior?"

The cat jumped down off the stove as Allan said, "Siring means to turn one into a vampire. And as for him being a cat..." There was a swirling of black smoke, and a man with deep black hair stood in the cat's place, "He's not."

Ray fainted.

Allan caught him and laid him on the couch. "Tory, I'm sorry for bringing him in without your permission, but he wanted to speak with you."

Foreman stepped forward, frowning. "Tory, I understand that you attacked Imelda a few weeks back." Tory felt nervous suddenly. What were they doing here? What do they want with me? They're not going to kill me or anything, are they? Tory gulped, and then nodded. Foreman smiled, "Good."

"What?"

"I said 'good'. I'm glad you did. She should know that not all human men enjoy a woman as ugly as she hanging all over them." Tory laughed, but Foreman didn't seem to be joking. "But thusly, she's out for blood. Yours particularly. I would have been okay with her killing you, I suppose, but then she attacked an innocent, and last night threatened to kill another. This is against the rules."

"What rules?" Ray asked. They all turned to see him sitting up and rubbing his head.

Foreman walked over and sat down on the couch opposite him. "The general rules of the common vampire. Imelda is a maybe worrisome, but nonetheless common vampire."

"Who's Imelda?" Ray asked.

"Uh, the chick who attacked us yesterday. Remember?" Tory told him, and Ray nodded unhappily.

Foreman continued, "When she attacked and injured the innocent she was finally labeled a 'dangerous vampire'. Just this morning, actually. Most of us breathed a sigh of relief when they did."

"When who did what?" Ray asked.

Foreman's frown became deeper, but he answered, "When the heads of the System labeled her a danger, she is now a wanted felon." Allan smiled and walked over and sat on the floor next to Foreman.

"Okay, so why are you here?" Ray asked.

"Because we have been appointed to guard you until the danger is over."

Tory asked, "Okay, but you're not going to follow us to work or anything, are you?"

Allan laughed, "Don't be ridiculous." Ray's face relaxed in relief.

"You won't be going anywhere," Foreman finished.

Chapter 5

Even one step outside was out of the question. Ray and Tory called in sick and then sat around the house playing card games, watching the T.V and making random dishes of food. Ray tired quickly and conked out on the couch. Tory sat and asked Allan questions about vampires, thoroughly intrigued. Allan answered most of his questions, (How old are you? One hundred fifty-five. Why is Imelda so mad about me punching her in the face? Women are strange creatures.) but left some things unsaid, which gave Tory an eerie feeling in his stomach.

There wasn't much to do, lazing around Tory or Ray's house. They had to alternate because of Ray's cat Eileen, who growled at the vampires and would hide until they left.

 Halfway through the second week, Ray began to worry about Crazy. He had called his brother every day and Crazy seemed to be doing alright. He said that his wounds were healing faster than any of the doctors had expected, but Ray still worried and he became irritable. Allan informed Ray that another vampire was healing Crazy daily, bit by bit.

Ray finally requested that Allan take him to see his brother, but Foreman denied his request. Ray had sat on the couch, fuming and silent. Tory had baked some pastries from a recipe that he looked up online and tried to give some to Ray, but his friend waved him away, glaring at the T.V's blank screen.

Tory was woken up that night by Ray shaking his shoulder harshly. "We're getting out of here," he growled and pulled Tory out of his warm bed.

"What do you mean?" Tory asked. Ray shook his head and pulled him to the window, handing him a coat and boots.

"We have to go see Crazy. I've been feeling weird about him and it's driving me, well, crazy."

Tory laughed nervously and rubbed the sleep from his eyes. "Okay but listen. You know how in those dumb horror movies the main characters leave the safe haven when they're not supposed to and they get in trouble? We're not the dumb main characters of some bad horror flick."

Ray scoffed as he shoved on his shoes, "Yeah, more like Twilight."

Tory screwed up his face in disgust, "How about no."

Ray stood jerkily, "Yeah well, I'm going and as my best friend, you are required to go. It's just one of those things."

Tory felt a child-like happiness. He hadn't had anyone call him friend for a long time. "Fine. But let's be quick about it," he said, and they rushed to go out the window and scale the wall.

Outside on the sidewalk, Ray spun in a circle, grinding his heels into the hard snow. "Freedom!" he shouted. "Freedom from those evil vampires!"

Tory shook his head, but looked up to watch his breath float merrily towards the black sky. "I wonder why they didn't follow us," Tory mused. Looking over, he was shocked to see Ray waltzing ahead. He ran to catch up. "I wonder why they-"

"You know? These past few days have been so weird. I feel like I'm in some sort of trippy nightmare," Ray said. Tory nodded in agreement.

"And you will soon be woken from this dream," said a demonic voice. Tory glared into the darkness, trying to see who had spoken.

Ray looked at him, "Did you say something?"

"I thought that was you."

"Yes, well, you are both wrong," said the voice. They looked about them, confused. Tory's heartbeat sped up in fear, but Ray seemed to just get upset.

"Why can't I just go see my damn brother in peace?!" Ray growled. In front of them the darkness seemed to open, and a whistling noise filled their ears before all went black.

~~~

Allan and Foreman were standing outside the apartment discussing who would go hunting first. They hadn't fed in weeks and Foreman's eyes had taken on a crimson hue that didn't soften his harsh features. Allan was exhausted and after fifteen minutes of arguing, he finally said, "Forget it, we can go together. It's not like they will try to go anywhere. They haven't tried that once."

Foreman nodded as his eyebrows furrowed thoughtfully. "I suppose that's not quite out of the question. Just in case, let's check on them before we leave."

When they went back in to the apartment, they were incensed to find the beds empty and Tory's bedroom window open. They leaped out the window, flying to find them, ignoring the snow billowing around them as they landed on the ground. Foreman searched for footprints, but any tracks had been covered by the newly fallen snow.

A whistling sound that ended in a thwack pierced Foreman's ears and he shot off in the direction of the noise. Under a streetlight that flickered yellow, he and Allan found a puddle of blood seeping into the snow, horridly dark.

He turned to Foreman who glared grimly at the blood and stepped forward to try and detect where the trail led to.

"Are they dead?" asked Allan, horrified.

Foreman shook his head, "No. They're both alive, but they're injured and very badly as well. We need to find them before the cold gets to them, or before they lose too much blood."

Allan walked in a quick circle. "But I can't smell them! Where are they?"

Foreman took a deep breath and looked to his left. "There," he pointed. The wind moaned and tugged at the trees as if begging to play with them, while the snow swirled down over the drying blood, softly covering it in nature's substitution of silence. And then the two lean figures under the dim street light were gone.

They found her in the lake. "I'm glad you came," she said. "These would be hard to finish all by myself."

Allan stared down at the limp bodies in the water.

"I told you that in the end, they would die," Imelda murmured.

Allan stepped closer towards the water, growling low and menacing. "Why do you do these things, Imelda?"

"My name is DRACULARA!" she howled. Her body tensed up at the force of her own voice. The power of her scream produced ripples in the dark water. She breathed heavily; smoke billowing about her small frame. "Why?" she whispered. "Why couldn't you just forgive me and come back?" The moon broke into view and bathed her in pale light, revealing her sorrowful face.

Allan stopped advancing into the freezing lake and stared at her, his face emotionless.

"I still love you," she said, her eyes pleading. Allan watched as she stroked the human's heads. "It doesn't have to be this way. We could run away. Together. You and me. I gave you all, Allan. Please don't betray me this way."

Allan took a step back as she reached for him.

"I don't want to be this way anymore. I'm tired of being angry, of hating all men, and I know it's my fault, but I just..." She lapsed into a silence that seemed to last forever.

She looked at Allan as Foreman walked into view. "Say something," she pleaded.

"I don't speak to felons," he murmured.

Then he walked into the water. Imelda hissed and stepped back, her hair falling in front of her face. She pulled Ray and Tory along with her. Foreman made a rush at her, his eyebrows furrowing slightly. He moved faster than the human eye could see, but Imelda dodged nimbly out of the way, releasing her grip on the humans and landing on the east side of the lake.

Foreman landed in the water next to Ray. He lifted him and put him over his shoulder, drenching his coat instantly. He lifted Tory as well and slung him over his other shoulder, his long hair getting soaked and freezing quickly from the cold. "Allan."

Allan turned his head to look at Foreman, "Yes Master?" He had been advancing towards Imelda with determined steps.

"Finish her." Foreman jumped out of the water, "I'm taking them to a hospital." Allan nodded as Foreman slipped out of view. Allan looked back at Imelda.

"You won't speak to lowly vampires like myself, will you?" Imelda queried him, her eyes wide, "how humiliating to know that you'll be killed by one."

She sprang like a lion, her hands like claws out in front of her. Allan held his fists up to meet her. A wave of air sprang away from their bodies when their hands met, and Allan lifted his leg up to kick Imelda. She made no noise, and simply skid to the ground on her feet. Allan charged, aiming a punch. She picked up a head-sized rock and threw it at him.

"Remember when we were kids Allan?" she shouted as he punched the rock into tiny pieces. "Remember when the light of the sun was a pleasure we took for granted?"

Allan came at her swiftly, but she swung around, dodging his punch and slapping him in the face. Her nails left four scratches. He cried out in pain, the poison on her nails seeping into his flesh.

She watched as he fell, his eyes closed tightly. "Do you remember when we were in love?"

The pain was excruciating and Allan worried about what kind of poison she had lined her nails with. Suddenly, he remembered that he had his gun with him. He stood slowly. "Imelda."

She laughed and stood with her arms akimbo, her right foot tapping on the wet ground, "It's Draculara."

"Imelda. I didn't stop loving you." He looked up to see her face softening. "You changed into a different person, and I found I didn't love her."

Her eyes grew wide and her hands fell from her hips. "Allan, I-"

He lifted the gun and pulled the trigger.

It hit her right in the eye. Blood spurted from the hole like something from a comic that wasn't comical. She fell, and Allan stepped over to her writhing body. He brought out a vial of what looked like normal water, but when he poured it onto her back she screamed in agony. The water hissed as it burned its way towards her heart.

Lighting a match, he dropped it onto her hair. "I'm sorry," Allan murmured as the vampire Imelda burned to death.

Chapter 6

Allan walked Crazy to the car. Jane the nurse, and now Crazy's girlfriend, walked close behind. She warned him about straining himself. "…and don't lift any heavy boxes or anything, okay?"

"Alright babe. I'll call you, okay?" Crazy kissed her on the lips and slid into the back seat of Tory's car.

Allan smiled at Jane. "Thank you for taking such good care of him," He said, and got into the car as well.

Ray looked back at Crazy from the passenger seat, "Hey bud."

"Hey man. Is Foreman at the house or something?" Crazy asked.

"Yeah, said he wanted to finish up his work."

"Ah well. That old bat can do what he wants. Are we going to go to watch a movie?"

Allan smiled, "Ah yes. Mountain Men, am I correct?"

Tory started the car and they drove off into the night, the cool wind blowing snow across the pavement.

About Dinah T.R. Shatter

Dinah T.R. Shatter was born in a telephone booth, traveling through time, towards the Great Perhaps. She likes to draw and bother her loved ones. In her free time, she can be found battling Bobbit Worms, and singing. Her siblings and friends like to say that, "She can eat you out of house and home!" (and she might just eat your house as well.) She lives in Palm Harbor Florida, and is training to control the weather so that she can make it snow. She has a brother named Merlin, and yes, he is a wizard. Her whole family, in fact, possesses magic qualities. That's why she's so weird.

Connect with Dinah:
facebook.com/DinahT.R.Shatter

Rain

By Désirée Matlock

Scaredy Cat stretched out in her favorite window as I washed the dishes. A deceptively warm shaft of yellow light shone from the western windows, cutting through the broad beams of my house with the kind of tangible directionality that remind most folks of heaven. I wiped my hands dry and looked out. The air lay heavy and hushed, and low clouds threatened to close off the last of the light. There was a storm coming in for certain.

Winter might have been technically over but night still fell whip fast, and the chickens needed to be looked in on before dark. I headed to the door, grabbed my jacket from the peg, slipped my arms in, and patted my hand against the waterproof inside pocket to check that my cellphone was still there. It was not much better than a paperweight this far out into the wilderness, but the camera worked.

Outside the valley seemed to be waiting in a hushed reverie. The quiet broke suddenly as three large dogs barked at once from a half-mile downhill. The foreman's dogs. I looked searchingly below to where DL's trailer sat. He kept the thing parked within shooting distance of the ranch gate at the northern border of the Flying M Timber Ranch. The gate crowned the road which snaked alongside the creek at the valley bottom, our lifeline to town. Those dogs were there to sound the alarm, but did a terrible job of differentiating real threats from civet cats or quail. DL must have looked into it and hushed them because they quieted down.

As Foreman, DL oversaw the logging during warmer weather. There wasn't much to oversee this time of year. Trees don't wander far. The old man mostly sat watching the road and the creek beyond, working his way through a respectable quantity of homebrew and cigars.

I watched my step off the mossy hundred-year old cedar porch, pulling my collar against the cold and ominous sky. The clouds were dirty and grey as washday water, and just as ready to spill.

It had already been drizzling all week and the creek was near full as it was. Nature didn't care. Judging by those clouds, I was in for a downpour that did its level best to pound my lonely hills down into silt, flood the creek, and slide the road out to sea. Cityfolk call for FEMA in weather that hillfolk just call rain.

I pulled gloves on and started crunching my way along the gravel path uphill toward the coop through the ever-present mud. There were no chickens pecking at the run, they were smart enough to be tucked up early for the night. Hens aren't really the risk-taking type.

I opened the coop door and ducked in. After waiting for my eyes to adjust, I checked the feeders, the water trough, and the heater. "'Night, ladies," I whispered as I secured the trapdoor to the run. I locked up the coop as I left. Another day down.

Out of habit my eyes rose up-meadow to the trees. On the closest fir along the tree line I spotted a loose tree limb dangling perilously from lower branches, a widowmaker. Normally, I'd leave it to crash down on its own, except it was hanging over my satellite dish. If the dish got bumped out of alignment when it fell, I'd be offline until they could get another truck out here. There was nothing for it but a controlled knockdown, and nobody but me to do it.

The sleek, white satellite dish was bolted nearly ten feet up a pole. It looked utterly alien against the rich green fir trees that climbed tall against the hill. Behind it was nothing but woods for a hundred miles, all the way to the interstate. My family, the Maylards, are one of the very few original homesteaders left out here. It gets harder every generation for anyone except hardheaded cusses or old-fashioned bumpkins to hold on to the land. I love my folks, but truth is we qualify as both.

When I got to the landing, I took a moment to stretch. I had a glorious view of my roof, the dusky purple-green valley and the opposing hills, now losing their details to the quickening night. I pulled out my phone, snapped a photo, and looked at the signal bars. None, of course. I tucked my paperweight snugly back into the waterproof pocket.

I turned my attention back to the widowmaker. Edging around to the climbable side of the tree I hefted myself up branch by branch. The cool wet moss that coated the entire tree soaked cold water through my pants as I scooted out above where the widowmaker was barely caught up on a knot. I reached down, my fingers just able to wrap around it, and it suddenly came free into my hand, cold and spongy. I tested the deadweight in my hands, fingers digging into the rotted flesh of it to get a better grasp. With effort, I lifted it completely free. I swung the branch slowly until it gained momentum and let go on the outside edge of the fourth swing, letting gravity do the rest. The rotten wood landed a satisfying distance away, shattering into bits of mossy shrapnel.

My eye caught on what looked like an animal track below. Clinging to the moss-coated branch, I shimmied back to the trunk and worked my way down to the ground, then went a little deeper into the trees to get a closer look at the tracks.

Not an animal. More dangerous than that; a human. An unfamiliar one that left boot tracks in the clay headed north to south. That could only mean trouble. It's not as though there's a Starbucks on the other side of the rise; there is just no good reason decent folks would be walking through the ranch without stopping in. Usually meant poachers or meth labs.

I backtracked the trail a few dozen yards, but it faded. I considered following further, but every generation of my family since the original homesteaders had lost someone to the land, and I wasn't going to be this round's loss. Wandering around with no gear and wet pants, especially near nightfall this close to winter, was a quick ticket to the Darwin awards.

I squatted and squinted. The track was smallish, not as deep as I'd expected, and no water pooled in it, which meant it was from today. The imprint was perfect, no nicks.

It ran north to south, parallel to the ridgeline. If I stood tippy toe, I saw the roof of my own house. If I were trying to not be seen from my windows, while keeping close enough to know where the house was, that was exactly where I'd choose. Doubt niggled me. I couldn't tell if my extra sense was perking up, or just paranoia.

My folks would want to see them, so I pulled the phone out, snapped a few photos and slid it back it into the pocket. I started picking my way back to the house, heavy with wondering.

If I were wrong about the when, our trespasser could be hypothermic or dead. I tried to heighten my extra sense, checking for anyone recently dead, but got nothing. Whoever he was, he wasn't haunting my woods. Yet. I didn't think. Better check.

I yelled out, "Mabel! You 'round?" as I crunched further down the hill, sliding awkwardly but staying top up.

"Maaaaabel! Mabel honey, you 'round?" I could feel her

listening. I wanted to enlist her help in this, and being a little extra kind would help.

I started to shout in the other direction, "Sweetie? Maaaay-" and spun round almost right into my great-great-aunt Mabel Maylard, who stood at my side in calico and no shoes, swinging a basket lightly. Gave me quite a start, despite myself.

"Hello, Loretta." Mabel smiled at me and said, "Would you like a blackberry?" Whatever memory she was reliving was a summer one, and happy looking.

"Yes, indeed." I obliged her, and she reached into her basket and handed me a ripe berry that vanished as it reached my hand. She watched as I raised the almost-berry to my mouth.

"Mmmm. Nothing finer," I said like I was playing tea party. It felt a touch ludicrous since Mabel was full grown when she passed, but truth be told, I understood looking forward to blackberry season. God's honest truth, if I could skip the rest of the wet season, I would too. So I played along. I'm not much for complaining on circumstances to someone worse off than me, and Mabel qualified. Go ahead and speak to the dead; like it or not, you'll learn humility.

"Mabel, I'm looking forward to picking berries myself, but for now, could you do me a favor?" I pointed uphill. "I need you to take a look-see in those woods for me. I think we've got us a wayfarer. Smallish man by the look of the track, and in brand spanking new boots."

Mabel muttered about damn fool city folks. That made two of us who thought hiking in new boots was a sin.

"I'm worried he may be lost or dead by now. Got tracks show he passed by this morning headed north to south just beyond the satellite dish."

"The what dish?"

"That there white thing, looks like a tipsy birdbath." I pointed, but I didn't know if she'd be able to see it or not. She was going to need a landmark that hadn't moved, and the tree line wasn't going to work. It moved with every generation of trees planted.

"Never mind. He was about 40 yards down from the ridgeline." She started looking in the right spot. "I don't know where he's at, but I need you to look around for me, find him, guide him this-a-way if he's still breathing."

She pulled a hair back behind her ear that had come loose in a soft summer breeze we didn't share. "Never did like me a trespasser. Do we have to bring him in?"

"If he's city folk, he'll die before he finds the road again," I said.

"I suppose that matters," she said as she nodded, rolled up her now woolen sleeves, and stood ready to go in her moccasins and pants. A useless rifle likewise showed up in her left hand, and I knew she was on the case. She understood the urgency, but whether she'd remember an hour from now or be back to blackberry picking was anyone's guess. Mabel wasn't the most reliable search party, but boot prints weren't enough to bring the law out here, so she was all I had to work with, at least until I could get DL or my father out here in the morning.

As she started off, I hastily added, "Mabel, don't bring him back to the house if he's passed. Just tell me where his body's at, so we can give him a proper burial." She nodded fiercely. A proper burial was something she could get behind.

I continued on down to the house, walking up to the gravel off the back door. Lord, half the hill had stuck to my boots. I stomped a bit to loosen the mud, then wiped my heels near pointlessly on the scraper by the door. There is a lot to be done just to keep mud from invading. I opened the door and quickly walked into my wood-heated warmth, shutting the cold outside.

Scaredy Cat saw I was home and she walked over to greet me. I petted at her for her efforts while I kicked off my boots and socks by the hearth.

I scurried all the way back to the mudroom, toes curled against the cold, grabbed some warm clothes from the dryer, and two socks. They even matched. I got them on fast, and then walked to my desk. I extricated my phone from the jacket pocket, plugged it into my laptop and quickly sent an email off to my father and DL about the tracks.

Scaredy followed me to the kitchen to watch me cook myself a plate of eggs and toast for one. When you live alone, you have breakfast whenever. I'd have made extra for Scaredy, but she's past the need for such things. She's been dead going on ten years now and still here. I don't have the heart to push her. Love that comes honestly is hard to find, and I won't be turning hers away. I don't judge her for staying.

Sometimes, when he's feeling philosophical over cigars, my

father likes to say that I had more run away than stay in me when I was growing up. I never like hearing it, makes me feel like my momma.

It's true though, I was hard to hold still. As soon as I felt old enough, I called him names and lit out. I would never have thought to come back if I hadn't been bottom dealt by life.

I headed to Cali first, working with horses. Found me a cat to come home to, then moved on to New Mexico with her to work on a cattle ranch, keeping up the horses. Not too long after, I met me a genuine rodeo rider, handsome as they come. We fell hard, traveled on the rodeo together. At first, it was the Turquoise circuit, then Texas. We got married somewhere along the way, not too long after Scaredy died.

Jimmy and I got pregnant so we settled in Jacksonville where he had kin. I stayed home keeping house while he rode off and I got to know his cousins. He wasn't home that much, but we were still over the moon, and he loved watching my belly grow.

Nature took its course and we had us a baby girl. I named her Abigail after his dead momma, and I loved her more than I thought a body could love anything. We both wrapped our lives around her.

At sixty-three days old, Abby just stopped breathing one night while we slept. No reason.

Both me and my Jimmy had a real hard time dealing, in different ways. Jimmy grieved with me at first, and spoke of how our mommas would guard over Abby. Words I couldn't get behind. When you see death the way I do, it's hard to pretend along. Heaven, angels, gilded harps, I know nothing of them.

I don't remember the funeral. I remember spending what turned out to be a week sitting with my eyes closed in bed, Scaredy purring on my lap, tethering me to this world. I had to know. At first I felt around lightly for Abby in the emptiness and then drifted further and further. I couldn't find her. My baby hadn't stuck, and I should have been thankful.

It was hard, but I made myself open my eyes again. Jimmy wasn't around. He'd found solace and comfort in another woman's arms. I wasn't up to fighting about it. He stopped working, and the money dried up. Over the next few months, he wandered farther and farther, drank heavily, started using drugs. By the time I stopped grieving and was ready to get back to living, he wasn't mine anymore.

On what would have been Abby's first birthday, I woke, picked wildflowers for her grave, and then realized I hadn't seen Jimmy at all. I laid flowers for her, and then said my goodbyes. It felt final.

Jimmy came home almost at dawn the day after, crazy high. When I tried to soothe him down, I got his fists in response. I lived, but our marriage didn't.

I had no one in Jacksonville that I trusted. All our friends were his friends, adopted. I knew Jimmy didn't know exactly where I was from. All I'd ever told anyone was that I hailed from out west in gold country. While he was still in jail I lit out, this time for home. I drove until I couldn't anymore. When the car broke down by a gas station, I sold it for bus fare but I still had to walk the last twenty-three miles to my father's porch. Before the bruises were finished turning yellow I was on my father's doorstep after a decade, with not a stitch to my name. I expected a tongue lashing, but my father and Linda had put me up in the old barn house without a sharp word, just forgave me quietly over a stack of blankets and some of Linda's old duds. You don't turn away family, Linda likes to say.

Scaredy had quickly settled into hunting disinterested mice. After a little downtime, I pulled myself out of bed and bought some laying hens for something to earn with. I was starting to sell some copper kettle lanterns I'd made from salvage as well. It wasn't much money, but it was enough.

About eight months ago, our family lawyer sent Jimmy divorce papers with my contact information obscured by judge's orders. Just six weeks past, the divorce was final. I'd gotten a second set of papers in the mail and that was that.

I sat down to eat at my kitchen table and Scaredy hopped into my lap. She purred away while I ate, and we two had us a moment of satisfied contemplation watching the sun touch the jagged tree line on the far side of the valley.

Mabel showed up on the couch wearing a flowered shift, humming to herself and carding wool.

"Hello, Miss May. Did you find him?"

"Who?" She looked up at me, her carding continuing without thought.

Patience grasshopper, I thought to myself. "Our wayfarer?"

"Heck, I forgot." She looked abashed. "I did enough looking

before I forgot what I was doing, though. I'm not finding any trespasser, but those tracks came over from the northeast border and I lost them at the fork in the creek. He headed a ways downhill to get there, too."

"I've got a hunch he means someone harm," I said. I was surprised to learn I meant it. I sometimes have to say a thing out loud to know if it's true. "I'd sure like to know where he's at."

She put down her carding, looked at me with worried eyes. "I'll keep looking," she said and then walked outside through the wall where the door used to be before the bathroom addition.

I took a moment to put another log on the fire, and sat back down on the couch. I snuggled up, hands wrapped around a hot mug of tea. Scaredy Cat curled herself up on top of my feet and we comfortably thought about nothing while the sun set.

There is nothing in this world so dark as country dark, or so goes the old adage. I silently agreed. Tonight, a cloud-smothered night quickly shrank the visible world to exactly the size of this house. The rain had just barely started, and a few drops landed on the glass here and there to prove the outside still existed.

Three loud knocks landed emphatically on the door and echoed through the barn. I hadn't heard a car.

I slid my feet out from under Scaredy and walked over to the bookshelf to get my gun off the top shelf. I knew all my closest neighbors' knocks, and this wasn't familiar. I clipped the holster onto my belt.

Scaredy looked right up at the door, like she could see through it. Probably she could.

Another set of loud knocks, and then "Hello, anyone home?" A man's voice. The knocking couldn't be ignored anymore.

"Coming!" Scaredy ran to hide under the piano, which set me on alert. Her instincts were as good as fact to me. She'd been worried about Jimmy from the beginning.

I opened the door to find a tallish man with wavy blond hair and light green eyes. Lord, he was easy to look on. I tried not to show any opinion, just smiled inquisitively up at him.

"Evening," he said. Then I spotted the uniform. I worked to keep the smile on. A cop only meant trouble had come our way. The buff-colored uniform he wore had a dark waterproof jacket and a pretty good pair of water-tight leather boots that meant business.

I noticed another man moved behind him, shuffled a touch at the edge of my porch, said "Evening," and then clicked on his flashlight and started shining it around my yard.

"Evening, Sheriffs. What can I do you for?" I smoothed my hair into place.

The deputy looked down, hand moving to the butt of his gun upon seeing that I was carrying. "First, I need you to agree to keep that in the holster." I nodded, snapped down the leather. "Alright, then. I'm Deputy Evans and this here's Deputy Bonner, ma'am." He gestured at the man behind him, who pointed himself my direction. Thick brown hair and brown eyes. I thought I recognized him from somewhere.

"Do I know you, Deputy Bonner?"

"Don't believe so," he said, turning to sweep my yard with the flashlight beam again. He sure seemed familiar. My folks wanted me to socialize so had taken to nudging me into town for monthly square dances at the Elks lodge. I was pretty sure Bonner was at the last one, a few days past.

"Elks dance, maybe?"

He looked at me, said "Possible," and then enigmatically returned to the darkness off my porch.

Deputy Evans continued, "I was wondering if we might take a look around your property?" I nodded. Every few years, the law comes to tromp around looking for someone who thinks this neck of the woods looks better than jail.

Deputy Bonner headed off wordlessly to poke around, following where the beam of his flashlight led. I called after him, "I saw strange boot prints up near the satellite dish."

"I'll keep an eye open," he said over his shoulder as he tromped off. Bonner was being followed around by another deputy. Not a live one. I tried not to follow with my eyes, instead looking at the hill in general as the deputy and his straggler walked off.

My door-knocking friend pointed into the house, "May I come in?" Not just a simple property check. Hmm. Taking my hesitation as a sign of alarm, he added, "Don't worry, we're just taking precautions." He smiled big right then. Lord, I couldn't help myself, I touched my hair again. Damn. I reminded myself not to fall for handsome. Plus, Scaredy was acting up and that needed heeding.

"Can I see your credentials first? Can't be too careful."

"Certainly, ma'am." he said.

I pinched my lips and said, "It's miss," without thinking it through. Twenty-goddamned-eight is not 'ma'am' territory.

He flipped out a plastic badge and handed it to me. Sheriff's Deputy Jacob Evans, the badge told me. His details were printed on top of an image of the familiar star. Name and face matched. Good enough for me.

"Welcome, Deputy Evans." I handed his badge back.

He looked at me past the brim of his hat, tipped it with one finger. "Thanks." Those eyes were just too pretty. I'd have to watch this one. He probably was used to getting his way, looking like that.

"I'd like to do a thorough search of these premises. Do I need to get a warrant?"

"No, that's fine. Go ahead, poke around." I moved out of his way.

"Where's your car at, Deputy? You walk all the way here from the county seat?"

He chuckled, kicked the mud off his boots and shuffled on the mat before he stepped in. "We left the cruiser down at the bottom of the driveway. Looked like too steep a grade to be passable while the clay's this soft."

"Sometimes," I confirmed. I smiled, but he wasn't looking anymore, he was scanning the room already.

He wasn't telling me straight, I could tell. "Is there some trouble I should be aware of, Sheriff?"

"Just taking precautions. Is there any part of this house, or this property, that someone could be in without your knowledge?"

"As far as the house goes, I don't think so. Plenty of outbuildings, though. Haven't looked under the porch in a while, but if he's under there, he's got an angry 'coon for company. And there is the hayloft. That's my room but I haven't been up there all day." He looked past me with a cop's eyes, assessing the house.

I chewed my lip. "I won't lie, you got me worried. Is there anything to be worried over?"

He said, "I'll explain as soon as I can, but I need to take a look around first. Won't take too long." He quickly worked his way through every corner of every room downstairs, checking corners, closets, doors and windows. I found it fascinating watching through the open doors, and I could almost hear him saying "clear" in his head each time he popped in or out of a space. There wasn't anyone else here, but he wasn't leaving until he'd checked. I left him to it, while I tidied my kitchen. Wasn't any point in worrying over it until he could explain what brought the law out this far. He climbed the ladder to the loft. While he was up there, I heard Scaredy Cat under the piano, making low noises, out of her wits. I'd never seen her so scared. She quieted down when he came back down the ladder into the living room.

Deputy Evans walked over, sat down on the couch and I joined him. He opened up a notepad and looked down into it. "Well, I'm hoping you can answer some questions, help us out." I nodded.

"What can I do you for?" I was sick of waiting to pass out my bushel of 'no, sirs' in order to find out what brought him out my way.

He looked down at his own notes. "Seen anyone around here lately you don't recognize, ma'am?"

"Just those boot prints I told your partner about. Hold on, I've got a photo." I walked over to the jacket, pulled the phone out and showed him.

"Anything else?" he asked, scratching in his pad.

"I haven't seen anyone on my corner of the ranch since the Jehovah's Witnesses come out Monday before last. "And it's Miss. Miss Loretta Maylard," I said again.

"Miss Loretta Maylard," he repeated quizzically, "You're one of the Maylards?" I had a hard time paying attention though, because right then, Mabel came in again, waving her arms with excitement. "Strangers on the homestead, Loretta, wandering all over the place. Circling about like they looking for some-at. Two up at the main house, two here. Oh, look, another one. That makes three here!"

I nodded. "M-hm. That's right." I looked at her for that part, then back to Deputy Evans. "Willis Maylard is my father, Deputy. He and Linda live thataway in the ranch's main house," I pointed farther up-mountain and to the south.

Mabel continued, talking a mile a minute, "...Tromping about making a racket to raise the dead. There's two of 'em in the meadow right now, and one's like me. He's following another one around that's looking for someone else. Keeps calling a name, 'Lester', he says. The live one, I mean. And now there's this handsome one, too." She was so excited she could burst. She was staring at Deputy

Evans. "Lordy, look at him." She raised her eyebrows at me, looked down her nose. "Be nice to this one, maybe he'll stick." Just like family to poke their nose where it doesn't belong.

Mabel was buzzing, eyes big and waiting for answers. "Give me a minute, please," I said.

She huffed and walked over by the woodstove. An old rocking chair materialized under her, the one that had fallen apart when I was three. Mabel sat down in it, muttering about how I could do worse.

Then to have some excuse for saying I needed a minute, I walked in the kitchen, got a glass of water, and came back out. I have to do odd things to keep from looking touched around the living sometimes.

"Deputy, what's going on here?" I asked as I sat back down. "We don't usually have whole house searches for something like this."

"To cut to the chase, we have reason to believe that a fugitive is headed this way, presumed armed and dangerous."

It was getting harder not to worry. "In what way is this fugitive you're out here looking for dangerous?"

"Well, he's a known drug dealer, suspected in a number of criminal activities in California, considered a 'loose cannon' amongst his associates, according to the Los Angeles county authorities." He looked at the notebook again. "Have you ever lived in Los Angeles?"

"Once, when I was eighteen. Not for long, though." He looked dubious but I continued, "Is there some expectation your fugitive might barge into my home, Deputy Evans?"

"There is cause to consider it. You should be alert." He settled in, looking comfortable on my couch. "Call me Jake," he added. Not likely while he was being all official. I decided he'd have to come out of "cop mode" before I'd even consider him. Here I was considering him. Damn fool.

I was looking at him too long, and I felt like he could tell exactly what I was thinking. I moved along, "What's the cause to be alert? Why here?"

He looked like he was thinking what to say. I could feel him being a touch sneaky. "A few days back, about ten miles that way," he pointed north, "a kid and his dad walked into their tree fort to find our boy smoking a cigarette. The trespasser took off, but the place was trashed. We had no luck with dogs; too wet. In the fort, they found a mattress, a makeshift toilet, dozens of empty red bulls, cigarette butts and a stash of oxy and meth. It looked like he'd been there for maybe a week. Poor kid."

It took me a second to get that he meant the tree fort's owner. I nodded.

He continued, "Kid and his dad both verified the ID from a photo lineup. But we'd lost the guy. Then, yesterday, out of the clear blue, he was spotted by a guy out fishing about a mile the other side of your northern border."

He pointed. That was awfully close to us. "So, you must have combed the spot with no luck. What makes you think he's here specifically?"

"No flies on you, huh?" The sneaky feeling built up big.

He reached into his jacket pocket. He took out a small piece of paper and looked at it. "Today, the forensics team finished combing through the mess in the tree fort. Found a photo."

He handed me the wallet sized photograph, watching my eyes as he did so. My stomach sunk. I recognized it as a cheesy photo booth shot I had taken for Jimmy when we were still in our honeymoon days. I remember when he'd tucked it into his wallet and kissed the leather, saying it was never going nowhere. And yet, here it was, in my hand. That wallet held nothing but loose things, apparently; money and promises.

The deputy was watching me closely to see my reaction.

"That's me," I said unnecessarily. "A handful of years back, but still me." I handed it back.

"Yes, we worked that one out." Somehow not said smugly, as only a lawman could manage. "Our dispatcher Roberta recognized you from the picture. She works part-time at the Shearing Shack salon. A hairdresser is better than facial recognition software around here, and a lot closer to our budget." I smiled at the joke. Every single person in town would be gossiping after me and my fugitive with Roberta knowing. Gossip spreads faster than fire out here.

I heard DL's dogs acting up fierce for a minute, but then they shut up again. I thought about the boot print. Jimmy wore a men's eleven. The boot prints must relate to the nameless-fugitive-probably-Lester that Mabel had mentioned.

"I am sure hoping this isn't anyone I know, deputy, but that photo tells me my ex-husband Jimmy may be involved. Last I knew, it was in his wallet."

"What's your husband's full name?" He pulled the pad back out and made a note again.

"Ex-husband. William James Cuess, goes by Jimmy. We're not married anymore. Papers came through six weeks ago." I may have said that too proudly.

"Congratulations." The corner of his mouth quirked upwards as he tucked the notepad away.

"Do you have any photos of him, Miss Maylard?"

"Not a blessed one."

"All right then. Are you absolutely certain you haven't seen anyone at all?"

I sighed, sick of the line of questions looping around. "Look, I haven't had a guest in months. I haven't seen sign of anyone, except that track I showed you. So," I stood up, spread my arms out to my sides, "wander away, Deputy. Check every corner of our land to your heart's content. But if anybody means me harm, and trespasses in this house, I am prepared to defend myself." He didn't need to know I was all hat and no cattle. I'd never shot anything more dangerous than a beer bottle in my life.

Deputy Straggler made a noise in the back of his throat from just beside my left ear, and I about jumped out of my skin. "Evans, you damn rookie, you got no sense. Can't you see the girl ain't involved?" I hoped that neither Deputy Evans or Straggler had noticed me jump. I wondered how long he'd been sitting next to me. I must have been quite distracted.

He looked at me, seemed to decide something, and relaxed. "Let's hope it doesn't come to that."

It suddenly occurred to me to say something I should have from the get go. "I know it's a day late dollar short, but you might want to get the ranch owner's permission before you search too much, since I don't own the place. The main house isn't too far up the road."

"Yeah, we've got a few guys already up at the main house, with your father and Linda." He added, "You know, I thought I knew all the Maylards."

I softened up. "I came home a few years back. We must have missed each other."

"Well, mighty nice to finally meet you, then." He seemed to

mean it, and for a brief moment he smiled genuinely. Too cute by far, this one. And unruffled by my rough edges. Then he took a breath, squared his shoulders, and his cop demeanor fell back into place.

If there were men at the main house, that explained all of Mabel's 'soldiers'. That meant there were at least four cops tromping around our land, five if you counted poor Deputy Straggler.

Deputy Evans pulled the radio off his belt, and started having a conversation into it. He got up and paced briefly, during which time I considered talking to Mabel, but he was still watching me too much. The other end of the conversation sounded like static to me.

His attention back to me, he paused and asked, "Miss Maylard, Do you know if Cuess has any ties to Los Angeles?" he said the name of the town like it was a disease.

"Jimmy's from Jacksonville. He hates California." Apparently, Evans agreed, as he nodded vigorously.

"Well, do you recall if any of his friends lived in Los Angeles?"

I sighed, "I barely recall his friends. If you want me to tell you what I know about a particular friend of Jimmy's, just ask. Maybe it'll jog something loose."

He looked apologetic, "All right. Do you know a Lester Mitz?"

Finally. "That's the fugitive?"

He nodded, unfolded a computer printout of a fuzzy old mugshot from his pocket. The soul tarnishes fast with drugs, eyes first. So, here was the Lester Mabel'd overheard. Lester Mitz. He looked like a grizzled sumbitch, and I was hoping they found him before he found me.

"Scary guy. No. I don't believe my ex-husband knew this man Lester Mitz while we were together. But I haven't seen Jimmy in a few years now. Can't vouch for his friends these days."

"All right then." He put the photos away and took a deep breath. Let it out like he was relieved to be done with those questions. He thought for a moment, spoke again and this time I didn't hear any sneaky in his voice.

"Do you feel that Mister Cuess is a danger to you?"

"Maybe he would be. It's complicated."

Somehow managing to sound more like a concerned friend than an interrogational cop, he sighed, "I need to understand how it is complicated." He looked me in the eye, and I felt his frustration. "Somehow his photo of you ended up in the care of a dangerous man. I need to work out how that photo ended up where it did, and why."

I agreed, nodded. "I left him a few years back. Drugs and the things men do when they're on drugs. I don't blame him particularly. The year before that had been really hard for us both." I'd never had to talk to anyone about it since I got here, outside of family. My throat closed over, but I tried to talk through the grief. "We lost…"

Unbidden, a memory washed over me of leaning over Abby's sweet soft head, and her scent bloomed into my nose, fresh and soft. It hurt like a shard of wet glass, cutting effortlessly as it slid past. Tears of fresh pain rolled into my eyes, and I closed them tight. Dammit, get a grip, Loretta.

I opened my eyes, kept talking. "We lost a child." I made myself finish it.

"It twisted him inside. He went downhill fast. Put me in the hospital. I didn't give him a chance to make a habit of it. I came home." I shrugged my shoulders. "And here I sit." There was something cathartic about telling Deputy Evans.

I breathed in deep, let it out, and realized that at some point, Deputy Evans had taken hold of my hand and I had not minded. Whatever he'd meant to do, lend support, show kindness, looking down at a man's hand wrapped around mine snapped me back to reality. My wall came back up. I couldn't help it.

"Thank you for your kindness, Deputy." I was back to my usual self now, and his hand retracted.

"Look, I'm not hiding from Jimmy here. It's simpler out here." I looked up again, "City life doesn't agree with me."

Deputy Jake looked at me with understanding, and I got a real smile. "It is a nice place to live when it isn't so cold out," he agreed. He'd decided to let me move on away from the rough topic.

"Okay, then," he said, standing up to stretch his legs. "I thank you for your hospitality, Miss Maylard. I guess we're through the questions. Thanks for cooperating. I'll be joining my partner but may check back here once more before we leave." He shrugged. "DL was pretty adamant about my staying up here with you."

I thought of something amusing, and laughed lightly, "I think maybe DL is trying to set us up. He's always trying to get young folks together."

He paused, "I think he might well be," he admitted, sounding less cop-like and more human now. "The guy means well. They all do."

"You get the set-ups a lot, too, then?"

"Well, yes. Comes with the territory." We shared a laugh. "But until my mom's okay, I'm not listening. She had an accident a few years back, and taking care of her is all I've had time for these days."

Oh my goodness. It was getting hard not to like this one. It certainly explained why an educated employed young man with all his limbs was still single. Every old lady at his church was likely fighting to marry him to their granddaughter.

"Well, good luck to you and your momma then, and you take care," I said as goodbye.

"Will do." He paused, touched his hat again, and then walked out the door.

I looked around for Deputy Straggler but he seemed to be gone again. It seemed safe to walk over to where Mabel sat in her rocking chair. "Looks like Lester the wayfarer is a fugitive from justice, Mabel."

She dropped her knitting in her lap, forgotten. "How exciting! I'm thinking of heading out to look around some more."

"Mabel, you don't have to. He'll turn up eventually. There are men here to find Lester now. They'll stop him." She tut-tutted.

"Since when do we leave it to them? Hmph. I'm going to gab with the dead one, at least." She disappeared on me before I could protest.

Next, I called my father to let him know what was up. The call didn't accomplish much, but it felt good. They hadn't found anything at his place, and were about ready to wrap. I wondered when these two would leave. I looked through the rain at two lonely flashlights bobbing among the trees in the vast dark.

I left them to it, put a new log on the fire, curled up with a book on the couch, pulled the throw over my feet and tried to relax. The holster dug into my hip and I unclipped it, tucking it into the couch cushions beside me. I dozed off without knowing it at some point before midnight.

I woke up unexpectedly, disoriented. Deputy Straggler was standing over me. I felt like he'd poked me awake, but that seemed unlikely. Not many dead were strong enough to do so. "Miss? Can you see me? Mabel said you would be able to see me."

Gee, thanks, Mabel. I was bleary. I looked up at him, and then at the front of the cable box. Damn, only 2:07 in the morning.

"M-hm. A-course," I responded. I woke up a bit more, looked up at my intruder. He was in his mid-fifties, and looked like the kind of cop you'd trust with your life. Looked like the kind of guy with more years on the job than both the deputies I'd met tonight combined.

He noticed I was awake. "Oh, thank-the-Lord-in-heaven. I'm saved," he intoned quickly.

"Can it wait until tomorrow? I'm exhausted." Rain was pounding loudly onto the roof.

He spoke hurriedly, eyes on the door, "Unfortunately not. I have to get a message to one of those deputies out there. Bonner. Bonner is the name."

"You need to get a message to Bonner? Fine, tell me in the morning," I said. I wasn't fond of midnight wake-up calls from pushy dead folks. I closed my eyes.

"No, goddammit. Me! I'm Bonner. Sheriff's Deputy Eugene Bonner!"

Okay, I was awake. If this was Bonner, who in hell was searching my outbuildings?

"That man out there wearing my goddamned badge bold-as-brass killed me a little over a week ago in my goddamned car." He looked mighty put out. I must have looked alarmed, because he calmed himself down for me. "Please, I need your help."

"Explain. You know what's going on here?" My heart sank, "Is Evans legit?"

I sat up on the couch, worried. The rain was really coming down.

"Naw, rookie's the real deal. But the man he's out there with is one dangerous cuss. Midway through my transfer from Josephine County, that asshole runs me off the road. I get to watch as he erases me from the computers. As he tails you around town. No one even knows I'm dead. It's like I never existed now." He paused and his eyes grew distant. He quieted down. "You never realize how little you leave behind. Not a soul knows me here. Except you now." He was trailing off on a tangent, as the dead will, and I needed him to get back on point before he got too far off track. This here was the kind of emotion that could trip him up and tie him here if we didn't nip this in the bud. I started patting where his hand was, hoping the comfort would help.

I nodded. "I'm sorry for your loss." He looked a little less dejected.

"He erased me so well that no one suspects. He's good." He had a lawman's appreciation of a good criminal that I didn't have. They're either clever stupid or dumb-as-a-stump stupid, but they all got one thing in common.

"Any idea why?" I asked.

He pulled out an imaginary note pad. "He's got business here, looks to be with you. Asked around about you before he showed up to duty. Followed you everywhere you went last two times you drove to town."

"Look, I don't know --"

"The other deputies turned in for the night. Those two men are all alone out there together. You're not safe with him here either. I need you to get up, right now, and warn the rookie out there that it ain't me he's working with."

Easier said than done. I started thinking on how exactly to go about it. He must have thought I was going to say no, because he panicked, saying, "Please, I don't want the rookie dead. I don't want you dead. I've never been so helpless in my life. Look," he tried to pick up my book. Nothing happened. "I'm sorry to be so anxious, but I need your cooperation, little lady." he said.

"It's okay, I understand." I looked right at him, pointed. "But when this is over and your partner is safe, don't get caught up in revenge. It isn't worth it." He nodded, slowly.

I went to the phone to call my folks. No dial tone. Tried the laptop. No satellite.

I sat down on the couch to think up a pretext to give the young deputy for how I knew what I knew about Bonner when I heard a gunshot too close to the house. I froze.

Then I heard a second shot, followed closely by a third. I was suddenly sober as a judge. I started digging in the couch cushions for my pistol. Then, I heard a thumping on the porch and couldn't remember whether I'd locked the door. I instantly rolled off the couch onto the floor. Bonner, the pretend one, came barreling through the door, shutting it hard behind him.

My couch and coffee table were going to have to do for cover.

Fake Bonner slammed the lock into place and leaned back. I tried to quiet my breathing. The only noise in the room was the sound of the rain, drumming relentlessly on my roof. The real Bonner tried 'shooting' him, probably not for the first time. When nothing happened, he looked at his gun, holstered it.

I got my first good look at Fake Bonner. He was completely nondescript. Brown hair, brown eyes, average height, weight, build. As innocuous as you get. No wonder he'd slipped in under the radar.

The scent of dust and cedar filled my nose as I pulled myself completely out of sight carefully. I focused on finding the shotgun under the couch. Fake Bonner started moving slowly into the house.

It felt like it took forever and then my fingertips slammed into the muzzle. The heavy gun made an inordinately loud scraping noise on the hardwood floor. I cringed, tried to be quiet as I wrapped my fingers around the gun.

He apparently hadn't heard, because he hadn't moved his feet. I could see them from under the couch. All I could think about was how his feet weren't small.

I lifted the gun and pulled it to me. Every motion screamed in my ears, but the drone of the rain hitting the tin roof saved me.

I almost screamed as the Real Bonner crouched over me to say, "I'm going to go try to find the rookie, get him in here." Then he ran right through the fake Bonner and outside.

Suddenly, Fake Bonner picked up his radio and started talking into it, sounding scared, "Shots fired, dammit! Repeat, shots fired! My partner is not responding on the radio!"

He put the radio back on his belt calmly and started heading toward the back of the house, carefully checking for me in every room.

What he'd said into his radio sank in, and I realized Deputy Jake was probably shot. I imagined the rookie lying somewhere bleeding out, and in that moment I realized I had a crush. Dammit, that was inconvenient.

Fake Bonner must have found the light switch panel, because the entire downstairs went dark. Only the loft light was still on. A small shaft of light shone on only the front wall of the house and a little of the living room. I found that I couldn't see beyond that circle of light. I turned my head and shaded the loft itself with my hand. I felt vulnerable while my eyes adjusted. The world formed into shapes in front of me again, and my heart jumped into my throat. I was looking right at Fake Bonner, halfway up the ladder to the loft. He noticed me at the same time, looked surprised as hell. He looped an arm through the ladder and wobbled perilously to the side, one arm freed up to grab the gun free of its holster. I broke the silence with chambering the shotgun.

"Drop it!" I yelled. He didn't. The gun was coming up too fast, and I saw the flash as it fired. I shot up at his center mass from the floor. It was deafeningly loud and disorienting for a moment. The shotgun slammed my shoulder into the floor pretty hard. Rock salt spattered small divots into the wall behind the ladder. As my vision cleared, I saw that he had fallen off the ladder.

He cussed as the rock salt kicked in. He was down, but moving.

My fingers were tingling from the impact of the shotgun on my shoulder. I was having trouble using my right arm, but I held the shotgun up through the pain and got my finger back on that trigger.

Before he could get up, I quickly picked myself off the floor and shot one more time. He stopped moving, but I'd just used up the only two shells I had. Besides, rock salt wouldn't stop him for long. He'd get up off the floor, and when he did, I wanted my pistol ready. I tried to search the couch for my pistol, but my right arm didn't respond. It hung useless, dislocated. I slammed myself into the coffee table hard, and screamed. It stung like liquid fire, but my arm was usable again.

I dug around deep in the couch and found my pistol at last. I threw the holster to the side and flipped the safety, chambered it, and focused the gun and all of my attention on the man writhing on my floor. I couldn't pull my eyes off him now and I was shaking like crazy. He was yelling obscenities, some at me, some at the pain.

I yelled, "Drop the gun!" but nothing happened. He started trying to get up again, and didn't let go of the gun. Stubborn cuss.

"Drop it! Last chance!" His shaky hand shot up toward me and I saw the flare of a bullet leaving the chamber. Terrified, I shot twice, this time aiming for his head. I got him on the second shot. He spun as he went down for good, crumpling into the corner of the room.

I scrambled to my feet, checking for bullet holes, positive he couldn't have missed twice. I was shocked to find myself intact but kept patting myself down until I was satisfied I wasn't hit.

I stared at the body in the corner of the room, waiting and

wondering. I watched as Fake Bonner's essence slipped away into the nothing. Never could make sense of who stayed and who left. Thank God for small favors.

I was shaking head to toe. I considered what to do now. Evans was lying somewhere shot, maybe dead, but maybe not. I couldn't wait for a search party, not if I wanted to find him alive.

On my way out the front door into the night, I grabbed my coat off the peg. I threw my feet into the boots, wrangled the coat on and slid right off the porch, banging my butt hard as my feet hit the gravel. Great start.

Where was Deputy Evans? My mind raced through dozens of ideas, but I settled on running downhill. It was completely pitch black, and I ran on memory, hoping I was right, adrenaline thrumming through my veins. I was already covered in mud from the waist down, and ice water was running down the back of my neck along my spine, sending off warning signals.

"Deputy Evans! Where you at?" I yelled as loud as I could to be heard over the rain. My eyes were adjusting and I could barely make out the ground.

"Deputy Evans! Jake!" I was practically crying.

"Over here!" It was Bonner, and he was leading me to my right. My foot bumped into something unfamiliar. I crouched.

It was Evans, shot in the shoulder and bleeding into the grass. He was half submerged in the muddy water rushing downhill. Out cold and sorry looking, but not dead. I pulled him up, slapped him on the cheek and rubbed his arms. It didn't work. Hell. I yelled loud. "Jake!" Bonner looked at me, guilty that he couldn't help.

"Go see if you can get DL to wake up, Bonner. We need back-up."

"Wake up, dammit!" I slapped Jake again, a little harder. He opened his eyes, looked dazed and reached out with his good hand to touch my cheek. "My partner shot me. Now you're hitting me? What's up with that?" Then he passed out again.

I rubbed his hands, hard, trying to wake him up again. "Wake up! Come on."

He woke up again. "Okay." He seemed out of it. "Okay," he repeated, and then shook his head. "Ow. Damn, that hurts." He tried to move his shoulder, and I stopped him.

"Quit it. We've got to get out of the cold." The rain was starting to feel warmer, and I wasn't minding it so much. I put my body under his other shoulder and crouched as he winced in pain. "Your partner? Not a real sheriff. Tried to kill me, too. Now he's dead."

"Mitz is dead, too. That's too many dead," he said groggily. Story of my life.

I lifted his weight off the ground. "Up you go. I can't do this without you. We're getting you back up to the house."

"Okay." He started helping me get him back up to the road. About halfway up the hill, he started needing less of my help. "What did you say about my partner?" he asked.

"Told me he killed the real Bonner to be able to look for Lester. Tried to shoot me. I shot him dead." I'd had to stretch that lie to fit the truth into it.

"Damn." He kept walking with me, but was leaning harder, struggling not to go under. "I'll need to get a statement from you," he actually said, then almost passed out again.

"Come on. Ask me when I'm warmer. We've got to get out of the rain. Walk. You can do it. Good." I coached him up the steps and struggled to hold him up as I opened the door to the house. The air felt hot against my cheeks, but these four old walls were a sore sight indeed.

The rain pounded away on the roof, safely out of doors. We flopped onto my couch and sat recovering, and it was hard not to stare at Fake Bonner dead on the floor in the corner. The body gave me the willies, all soulless and empty. I'd never shot anyone before.

I laid back, and a powerful urge to sleep hit me. I made myself get up off the couch, throw another log on the fire, and fetched the medical supplies. I looked in the bathroom closet, finally finding it on the high shelf. On my way back to the living room, I took a look at the thermostat on the kitchen window, 41 degrees. It would get colder before the sun came up.

Jake seemed to be doing better, if pale. He'd gotten up and was steadying himself at the desk, trying to call out.

"He cut the phone line," I explained, "I'm sorry."

We really needed to warm up. Hypothermia needs to be fought before you stop caring.

"Damn. Radio's full of mud, too." He planted his hands on the desk, looked down at them, "I need to get a move on as soon as you can patch me up."

"Not 'as soon as', Jake. The worst of the danger is past. We just need to get out of these clothes."

He looked at me and his color rose. I corrected myself. "I mean-- you're no good to anyone dead. Danger has passed. We need to peel out of the wet clothes and get dry things on. I have some of my dad's old clothes around here somewhere you can change into." Only a man could think I meant something like hanky panky after being shot and passing out several times.

"You need to lay back and let me dress that wound. The faster we do this, the sooner we'll be in front of the fire, warming up." He got more compliant, pulled off the bloody, muddy, torn mess that used to be his shirt and undershirt, and I followed his directions until the wound was clean and dressed. I grabbed the couch throw and wrapped it around his shoulders.

"Thank you," he said, looking at me intently.

"No problem. Just help me figure out what the hell this has to do with me. Deal?"

He nodded. His lips were almost blue, and I didn't want to know how bad I looked. We needed to get to the business of warming up.

I went up the ladder to get a change of clothes for myself, then went into in the back room. While I was back there, I found a box of old clothes and lugged it out for him.

While I was gone, he'd covered the body in the corner with a small tarp from the back porch. I doubted it was accepted practice, but we couldn't leave yet, and I understood him trying to protect me from the dead.

I walked back into the back bedroom and found every blanket I could. He called out to me to let me know when he was all done. When I came out, he was clean and dry. He looked pretty good in a turtleneck and jeans, albeit still hunched up with cold. We sat wrapped in old blankets by the stove, talking about whether or not it was possible to warm all the way up ever again. I bet on yes, he bet on no. I told him stories of falling into the creek, and he told me about an ice fishing trip. I declared him winner. Scaredy curled herself around my feet and purred. It wouldn't warm me up, but her trying was sweet.

"So, what happened out there?" I asked. "How'd you end up shot in the shoulder?"

"It's a crazy story. I was just about to wrap it up when I found

Mitz hiding in the shed, scrawny little guy decked out for hiking, maybe, or rock climbing? You know, pick axe, rope. Raving on and on about a goldmine."

I interjected, "If there were gold out here, we'd all be a lot richer."

"Tell me about it. Anyway," he continued, "I didn't see a gun. Tried to put him under arrest, but he ran. I radioed my partner to back me up, ran Mitz down to the mill, cornered him. Had my weapon on him. Then Bonner runs in. Lester stops, gets on his knees and starts begging my partner for more time, like he knows him. Then Bonner says, 'You screwed up, Lester.' Out of the blue, he shoots Mitz in the head. Bam!" Evans paused, looked down at his shoulder for a minute. "Damn. I got off one shot, but he was already headed back uphill. I tried to follow him, but I passed out. The rest you know." He added quietly, "Thanks for coming to find me."

"Any time." I smiled to lighten the mood.

He rubbed his hands together, smiled back. "You win the bet. I'm finally warm."

"I'm not sure I'll ever warm back up, so I'm thinking you won the bet." We grinned at each other.

"A draw then."

"So what's next?"

"I guess it's time to head down to my cruiser and call in for support. See if the roads are passable. You stay here. Don't touch that body."

I wasn't planning on it. "Gotcha. Check on DL, will you? He'd never stay quiet this long with shots fired. Something's wrong."

"Sure thing. I'll be back as soon as possible." Jake, Deputy Evans, grabbed up an old coat from the box, and I helped him pull it over his hurt shoulder. He headed out, back down the hill toward his car.

It occurred to me that we hadn't worked out how come Lester had my photo. I watched him walk away and wondered how long until he came back. Was this me missing him already? Not smart, Loretta. I was getting that he was more than I'd figured him for, but falling this early was just plain stupid. Scaredy started up a low yowl again, creeping me out.

I looked at the cable box. Lord, it was only 3:23. How had so much happened in just a few hours?

I set to work. After finding the holster, I clipped my gun back on but didn't feel much better yet. To fight the heebee jeebies, I went through the house checking locks, found a few windows to secure. I was locking the bathroom window when I felt someone behind me, and I made myself turn round.

My ex-husband strolled up, looking dangerous. "Hello, Lorrie."

"Jimmy!" My hand flew to the butt of my gun. He was alarmingly shrunken, stringy and lean. The drugs had obviously been rough on him. He laughed mockingly, took a step toward me.

"I'm not here to hurt you. I came to warn you. But judging by the state of things, looks like you didn't need warning after all." He paused, sniffed, looked at me sideways. "How'd it feel to kill the mercenary?" He smiled coldly, didn't wait for an answer. "You never did need anyone else, did you, Lorrie? Always so high and mighty, thinking you're above me." He was edging closer, a bite in his voice, the once-strong muscles in his arm bunching with the ache of wanting to hit me.

"I followed you, Lorrie, when you took off, you know. Not so much as a word. I looked for you everywhere but turns out all I knew about you was nothing. So, I waited in LA, hoping to catch a break, had some run-ins with the law instead." Drugs, obviously. He paced, curling and releasing his fists.

"Then you send those first set of papers to my folks and they sent them to me. I wanted to get you back." His eyes hardened, and I don't think even he knew if he meant revenge or reconciling.

"And then the next set of papers came, your handy dandy address stamped right on it. I was looking in the wrong goddamned state. I didn't even know Oregon had 'gold in them thar hills'." He said it like he was making fun of an old western. "Damn!"

"My address wasn't supposed to be on those papers, Jimmy," I said, stating the obvious.

"Then, I guess I am just a lucky duck, ain't I?" He smirked, didn't wait for me to answer. Instead, he pulled a gun from his waistband, and absently pointed it in my general direction.

I shut up, hand gripping my gun tighter. I didn't want to anger him, I wanted him gone. I watched his eyes for trouble but they were far away. "Lester's someone I got in business with in LA. He scares me." Eyes wide, like he wants me to be on his side. "You gotta understand, I was so mad when I got those papers. You can't treat people this way, Lorrie-my-love. Use them and run like that." He gestured plaintively and then his eyes narrowed. "It's very rude, and I don't abide rude. I talked with Lester about teaching you a lesson. And then I thought about it more, about finding you, getting you back for what you done. He offered to kill you, said you deserve it. It was do or die, Lorrie. And I decided. I couldn't pay him cash, so I said you were sitting on a goldmine here, a big juicy vein exposed that you didn't tell anyone about. Got the idea from your 'gold country' thing. I told him we could split it between us."

Jimmy continued walking toward me, "Now, what was I supposed to do without you?"

I stepped back again, right into the bathroom wall. His mouth curled up in an angry, feral way and to me he lost the last of his handsome right then, as ugly rage twisted him up.

"Jimmy, we're divorced."

"One time, Lorrie. It was one goddamned time." The gun came up, and he started pointing it at my gut. I raised mine right back. He didn't shoot, just walked closer.

"Drop the gun, Jimmy. And it's Loretta."

"What?" His eyes were scaring me.

"You know how many times I told you call me Loretta, not Lorrie. But you didn't listen." I grabbed his arm, cold and wet, and tried to push him away. "You're free. So am I. Go live your own life." He didn't budge.

"No, I am not! I can't!" he roared. He was right up against me now, pinning me against the wall. "Don't you get it, Lorrie?"

He drew back to point his gun at my chest, pulled the trigger fast as a blink. I screamed, but nothing happened to me. I pulled my trigger and the bathroom boomed and rattled. Damn gun kicked almost out of my hand as my vision whited out for a second and then flared back in from the edges.

I felt his hands on my throat and started kicking at him, but couldn't seem to do any damage. Scaredy Cat rushed in and tried to claw at his feet, bit him in the leg. He kicked her away.

A rush of adrenaline pumped through me as I realized that Jimmy was dead. Lester Mitz must have done more than just 'mess him up'. I had a homicidal poltergeist in my house. And my ex, no less. Aw, hell no.

My vision was blacking out. I needed air. I closed my eyes,

ignored my lungs, and clasped both hands in front of my heart. I reached out with my extra sense, and pushed. Hard. At first he seemed surprised, but then he bucked, held on tight, and started kicking. Sometimes, really angry souls could move things or knock stuff over around the people they had been closest to, but I'd never seen anything like this. My throat wasn't imagining the pain. He was realer to me, and I was realer to Jimmy right back, than the others ever had been. My eyes popped back open and I looked right at him, intensified my purpose.

Push.

Jimmy held on even tighter, looking at me with coal-hot wide-eyed fury, "Your eyes are trying to kill me, just the same as Abby. You and them spooky eyes are the reason she's dead."

"No I am not, Jimmy! I never hurt you, and you know damn well I had nothing to do with her dying." I said it without thinking. And I knew then, I was right. All the worry I'd worn thin and all the doubt left me. I was done. I had the truth.

I pushed with all my might. I'd never known I could push so hard. The pressure on my throat released and I realized I could breathe again, so I concentrated on breathing, and with every breath I intensified the push.

"You can't undo what you done, Lorrie!" he sounded panicked, thready, stretched a little thinner.

From searing lungs, I yelled, "I'm Loretta!" My arms flew back, and through my own rushing pulse I heard the clatter as my gun fell behind the tub. I clenched my fists to anchor myself to the here and now and I welled up a brightness from deep inside. My feet lifted right off the ground as my toes splayed out with the strength of the light rushing through me, swirling through me, pounding Jimmy's lost soul into the next life, and for a moment, the sound of rain hitting the roof stopped completely.

The bathroom grew quiet, shallow, and I could again feel cold tile beneath my feet. Suddenly, the tide turned. I could feel Jimmy grasp me, trying to pull me in, pull me under with him. Like getting your hair tangled up in something underwater, it hurt to pull myself free.

Quick as a wink, he was swallowed up and gone. The bathroom went black, and I could again hear the rain rattling the old tin roof.

I fell back against the wall, panting and holding my throat for a minute. That was going to bruise. Sweating with the heat of it, I crawled in the cool bathtub and passed out.

The sun came up, and steely unforgiving light poured into the bathroom, reflecting down into the tub, waking me. Scaredy was standing on my chest and kneading me as best she could. I sat up and petted her for a minute to let her know I was okay and realized my arms were freezing cold. The bathroom door had swung shut and since I'd gone and shot a hole in the window last night, cold air was whistling in. I made myself get up, wash up, and walk out.

Every muscle ached. I went to the kitchen, rubbing my arms for warmth, and started the percolator going. There. Coffee. Life could commence again.

I headed to the living room to put another log on the fire. Make that two. Deputy Bonner must have come back sometime in the night, because he and Mabel were sitting together in the living room. She was knitting and he was drinking a beer. They looked oddly content, all things considered. Happier than me, I reckoned.

I picked the duct tape off the counter where I'd left it, and made my tired feet walk back in the bathroom, slapped some tape over the hole where I'd poked the window with a bullet last night and considered climbing back into the tub.

I made my way over and tried the phones. No joy.

Feeling like a sack of old bones, I sat down at the table to sip my coffee and hoped it could miraculously help me feel like I'd gotten a restful night's sleep.

I thought about Jimmy. It was the first time I'd ever pushed someone unwillingly. I might not know where he'd end up, but I knew he wasn't welcome here.

I considered food, but couldn't drum up an appetite. A few minutes later, a car struggled up my driveway, gravel sliding in clay. I peeked out the front window at the cruiser parked between my truck and the road. Deputy Jake stepped out into the mud, looking a touch forlorn with his hat in hand.

He wiped his feet on the mat and came in, still in the clothes I'd given him to wear the previous night. He greeted me, sounding near as tired as I was. His eyes wandered to the tarp in the corner of the living room and laughed softly to himself in a sad way. "Damn. Wicked web, no?"

I didn't know what to say, so I nodded.

He smiled at me, dog tired but real. I liked his real smile.

"I've been looking 'round, and I'm pretty sure we know all the damage done last night. Main road's washed out and the four mile bridge is underwater. The main house saw not a peep of trouble, and DL says he wants to come up and check on you as soon as he's gotten some sleep. I told him you were just fine and that seemed to calm him down." Unexpectedly, he chuckled, eyes half closed, hand over his forehead with exhaustion. "Uhm, DL asked me to stick around here for a while to keep you company, calm your nerves so's he could 'rest easier'."

This time I chuckled with him. "That's real nice and neighborly of DL. Always thinking of others, that one."

I caught him eyeing my coffee cup. "You want some coffee, Jake?"

"I'd love some, thank you, Loretta. Could you Irish it up for me? DL's first aid kit is woefully low on painkillers."

"Okay, but I thought you couldn't while you're on duty?" I looked at him inquisitively.

He smiled weakly. "Yup. Not on duty now. I think I've earned a break." He sagged in his chair, long legs stretching out to fill the space under the table. Looked about ready to drop right there in my kitchen.

A little leeway was in order on account of the hole in his shoulder, put there by his partner. He started up talking shop again, "There's not much we can do about the bodies here, until the crime scene techs can come out. And we may never find out why Lester had your ex-husband's photo on him."

His good arm came up, and a hand ran through his hair. "I'm going to need to stick around for a bit. I reached them on the radio, and they're mighty interested in helping out up here, but dispatch says the helivac is not coming out until she's repaired. Plus, they don't see the point in risking it while I'm stable. There are -- and I quote -- 'more important evac problems right now'. Landslides on the coast."

I squinted out the window, worried about people I didn't know. I thought on all the trouble Jimmy had caused, dredging his criminal friend up to help him when he should have had the gumption to come out himself and have a go at me. Probably wouldn't be dead then. I felt sorry for him, but I had nothing to regret.

I looked at my guest again, who'd been watching me think. I shrugged myself clean of that line of thought and moved on to more practical matters. Wiped my hands on my pants, and stood.

Pain hit my shoulder where I'd held the shotgun. I put my arms out and stretched.

He piped up, "I'm going to need to stay here until the roads clear or evac shows up, and they're saying that'll probably be 24 hours at least. They need me to stay here. With you."

"Sure," I agreed. "Don't worry. You're plenty welcome, and there's provisions enough." I smiled at him, hoping I didn't look too pleased.

If he noticed, he didn't show it. He sat in my kitchen sipping coffee, looking out the window at the water sheeting down, then at me for a while. His eyes on me didn't bother me none. I felt comfortable with him there, in a way I couldn't put my finger on.

I was planning to go curl up somewhere and take a much needed nap. I stood, and he spoke up. "Can I speak plainly with you, Loretta?" He stood up, too. The cop attitude was gone. He sounded like just Jake talking to just Loretta, and I was glad of it.

"Sure." I smiled, honestly just too bone tired to put up a wall, and half past too tired to pretend I wasn't happy he was here with me. He took my hand up into both his.

"Look," he said, eyes up to the ceiling for a second, then looked at me, hard. "I'm going to have to get someone else assigned to this case when I get back."

"All right. Why so?"

He placed his hands on the sides of my face, and those startlingly green eyes came right up close. I understood why he'd been agitated then. He was going to kiss me. Men always get all riled up about simple choices, don't they?

I looked for reasons to complain and found none. Then his mouth came down towards mine carefully, like he was double checking, and I surprised myself by leaning up into it and kissing him. We fit together perfectly.

He pulled me closer to him, and took over the kiss, deepening it. Near everything in my life tumbled about and rearranged itself. Sounds impossible, but I felt a part of myself settle into this man in a sort of permanent way. The scariest and most magical thing I've ever felt in my life.

Then he dragged his mouth from me, touched his forehead to mine. "See?" he breathed.

"I see," I murmured into his cheek. Didn't move an inch, just stood there feeling changed, letting him soak in.

I broke free to look down at Scaredy, who was doing figure eights around our legs, purring. He looked down, too, slightly bewildered. There was a discussion for another day.

Outside, the rain came down even harder. Pounding on the tin roof, sheeting off like a waterfall, digging trenches into the ground at the eaves of this old house. I'd never been so grateful for rain.

About Désirée Matlock

Désirée Matlock presently lives in a beach town with her beau, twin daughters, two cats and a dog, where, whenever she gets two seconds to rub together, she writes by a window overlooking a lake. She loves to travel and play the piano, although never at the same time. She won't bore you further with the mundane details of her simple life unless you visit her blog.

Connect with Désirée:
www.DesisTwoCents.com

Gravity of Love

By Angel Woolery

Innocuous is how
she desired her visit to be
as she embarked upon
that day trip
through his soul.
She resolved to traverse
his tender feelings
as lightly as she was able.
Expecting
even as she took such care
that bruising was
inevitable.
The ache to caress
the source of his admiration,
overwhelmed any sense
she might employ.
And needing
just once
to bathe in the purity
of his affection,
she mouthed a silent apology
and immersed herself
in his warmth.
He held still his racing heart
mid beat,
not wanting to startle her.
His breath paused
awaiting her judgment
as painful moments of uncertainty
consumed him.
A lifetime of wanting
balanced on the perilous edge
of her acceptance,

far from his reach.
Never would this lady
have known
what his heart held
had she not trespassed.
Never would he have
braved an invitation.
He, ever at her mercy.
She, now unwittingly at his.
Surrounded by
the sheer intensity
of his regard,
she had never felt
so vulnerable.
His whispered yearnings
became a part of her
as they bypassed her ears
to slip through the hairline cracks
of her neglect.
Raw honesty
chipping delicately
at her defenses
'til they lay in ruins
at her feet.
A pile of useless assurance.
She had noticed naught
until 'twas far to late.
Attempting a hasty escape,
her footfalls only serve to
churn unexplored emotions
like autumn leaves in
a late season storm.
And her
the mightiest of Oaks
taken by surprise,
finds herself bared
without consent.
Left exposed
by the most elemental of forces.

Her once sure steps falter
as she struggles
to find purchase.
Knowing
he cannot let her fall,
he must let go his insecurities
to grant the safety
of his embrace.
She surrenders to
the inevitable
and in the yielding
of willfulness
finds the key to her survival.
Acceptance.
The brilliance
such freedom of emotion
fills her with
serves to light her path
through eternity,
no longer trying to escape
the gravity of love.

About Angel Woolery

Angel's work has been described by other poets as "gritty" and "sweetly sensual". Poetry in particular is gratifying for her as a writer as it is a personal, yet formal, artistic exercise. She finds the intellectual challenge of shaping thought into a predetermined format, a pleasurable way to while away some hours. Though what intrigues her most is that the emotional intent behind each piece is transmuted beautifully into something different by each reader, allowing the creation to become as meaningful and personal to them as it is to her.

Connect with Angel:
Facebook.com/AngelWooleryPoet

Other books by Angel Woolery:
The Taste of Innocence

Thank you, dear reader, for taking the time to enjoy our handy work. Look out for more books from the Ink Slingers, both as a group and as individuals!

And as always, may your world be filled with adventure and the stuff that dreams are made of.

Cheers!

The Ink Slingers Guild

www.ingramcontent.com/pod-product-compliance
Lightning Source LLC
Chambersburg PA
CBHW070915180626
46817CB00003B/1068